He was enca...

A mailed hood, ... Hugh's tall body ... hidden by the ... helmet. Only his ... frightened Rowena more than the long sword he held. They were as cold as ice, a strange silvery grey.

For an instant she wanted to shriek in terror and then her chin came up and she forced herself to meet his contemptuous stare.

Dear Reader

Treats this month, as the autumn evenings begin to shorten. We welcome back Gail Mallin with CONQUEROR'S LADY, as Rowena and Hugh battle it out, and give you another Regency from Paula Marshall — how *will* Cressy cope with Society's rules? Patricia Potter is back with DRAGONFIRE as the Boxer Rebellion sweeps Peking, and THE DOUBLETREE by Victoria Pade offers a variation on the mail-order bride. Four books offering fascinating characters we know you will love. Enjoy!

The Editor

Gail Mallin has a passion for travel. She studied at the University of Wales where she gained an Honours degree, and met her husband, then an officer in the Merchant Navy. They spent the next three years sailing the world before settling in Cheshire. Writing soon became another means of exploring, opening up new worlds. A career move took Gail and her husband south, and now they live with their young family in St Albans.

Recent titles by the same author:

DEBT OF HONOUR
THE DEVIL'S BARGAIN
A MOST UNSUITABLE DUCHESS

CONQUEROR'S LADY

Gail Mallin

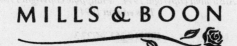

MILLS & BOON

MILLS & BOON LIMITED
ETON HOUSE, 18–24 PARADISE ROAD
RICHMOND, SURREY, TW9 1SR

MILLS & BOON, the Rose Device and LEGACY OF LOVE are trademarks of the publisher.

First published in Great Britain 1994 by Mills & Boon Limited

© Gail Mallin 1994

Australian copyright 1994   Philippine copyright 1994 This edition 1994

ISBN 0 263 78727 3

Set in 10 on 12 pt Linotron Times 04-9409-81085

Typeset in Great Britain by Centracet, Cambridge Printed in Great Britain by BPC Paperbacks Ltd

CHAPTER ONE

THE long-haired star blazed across the heavens.

'What think you, Odo? Is it a sign of victory or an omen of evil?'

Light showering from the comet's fiery tail threw the austere planes of Hugh de Lacy's face into sharp relief.

Odo de Nevil turned from contemplation of the strange blood-coloured sky to glance in surprise at his tall companion. It was rare to hear a note of hesitation in that deep voice.

'Why, victory, of course!' he replied with a hearty laugh. 'All Normandy is arming for invasion. England is as good as ours.'

Hugh's black eyebrows quirked. 'So you think our Duke's cause just?'

'Hush, lad, not so loud!' Odo laid a large, meaty forefinger to his lips and glanced about them warily, peering into the April darkness. The courtyard appeared deserted but one never knew.

'You don't want some tattlemonger running to William with a tale of treachery.'

'Treachery!' Hugh spat the word, his amazingly light eyes narrowing. 'I am the Duke's man, body and soul. If he ordered us to march into hell, then I would obey!'

Quailing before the fury he had inadvertently aroused, Odo apologised. 'I meant no slur on your honour, my lord,' he said with stiff formality. 'Only that there are those who are jealous of the favour shown you by the Duke.'

The anger died out of Hugh's face. 'I know.' He nodded ruefully.

He was the fourth son of an impoverished noble family of Caen. At the age of ten he had been sent off to another household to serve as a page. It was the custom but from that day Hugh knew he would have to make his own way in the world.

When he attained his knighthood on his nineteenth birthday, his father had scraped together the money for a sound horse and armour and handed them over, saying, 'This is all the patrimony I can afford, my son. You'll have to take service with one of the great lords. Why don't you try the Duke of Normandy?'

It was good advice.

William was a hard taskmaster but fair. He had soon noticed how Hugh tackled even the lowliest task with unstinting concentration and he had begun to reward the young knight with greater responsibilities.

Ten years had gone by and Hugh had risen high in the ducal service but there were still those who remembered his undistinguished origins.

'Forget my maundering, Odo,' Hugh said, burying the uncharacteristic pang of doubt which had arisen out of nowhere like a demon to plague him. He reached out to grip Odo's shoulder in a silent gesture that begged forgiveness.

The older knight's affront melted. 'This business isn't work for a fighting man,' he muttered with a sympathetic growl and jerk of his head at the elegant manor-house behind them.

'Aye, but the Duke needs volunteers,' Hugh observed drily.

A snort of irritation exploded from Odo's heavy frame. 'For all the good we are doing, we might as well have stayed at home. We have been here three days already and still my lord Count bleats of caution and hesitates to open his purse!'

'He's been listening to the doom-mongers who warn that nothing but disaster will come of invading England. They think William is mad to attempt it.' Hugh shrugged his broad shoulders in irritation. 'I'll try to arrange another audience in the morning.'

Odo swore.

'At this rate we'll never gather enough ships in time to cross the Channel before summer ends!'

'Then we'll all have to swim.' Hugh grinned suddenly. 'Make no mistake, Odo. Milksops like Count Brian won't deter the Duke. He is determined to succeed.'

He paused, his smile fading. 'And, by God, so am I! Our Duke is going to get all the ships he wants even if we have to build them for him.'

It was the task William had set them, to gather an armada so that he could sail across to England and avenge the insult that the new English King had offered him.

'And when we do,' Hugh continued grimly, 'we are going to teach Harold Godwinson a lesson.'

'Aye, we'll throw that oath-breaker off his ill-gotten throne and win our fortunes into the bargain,' Odo chimed in eagerly. He chuckled, rubbing his hands together in anticipation. 'Think on it! There'll be fine estates going a-begging, enough surely for William to reward even the likes of you and me.'

Hugh flashed him a startled look.

In his single-minded pursuit of duty, Hugh de Lacy had not allowed himself to think beyond solving the problems of the moment. God knew there were enough of them! But Odo de Nevil's chance remark hit a nerve.

Land! Land of his own!

'So there will,' he answered slowly, an enticing vision of the future suddenly gleaming before his eyes.

'My lady, I do not think you are concentrating.'

The gently reproving voice of Father Wilfrid made Rowena jump and slacken her hold on the parchment scroll she was meant to be studying. It snapped shut and the force of the movement sent it skittering off her lap to the floor of the bower.

'I'm sorry, my wits were wandering,' Rowena apologised, her cheeks pinkening with guilt as she bent to rescue the precious document.

'Perhaps we should abandon our lesson for today,' the little priest suggested, a twinkle in his eyes. He glanced at the June sunlight streaming in through the open door of the small one-roomed cottage which was Rowena's personal domain. 'It must be nearly noon. Your father's guests will be here soon.'

A radiant smile lit up his pupil's face.

'Thank you, Father,' she cried, springing to her feet with a youthful vigour that made the old priest's bones ache. 'I promise I shall pay more attention next time.'

'I think French verbs can wait until Godric has returned home.'

The elderly priest smiled at her sudden blush. It was a secret known all over Edenwald that today was the day that the thegn intended to announce the betrothal of his only daughter, his sole surviving child, to Godric Athelstanson.

A plump figure, garbed in coarse grey serge, appeared in the doorway and Father Wilfrid announced, 'Ah, here is Elgiva, come to scold us for lingering so long over our books. I shall leave you in her capable hands, my child.'

A squawk of flurried apology greeted his remark but Rowena mercifully intervened. 'Father Wilfrid is teasing you, Elgiva. You are not interrupting. We had already finished.'

Elgiva nodded stiffly, but when the door closed behind the priest she sniffed eloquently.

'If you ask me, too much book-learning has addled the good father's wits,' she muttered indignantly. 'You'd best watch out you don't go the same road, my lady. It isn't natural, taxing your brain with all this reading and writing——'

Rowena had heard this homily before and hastily sought a diversion. 'Shall I wear my blue roc for the feast or my red?' she interrupted.

Elgiva bustled over to the wooden clothes chest that stood against one white-washed wall and held up a fine woollen over-gown dyed a deep crimson. It was decorated with bands of gold embroidery around the edges of the neck, hem and wide, loose sleeves.

'This one shows off your skill with a needle. Come, let me help you into it or they'll be here before you are ready.'

Rowena stood obediently while Elgiva fussed, arranging the three-quarter length crimson roc over a longer pale green under-kirtle until both gowns hung to her satisfaction.

'Now for your hair, my lady.'

Elgiva seized Rowena's wooden comb and pushed her charge down on to a stool.

'Oh, Elgiva, must you? I am well enough as I am!'

'For shame, Rowena Edwinsdaughter! You are almost sixteen—too old to romp around like a churl's brat. I intend to see to it that your mother is proud of you when she looks down to watch your betrothal from her place in heaven.'

'Godric doesn't care what I look like!' Rowena muttered rebelliously, but Elgiva ignored her and firmly removed the plain head-rail, loosening the heavy braids concealed beneath.

A silken mass of gold rippled free.

Elgiva drew the comb through the glinting strands with fierce pride. Such glorious hair her darling had! It fell below her knees like a living cloak of sunlight.

In fact, it seemed a pity to hide such loveliness, but custom demanded that women cover their hair, so Elgiva braided it again into a thick coil at Rowena's nape, where it would stay concealed by a long muslin veil, held in place today by a silver headband.

'Stand up, my lamb, and I'll fetch your best summer mantle.'

Elgiva carefully placed the bright green cloak around Rowena's slim shoulders.

'If your father had agreed to Lord Godric's proposal when he first asked for you two months ago, you could have worn your fur-trimmed mantle for the betrothal ceremony,' she lamented, fastening the silver cords of the green cloak across Rowena's breast.

'Well, I should be far too hot in that today, even if it is the finest garment I own,' Rowena laughed. 'Anyway, you know there was no hurry. Father won't let us marry before my birthday.'

She would be sixteen in August and the thegn had told Godric that he must wait until after the harvest to make her his bride.

'Aye, he is reluctant to lose you, my lamb.'

'Wynburgh is only three miles away,' Rowena

replied, but there was a catch of uncertainty in her voice.

Much as she loved Godric, the thought of marriage was rather frightening. She would have to leave her beloved Edenwald, where she was mistress in all but name, and learn to share a home with Godric's mother and sisters. It would all be new and unfamiliar, and she would be subject to her mother-in-law's dominance.

And Ethelwine Alfredsdaughter doesn't like me!

Quickly Rowena pushed the unwelcome thought aside.

'Three miles is far enough,' Elgiva sniffed. 'Why, I remember when we travelled to Hertford, my lady. I was that sore I couldn't sit down for a week!'

A giggle escaped Rowena at the memory. Hertford was their nearest town, some five miles to the north. Lord Edwin had permitted her to accompany him on a trip last summer. The roads had been hot and dusty, but Rowena had been fascinated. It was the furthest she had ever travelled in her life.

'I wish Father would take me with him to London when he attends meetings of the Witan,' she murmured wistfully.

'And why should he, when he is busy with state business?' Elgiva demanded tartly, bringing out Rowena's best leather shoes. 'The King summons his nobles to help him rule the country. Your father would have no time to spare for you, my lady.'

'But I should enjoy hearing of what goes on in the councils,' Rowena protested. She tilted her chin in a characteristically determined little gesture. 'I might even have learnt whether these rumours that William of Normandy means to invade us are true.'

'Bah!' Elgiva snorted at this unseemly talk. 'War is men's business, child.'

Rowena bent to put her black shoes on, curbing the retort that rose to her lips. The whole village had been buzzing with speculation for weeks, but there was no point in arguing with her nurse. Elgiva insisted on treating her like a baby!

Elgiva eyed her warily. She knew that particular expression! What wayward thoughts was the child dreaming now?

A little sigh escaped her. Oh, why had Lord Edwin reared the wench as if she were the son he had always longed for? His indulgence had bred this unhealthy interest in masculine pursuits like politics and reading. Saints defend us, but the child was even learning to speak French!

Elgiva frowned.

The loss of his wife, Lady Hilda, nigh on two years ago hadn't helped. The thegn had turned to his daughter for companionship, with the result that she had spent even less time at her loom. Now, although she could weave and embroider as beautifully as a noblewoman should, she was far too outspoken and too fond of getting her own way. It wasn't proper for any woman to behave so boldly!

Still, perhaps marriage would steady her. Godric Athelstanson was a fine young man and related to the new King. No matter was troubles befell—and Elgiva *had* heard the worrying rumours—at least the child's future was now assured.

Rowena straightened and Elgiva let out a crow of satisfaction. 'There! For once, you look the way a thegn's daughter should!'

Rowena merely grinned. She cared more for comfort

than for finery, but when Elgiva brought her the beaten
silver handmirror that had been her mother's she was
pleasantly surprised by the change wrought in her
appearance. She was still too thin, of course, and sadly
lacking in bosom, but the elegant gown gave her a new
dignity. Perhaps Godric's mother might even think her
improved enough to keep her barbed comments to
herself?

'Listen! I hear the sound of new arrivals!'

Rowena's quick ears caught the blast of the horn
coming from the direction of the palisade gate.

'They are early! We must hurry, Elgiva,' she urged.

However, when they reached the Great Hall, to
Rowena's surprise they found it almost empty. Instead
of the usual throng of people, only a reluctant-looking
messenger stood before the raised dais where her father
was seated.

One glance at the thegn's bearded face told her it was
bad news.

'Come, daughter!'

The thegn stood up, nodding dismissal at the man and
beckoning her to follow him.

Behind the dais, the far end of the hall had been
partitioned off with a curtain of deerskin, a modern
custom in a rich man's household to provide comfort
and privacy for his immediate family.

With a quick worried glance, Rowena waved Elgiva
aside and obeyed her father's summons.

The small room formed behind the deerskin curtain
was pleasingly furnished but the thegn of Edenwald did
not sit down. Instead he stood, drumming his fingers
against the arm of his carved chair.

'May I know what is wrong, Father? Is Godric not
coming?'

The thegn glanced up and for an instant a smile split his worried face. He liked the way his daughter used her intelligence and came directly to the point. He had taught her to eschew foolish feminine timidity and prevarication.

'Godric has received an urgent message from his kinsman. Harold wants him to take part in the command of our shoreline defences.'

The thegn paused, allowing her time to digest this unexpected news. 'He left early this morning. The messenger came to bring us his apologies. He asks that you forgive him and promises to visit Edenwald as soon as he is able to do so.'

Rowena clamped her lips shut on the protest that clamoured for freedom and said stiffly, 'It is a great honour that King Harold does him.'

Lord Edwin nodded his blond head slowly. 'Aye, but it pleases me as little as it pleases you, my dear.'

Astonishment made Rowena's mouth fall open.

'When I agreed to Godric's request for your hand in marriage, I saw in him a son-in-law who would look after you and Edenwald when I am gone.' He frowned. 'It was no part of my plan to find you an ambitious husband.'

'No man can refuse his king!' Rowena rushed to Godric's defence.

'Perhaps you are right.' The thegn let out a sigh. 'We must all do our duty.'

He was silent for a moment, his tall, heavily muscled frame rigid with tension, and then he said abruptly, 'Do you remember me telling you what King Edward said on his death-bed?'

Rowena nodded in puzzlement. Edward had prophesied evil falling over the land in a welter of blood.

'He was barely cold in his grave before these angry rumblings from Normandy began.' The thegn's blue eyes were bleak. 'And there was that strange star only two months ago.' He shook his head. 'I am beginning to fear for the future, my dear.'

'Then you think Duke William will invade, Father?' Rowena's voice wobbled uncertainly. She had never seen her father look so sombre and suddenly all the rumours she had heard no longer seemed comical.

'He claims that his cousin Edward promised him the throne,' the thegn replied, a measure of calm returning to his manner. 'I don't believe it myself, any more than I believe that Harold Godwinson swore an oath to help him uphold that claim.'

'Godric says it was a trick.' Rowena forgot about superstitious omens and her eyes, a deep speedwell-blue like her father's, sparkled with indignation.

'Harold told him about it when Godric visited him at Waltham last year. Apparently, Harold thought he was just taking an oath of knightly loyalty, which he had only agreed to in the first place because William was holding him prisoner and wouldn't let him go unless he did so.'

'Aye, that sounds like William. Always out for the main chance.' Her father snorted in derision. 'Normandy's ambition is overweening and that's the problem, my dear. He's been made to look a fool and he's not the man to stand for that kind of humiliation.'

Rowena turned chill. Her father had answered her question. Invasion was no longer a possibility. It was a certainty!

Wherever Rowena looked the palisaded courtyard was full of armed men.

Some were already mounted, others milled about in the September sunshine, shouting and swearing in a frenzy of last-minute preparation. In the midst of all the confusion, Father Wilfrid hurried from one man to another, dispensing blessings and hearing hasty confessions.

Rowena had eyes for no one but her father. Forgetting all notions of dignity, she ran to him and flung her arms about his waist. All she wanted to do was cry like a baby!

'Tears, my daughter?'

Lord Edwin tilted up her head with a gentle hand. He smiled down at her with understanding but his voice was firm. 'Always remember you are a Saxon of noble birth, Rowena, and Saxons do not weep when their King commands them to follow him to war.'

Rowena nodded, sniffing back the sobs that threatened to choke her. After a moment she managed a watery smile.

'That's better.' The thegn permitted himself a broad grin. 'Don't fret, my dear. We will be home again before the harvest is finished and then you shall have the most splendid wedding ever seen in this shire.'

'I'll hold you to that promise, Father,' Rowena replied, forcing lightness into her tone. 'And you can tell Godric Athelstanson when you see him that he is not going to escape marrying me no matter how far away he runs!'

The thegn gave a roar of delight. 'Aye, I'll tell him, girl! It will take a better man than Tostig Godwinson to thwart your plans.'

A shadow flitted across Rowena's fine-boned face.

'It seems so strange, Father, that you are bound for the north. All summer long Godric has been away guarding the coast while we fretted Duke William would invade and now King Harold's own brother rebels against him, bringing an army of invasion down on us from Norway!'

'England is a ripe plum, drawing the wasps,' the thegn answered heavily. 'Harold must beat them all off or we'll have no peace.'

'But the messenger who came to summon you to join the fyrd said three hundred Viking ships had sailed up the Ouse!'

Rowena shivered at the thought. King Harold was hastily summoning the army, but would he have enough men to deal with the renowned Harald Hardrada of Norway?

'Hardrada's a fierce fighter,' the thegn said, confirming her fears. 'But Tostig Godwinson is a fool to trust him as an ally. Hardrada wants the English throne for himself, but we shall prevail and send him packing back where he belongs.'

Rowena nodded, recovering her poise. Her father's calm confidence was soothing but she couldn't prevent herself from saying sadly, 'I wish the King had permitted Godric to come home when he dismissed the rest of the fyrd.'

Strong northerly winds had been blowing for weeks, imprisoning the fleet which William of Normandy had gathered across the Channel in the port of St Valery. Knowing this, King Harold had reluctantly decided to disband his militia so that the men could return to their villages to gather in the harvest. But Godric Athelstanson had withdrawn to London with the King.

Rowena had been hoping that he would return soon, but instead the news had come of fighting in Yorkshire.

'It is months since I have seen him and now there isn't

even a chance to say goodbye before he goes into battle!'

'Godric is a fine warrior.' The thegn tapped her cheek lightly with one forefinger. 'You must not worry so, daughter,' he added in a kindly voice, but his gaze slid away to check on the progress of his men and Rowena sensed his masculine impatience with her nervous qualms.

Father Wilfrid approached to say that he was finished hearing confession and Rowena seized the chance to school her fears. By the time her father turned to her again, her expression was serene.

'Here, my dear; I want you to have these.'

Lord Edwin held up a heavy bunch of keys and Rowena gasped. They were the keys of the coffers and storerooms that held all the wealth of Edenwald. It was customary for the lady of the household to guard these keys, but the thegn had held them himself since his wife died.

'It is time you took charge,' he said gruffly, holding them out to her. 'I am leaving Edenwald in your hands.'

Her spine straightening, Rowena accepted the keys with a proud smile. 'I'll take good care of them,' she said, delighted by his gesture, which proved beyond all doubt that he considered her capable of responsibility.

Lord Edwin nodded in satisfaction.

'Father Wilfrid and Oswald the reeve will help you, but I must take every able-bodied man with me. It will be no easy task to gather the remaining harvest in.'

'We'll manage, Father,' she replied confidently.

His bearded face grew solemn.

'You are the last of my blood, Rowena. If anything should happen to me, promise that you will do all in your power to keep Edenwald safe.'

'I swear it. By the Holy Cross, I swear I won't fail you,' she replied fervently.

Together they knelt for the priest's blessing and then the thegn bellowed for his housecarls to mount and for the men on foot to line up in good order.

'God keep you, daughter, until I return,' Lord Edwin murmured, and pressed a swift kiss upon Rowena's brow before mounting his own horse with a lithe ease that belied his forty-seven years.

Rowena's heart swelled with pride. At an age when most men were content to sit by the fire, her father looked every inch a warrior!

Clad in a byrnie of interlocking iron rings, the thegn wore a pointed leather cap stiffened with iron bands to protect his blond head. His sword hung from his belt and he carried a round shield and the fearsome Saxon battleaxe. It took great strength to wield this weapon, but a skilled fighter like the thegn could bring down a horse and rider with one blow of its heavy curved blade.

'Goodbye, Father, goodbye!'

Rowena waved farewell, a brave smile pinned firmly to her lips.

The days slid slowly past, each anxious hour filled with toil. Rowena's fair skin spoiled as she worked in the fields but her unceasing labour earned her the respect of the villagers. Her willingness to listen to any problem they brought before her further enhanced the opinion that she was a worthy deputy for her father, but Rowena found the waiting hard.

'I wish we had news!' she exclaimed to Elgiva as they made ready for bed one evening.

'It's only been two weeks, my lamb,' Elgiva soothed, offering her a hot posset.

An hour later, tossing restlessly in spite of her weariness, Rowena stared into the darkness. She could hear Elgiva snoring faintly upon her pallet and she longed for the oblivion of sleep.

A faint clinking sound brought her sitting bolt upright.

There it was again!

'Elgiva! Elgiva, I can hear the sound of horses!' She shook her maid awake. 'The men have returned.'

Too impatient to wait for Elgiva's assistance, she began scrambling into her own clothes. 'Follow me when you are dressed.'

'My lady, wait. . .'

Snatching up her mantle, Rowena ignored this protest and sped from the bower.

Flaring torches lit up the courtyard and Rowena skittered to a halt, her eyes widening in dismay.

Instead of noise and commotion only a dozen or so horses stood there, lathered and sweating in the chill October air. They looked as if they had been ridden to exhaustion and the men dismounting were so travel-stained that Rowena scarcely recognised them.

'What has happened?'

Their weary, dust-caked faces stared back with a blank numbness that terrified her.

'Tell me, oh, please tell me!'

She plucked in desperation at the sleeve of the nearest man, but he shook his head, mumbling incoherently. Realising he was practically asleep on his feet, Rowena abandoned the attempt and hurried on into the Great Hall.

On the threshold she paused in disbelief. Everywhere she looked men sprawled on the benches that lined the room or lay collapsed on the floor.

'My lady!'

Aldith, the most senior of the household wenches, rushed up, her face awash with tears.

'Calm yourself, Aldith. Have you ordered ale to be served? No? Then see to it now. Rouse the rest of the maids and bring food for any man that wants it.'

Rowena gave the order calmly, curbing her own panic as she dispatched Aldith to the kitchens.

Hurrying down the long hall, she searched the travel-stained throng for familiar faces, but many of them were unknown to her. By the time she tugged aside the deerskin curtain her heart was beating wildly.

The man slumped in the thegn's carved chair lifted his blond head at her abrupt entrance.

'Godric!' His name burst from her lips.

Godric Athelstanson's eyes were almost as blue as Rowena's own, but now they were bloodshot and filled with grief as he gazed wearily at her. A filthy bandage swathed his right thigh and he winced as he rose to greet her, a young giant of a man in his twenty-first year, his long flaxen hair and beard tousled, his fine clothes stained by mire.

'Godric, sit down. You look exhausted.' Rowena moved quickly towards him, joy at finding him here so unexpectedly mingling with dread of what it might mean.

'There is something I must tell you first.' Godric's voice was hoarse with strain.

Rowena felt her scalp prickle.

'Your father——'

'Was it victory for the King?' she interrupted hastily, afraid to hear what he might say.

He nodded. 'We fought at a place called Stamford Bridge, near York. Tostig Godwinson is dead and so is

Harald Hardrada.' A grim smile touched Godric's mouth for an instant. 'King Harold gave him the seven feet of English soil which he had promised him for his corpse.'

There was pride in his voice but Rowena sensed Godric's reluctance to continue. Summoning all her courage, she managed to say, 'And my father?'

In the flickering torchlight she saw a muscle twitch in his cheek.

'He is dead. We were fighting hand to hand and he was cut down by one of Hardrada's axemen.'

Rowena swayed and Godric put his arms around her.

'Don't weep, sweeting. He wouldn't want it. He died the kind of death a warrior would choose. You can be proud of him.'

Rowena was scarcely aware of the tears pouring down her cheeks and she stood like a statue in Godric's awkward embrace. Yet in a corner of her mind she knew Godric was right. Her father had given his life to achieve victory, a bargain he would have accounted well-made.

'The King has asked me to convey his sympathy and give you his grateful thanks,' Godric said at last, patting her shoulder and gently releasing her.

Rowena choked back a final sob. She lifted her head. 'It was kind of him to think of me,' she murmured. Swallowing hard, she added, 'I've sent for food. Won't you sit down and tell me all about it while you eat?'

Godric shook his tousled head. 'Rowena, I've more bad news,' he said gently.

She stared at him. 'What could be worse than this?'

'Duke William has landed at Pevensey.'

Rowena opened her mouth, but no words would come and she had to struggle for breath in long rasping gasps. The shock was so great she could scarcely make sense of his explanation of how a weary messenger had burst in upon their victory feast at York to present the King with news of this latest calamity.

'From that moment we have ridden with all speed. Those who could not keep up the pace were left behind. It has taken me only four days to get here.'

Rowena's eyes widened at this incredible feat.

'But it is almost a hundred and sixty miles to York!' she exclaimed. 'I asked Father Wilfrid.'

A faint grin lightened Godric's weary face.

'Our outward march was just as fast! When Harold puts his mind to it, everyone jumps!'

His smile faded. 'That's why I could not bring your father's body home for burial, but I gave orders that two of his men stay behind. They will see to it.'

Rowena nodded. There was no need to ask why he had not arranged a larger escort. Every man would be needed in the struggle to come.

'The King has gone on to London. He intends to march on William as soon as he can.' Godric's quiet statement confirmed Rowena's unhappy thoughts.

'I must rejoin him. Unless you object, I shall take command of the men from Edenwald.'

'My father would have wished it,' Rowena nodded.

'Aye, I like to think so too,' Godric muttered gruffly.

He stared down at her and then said abruptly, 'I should not have left Harold's side but I knew you would be desperate for news.' His expression softened. 'And I wanted to see you again.'

Rowena squeezed her eyes tight shut to prevent any further foolish tears. After a moment she was able to control her voice. 'I'm glad you did,' she whispered.

His arms came around her and she laid her head

against his shoulder. Silently they clung together, holding each other close for comfort.

'My lady.'

Elgiva's voice roused them and Rowena turned.

From her maid's reddened eyes, she knew that Elgiva had heard the dreadful news. 'Does everyone else know?' she asked, slipping from Godric's hold.

'Bad news travels fast.' Elgiva sniffed and dabbed at her wet face with a corner of her apron. She was dressed as usual in her workaday tunic and kirtle of grey and the sight of her plump familiar figure heightened Rowena's sense of unreality.

Surely she was merely asleep and dreaming! This nightmare couldn't be real!

'I must leave at first light.'

Godric's words snatched her back into the present and, pulling herself together, Rowena declared, 'Then we must prepare food and drink ready for your journey.' She turned to Elgiva. 'Will you tell Aldith I'll be along in a moment?'

'Aye, my lady.' Elgiva slipped out.

'Do you really have to go so soon?' Rowena swung back to confront Godric, a pleading expression on her face.

'I must.' Godric's tone was harsh and Rowena knew it was no use to protest.

'I'm sorry. It's not what I want.' Clumsily, Godric gathered her hands in his and held them tightly. 'If we had even one day I would beg Father Wilfrid to marry us, but I owe loyalty to my kinsman. He needs every trained fighter he can get.'

Rowena nodded her understanding. It would be wrong to try and change his mind. She must prove herself worthy to be her father's daughter and not whine.

Godric produced a smile. 'Don't fret, sweeting. I'll be back before you know it and I'll bring you a Norman in chains to be your field-slave,' he announced with deliberate cheerfulness.

Rowena barely repressed a shudder.

Her father had promised to come home once the harvest was finished. The grain was safely gathered in, but the thegn of Edenwald would never return to dance at his daughter's wedding.

Dawn had scarcely broken before Godric was rousing the men from their heavy sleep.

Father Wilfrid was waiting for them in the small church hard by the Great Hall where he conducted a Mass for their safety. When the hasty service was concluded he accompanied them back to the hall where Rowena was waiting with her maids to hand round bowls of broth and barleycakes.

Rowena was hollow-cheeked and pale, but the elderly priest noted her steady hands with a smile of approval. Young though she was, the thegn's daughter was living up to her responsibilities.

'Thank you, sweeting.' Godric accepted the horn beaker she handed him and downed the contents. He smacked his lips. 'You brew a fine ale.'

Rowena tried to smile.

Aldith came hurrying up to say that the oatcakes and cold meats had been given out for the journey.

All that remained was to say goodbye.

A thin drizzle came spattering down as they emerged into the courtyard.

'Tell my mother that I was sorry I could not spare the

time to visit Wynburgh,' Godric asked while his men were mounting. 'She'll understand your need was greater.'

Rowena doubted it. Ethelwine would be furious, but Rowena found she no longer cared.

'Farewell, my sweeting.' Godric drew her to him and for an instant Rowena hid her face against his shoulder, holding him as tightly as she could. Then she stepped back quickly.

'Take care,' she said, her voice brave but ragged.

'I will.' Godric smiled at her steadily.

Rowena's fingernails bit deep into the soft flesh of her palms as he mounted. She would not shame him with her tears!

But Elgiva and the other women wept openly at the sight of their tired and depleted force marching away into the grey misty morning.

'My lady, the pedlar is here.'

Elgiva erupted into the store-house, a look of fearful anticipation on her plump face. 'He awaits you in the bower.'

Rowena thrust the stone jar of honey she had been counting into Aldith's hands and ran.

Wulfric would have news of the outside world and her feet scarcely touched the earth as she ran, her veil fluttering in the icy breeze. December had brought bitter weather, but Rowena didn't notice the cold in her haste.

Wulfric the pedlar was hunched over the fire. His shaggy red head swivelled round when a blast of chill air announced Rowena.

'My lady.' He straightened to give her greeting.

Impatiently Rowena motioned him to take a wooden stool by the brazier and sat down opposite him.

He pointed to the leather sack at his feet.

'I have fine silken threads this time, my lady, and I've brought the salt and those iron nails you asked for ——'

'I don't want salt, I want news!'

His patter interrupted, the scrawny little pedlar gaped at her. 'News, my lady?' he asked cautiously.

'Don't worry, I shall pay for it,' Rowena informed him swiftly. 'Just tell me if there has been a battle with the Normans yet.'

Wulfric's face fell.

'There was fierce fighting near Hastings, my lady,' he muttered. 'Hadn't ye heard?'

'We've seen no one since our men returned from the north bringing my father's body home for burial.' Rowena's voice was stiff with anguish.

Wulfric bit his lip. He hated being the bearer of bad tidings! So far as he knew the battle had taken place in the middle of October, almost seven weeks ago. If no survivors had come straggling home to tell the tale. . .

'Wulfric, tell me what you know!'

He jumped and blurted, 'The Normans won.'

The blunt answer made Rowena gasp.

Avoiding her eyes, Wulfric continued hastily, 'I was told the battle raged all day. Time after time the Normans charged those damned horses of theirs, but they couldn't break our line. Then Duke William tricked some of our raw lads into thinking he was retreating and they chased after him.'

'Did the rest of the army follow?'

'Nay, my lady, but the Normans began firing arrows into the air. Thousands died in the panic and confusion.

The King's housecarls fought like demons, but Harold
himself was slain.'

Rowena could feel her heart thudding against her
breastbone like a wild animal. Godric would have been
standing close to the King, his banner next to the royal
standard of the Fighting Man.

'He must be dead,' she whispered, turning pale.

Wulfric thought she might faint.

'Some escaped, my lady,' he said in an encouraging
tone, wondering for whom she grieved.

Rowena shook her head violently. Godric would
never have left the King's side.

'Where are the Normans now?' She forced the question through stiff lips.

'I've heard they are heading north.'

Wulfric shuddered. He would not tell her how Edith
of the Swan's Neck, Harold's mistress, had pleaded in
vain for the return of the King's mutilated body.
William had ordered him buried in an obscure grave
before beginning a campaign of destruction calculated
to destroy all opposition to his rule.

'Is there no one left to stop them?'

'Nay. Both of the King's brothers fell at Hastings and
I've heard it said that the Aethling will surrender soon.'
Wulfric shook his shaggy head dismally. 'William has
threatened to burn London if it resists.'

Rowena pressed a hand to her hot forehead. She was
beyond the easy relief of tears, but her head felt as if it
might burst. If Edgar, the rightful Prince, was ready to
give in, then it must be true. The Normans had won!

'The Duke has been garrisoning every town he has
taken, my lady.' Wulfric sighed. 'He is taking hostages
and making everyone swear oaths of loyalty.'

'Edenwald will never acknowledge that Norman upstart as King!'

Rowena sprang to her feet in fury, her eyes a blaze of sapphire in her white face.

'I cry shame on those who surrender so easily to William the Bastard, who is nothing more than a stinking tanner's grandson!'

'Hush, my lady!' Wulfric's eyes bulged with fear. 'No one dares use that name. His vengeance is too harsh. He cut off the hands and feet of every man in the city of Alençon for that very insult!'

Rowena's slim fingers flew to her mouth to stifle her cry of revulsion. 'What manner of man can he be?' she demanded shakily.

The pedlar shrugged. 'Monster or not, he will be our new king, my lady. We can only accept it; we have no other choice.'

Angrily, Rowena turned away.

She would not, could not, accept Wulfric's practical philosophy!

Truly her father had been right to fear that the long-haired star had portended disaster.

Her world had turned upside-down and love had died forever.

But hatred remained.

She would never bend the knee to any Norman. No, not even at the cost of her life.

'So. The resistance is over. Now I can begin.'

Hugh de Lacy cast a glance at his liege lord and read the satisfaction in William's strong face.

He had just received the submission of the Londoners and the keys of the city lay clasped in his hand.

'Here, take these and guard them for me, Hugh.' The

Duke stretched and flexed his shoulders wearily. It had been a hard campaign.

Hugh came forward and took the keys.

The Duke smiled at him. He had made a wise choice in favouring this penniless knight. Now it was time to reward him.

'I have something else for you, Hugh.'

He snapped his fingers at one of the scribes who sat quietly at a table on the far side of the room. A whispered word and the man brought a parchment.

The Duke glanced at it quickly and nodded.

'An estate for you, Hugh de Lacy. A nice rich one.'

Hugh swallowed hard, controlling the excitement rising in him. His face impassive, he said quietly, 'May I know its name, my lord?'

'Edenwald.'

CHAPTER TWO

'How much further, Hugh?'

'By my reckoning, no more than a mile or two.'

Odo de Nevil groaned. 'God damn this rain. Does it do nothing else in this accursed country?'

Hugh de Lacy laughed.

'Your trouble is the English mead, my friend, not the English weather!'

Odo acknowledged this sally with a faint grin. 'My head feels as if it is splitting asunder.'

'Bear up. There's a patch of blue sky yonder.' Hugh raised an arm to point in the direction they were heading.

Odo surveyed it with a prejudiced eye. 'I can't think why I left Normandy,' he said plaintively. 'To think I might be snug at home in bed with Arlette.'

'Or Isabelle or Matilda or Adeliza——'

'Peace!' Odo flung up an entreating hand. After a moment he continued thoughtfully, 'I wonder what the women will be like at Edenwald? Plump and willing, I hope.'

Hugh's amusement faded. 'I'll countenance no rape,' he said, a sudden sharpness in his tone.

Odo glanced at him quickly, but decided against protesting. Hugh was strangely fastidious in such matters but in this instance perhaps he was right.

'Aye, it's as well not to sully one's own nest,' he replied sagely. 'But if you want no wenching, you'd best warn young de Beaumont now.'

Hugh nodded, casting a swift glance at the retinue of armed men who followed in their wake.

A fresh-faced young knight rode at their rear but that angelic expression was deceptive. At nineteen, Gerard de Beaumont was a seasoned fighter and a renowned rake, whose weakness for pretty girls was forever landing him in trouble.

'They can't resist that baby face of his,' Odo jested, echoing Hugh's thoughts.

'Hard work will cool his blood,' Hugh said drily. 'There'll be a great deal to do since the place has been masterless these last two months.'

A frown creased Hugh's brow. One of the Duke's clerks had told him that the thegn of Edenwald had fallen at Hastings so God knew who had been in charge since then. His first task would be to bring order to the thirty hides of land he now owned, an extensive area.

His frown deepened.

No doubt the Saxons would resent him. He would have to teach them his word was law. Fortunately, William had allocated him a dozen well-equipped men to help him achieve this task, part of his reward, and both Odo de Nevil and Gerard de Beaumont had elected to join his service.

Hugh knew that they had hoped for land of their own but William had not offered to enfeoff them. Hugh suspected that the Duke thought Gerard too young and Odo too fond of the bottle, but their ill luck had been his gain. They were both good, experienced men and he could rely on their loyalty.

'Look, we must be nearly there. Some of these fields have been recently ploughed.'

Odo's voice broke into his concentration, alerting

Hugh to something his unconscious mind had already noted.

'It looks good rich earth,' he said with satisfaction, eyeing the long narrow strips that made up each field.

Winterstock cattle were grazing on the common pasture, which had been hacked away from the edge of the surrounding woods, and in the distance Hugh could see swine rooting for the last few nuts and beechmast under the trees.

A water-mill stood on the banks of a stream. They forded it and rode on, passing a forge on the outskirts of the village.

'It must be a prosperous place to support a mill and a forge,' Odo commented.

Hugh nodded briefly. 'But where are all the peasants?'

Odo gaped at him and then turned to study the village once more.

It looked like dozens of others that they'd seen. There was the usual cluster of round wattle and daub huts, each standing in its own tiny garth planted with a few winter vegetables. Fowl scratched in the dirt and a couple of dogs dozed under the shelter of a mulberry bush.

But it was deserted.

At their approach, the dogs barked, geese cackled and hens flew up squawking, but even this frantic alarm didn't bring anyone running to investigate.

'Are they all fled or lying in a drunken stupor somewhere?' Odo demanded uneasily once the clamour faded.

The silence was uncanny.

Behind him, Hugh could hear someone muttering a

prayer to ward off evil. Swiftly he raised a hand and the
murmuring ceased.

Ahead lay a palisade. Inside it, he knew there would
be a large, log-built hall surrounded by several smaller
buildings. A rich man's home usually had a separate
kitchen, private sleeping quarters for his family, one or
two guest-houses, stables for his horses, a mews for his
hawks and often other attributes like a chapel.

'The answer must lie behind those gates,' he said
tersely, urging his mount forward.

To his astonishment, the gateway appeared
unguarded, but as they halted he heard the faint sound
of chanting.

'They must be in the church!'

With a flick of his hand, he motioned two of the men
forward to test the gates.

'God's teeth, they are unbarred!'

Odo's muffled exclamation was echoed by a low
ripple of astonishment from the troop as the gates swung
inward. Signalling for caution, Hugh led them forward,
his sword out in readiness for any trick, but the enclo-
sure was deserted, save for an old man lying asleep at
the foot of the palisade.

'Snoring on guard duty!' Hugh's lip curled in scorn. If
this was an example of the way things were being run,
then it was high time he took charge!

Issuing orders to his men, he dismounted and beckoned Odo to follow him. Together they advanced on the
small building, which, from its spire, must be the chapel.

The singing grew louder.

For an instant Hugh paused in the shallow porch.
Then, gritting his teeth at the necessity, he flung open
the door.

* * *

The singing died in mid-note.

For one dreadful moment, Rowena thought she might faint. The two figures advancing towards her seemed to sway before her horrified gaze. She had never seen Norman knights before, but she knew what these men were!

An appalled silence fell over the church and Rowena caught a creak and jingle of harness, warning her that more of them must wait outside.

Shock dried her mouth so that she had to swallow hard before she could speak.

'Who are you?'

The taller one stepped forward and spoke in heavily accented but intelligible English.

'I am Hugh de Lacy, lord of Edenwald.'

A surge of incredulous anger swept over Rowena, restoring her wits.

Stepping away from the altar-rails, she carefully handed the new-born baby she held back to its mother and motioned the frightened woman to rejoin the rest of the congregation.

'How dare you interrupt our prayers with your lies? Get off my land at once!'

Her voice rang round the church and brought an angry flush to Hugh's face. Automatically, his grip tightened on the pommel of his sword and it gleamed in the dim light as he strode down the nave to confront this challenge.

At his approach, her Saxons scattered out of his path, but Rowena did not flinch. She held her ground, remaining where she stood before the altar, but behind the shelter of her concealing skirts her knees were quaking.

She had never seen anyone so strange and terrifying-looking in her life!

He was encased in steel. A mailed hood, hauberk and hose shielded his tall body and his lean face was partially hidden by the ugly nasalguard of his metal helmet. It bisected his features, obscuring them. Only his eyes could be seen and they frightened her far more than the long sword he held. They were as cold as the ice that formed at the edge of the reedbeds when winter took the stream and almost the same colour, a strange silvery grey she had never encountered before.

He drew nearer and Rowena could feel the hard, pulsating anger emanating from his powerful figure. It washed over her in an overwhelming wave. For an instant she wanted to shriek in terror and then her chin came up and she forced herself to meet his contemptuous stare.

He halted, a bare yard away. Their eyes locked and Rowena felt the shock of it go through her like a knife.

'My lord! Remember where you are and put up your sword, I beg of you.'

The gentle voice of Father Wilfrid broke the spell that held Rowena in thrall and she tore her eyes free, her senses screaming.

'You, come with me. The priest is right; we cannot talk here.'

Rowena's lips tightened at his arrogance but she nodded her consent.

Without waiting to see if she followed, Hugh headed for the door.

'Father.' Rowena beckoned the priest to accompany her. 'Everyone else remain here until I send word it is safe.'

Emerging from the church, Rowena bit savagely on her lower lip to still its trembling.

He's got trained housecarls!

Her dismay swelled as she noted their well-polished weapons and efficient discipline. How could her pitifully few Saxons repulse this well-organised force?

A banner whipping in the wind attracted her attention. It bore the device of a silver swan held in a mailed fist against an azure background.

'What I have, I hold.'

Reading the words emblazoned on the banner, Rowena shuddered.

Edenwald had lost its best men in the two battles which had also destroyed her happiness. Most of those who had finally come straggling home were still recuperating from their wounds. It would be suicide to take on this professional troop!

'Shall we step inside the hall and talk?'

Rowena glowered at him, resenting his crisp demand. Did he think he could order her around?

But before she could correct this mistaken assumption, an elderly man ran forward and flung himself at her feet.

'My lady! Forgive me!'

'It's all right, Wulnoth,' Rowena said stiffly. 'Get up.'

'You ought to have him flogged.' Hugh spoke dispassionately. 'He was asleep at his post.'

God rot the man! Why did he have to be right?

'I would not dream of inflicting so harsh a punishment on such an old man.'

Embarrassment tinged Rowena's angry reply. Wulnoth's laziness had allowed the enemy within their gates, but she knew the real fault was hers. She ought to have assigned the task to someone more capable. It was no excuse to say that she had been too preoccupied arranging today's celebration to mark the birth of the first child born since the men marched away.

Rowena's hands clenched into fists of anguish. She should have been more vigilant!

The pedlar had warned that the Normans were in the vicinity and she'd ordered a strict watch to be kept. After a while they had heard that the enemy had left for London and they had thought that danger had passed Edenwald by. Their guard had slackened.

Now they must pay for that folly.

'Well? Do we stand out here all day?'

The impatience in Hugh de Lacy's tone forced Rowena to concentrate. She needed to know his plans. There was no chance of beating him in a straight fight, but perhaps she could outwit him?

For the moment, she must not antagonise this man. He held every advantage and they both knew it.

Silently, she turned and led the way to the Great Hall. Reaching its wide doors, she halted.

'Just you. He stays outside,' she said curtly, pointing at the shorter knight who had dogged their footsteps.

Hugh frowned. 'Very well, but the priest waits outside too.'

Rowena hesitated and then nodded, smiling reassurance at the worried-looking Father Wilfrid, who mouthed, 'Be careful,' at her.

Hugh issued a rapid stream of orders and Rowena listened, catching the odd word here and there and wishing her knowledge of French were greater. There had been no time of late for lessons with Father Wilfrid. Those halcyon days had ended when she had taken up her father's duties, but she would have to resume her studies. It put her at a disadvantage not knowing what was being said.

Hugh followed her into the hall and Rowena immediately turned to confront him.

'Why are you here?'

'I told you. This is my land. I have come to claim it.'

Rowena's eyes blazed with rage and for an instant Hugh half expected her to spring at him, but she managed to control herself. 'You have no right to do so,' she said coldly.

Hugh raised his eyebrows.

'You are lying,' Rowena added desperately.

He decided to ignore this insult and proceeded to remove his helmet and mailed hood with a leisurely air that infuriated her. Did he think himself so safe that he could dispense with precaution?

Of course he felt safe! He had armed men guarding the hall!

Rowena watched helplessly as he placed his weapons on one of the benches. His calm certainty made her afraid.

'Now, why on earth did they pick a little hellcat like you as their leader?' Hugh enquired pleasantly, folding his arms across his broad chest and surveying her with interest.

Rowena gasped as his meaning sank in.

'My father was the thegn of Edenwald,' she answered indignantly, forgetting her resolve not to antagonise him. 'Now it is mine and you have no right to be here, Norman dog!'

His mouth tightened. 'That's the second time you've insulted me, wench. I advise you to watch your words more carefully from now on. There is a limit to my patience.'

Rowena stared back at him defiantly, hiding her fear. She longed to continue hurling abuse at him, but there was something in his expression that prevented her.

'Good. I'm glad you can see sense,' Hugh remarked drily. 'Since you doubt me, believe this.' He withdrew a scroll from beneath his hauberk and held it out to her. 'Edenwald and all the land surrounding it, including the small manor named Wynburgh, have been gifted to me by Duke William of Normandy.'

Rowena scanned it rapidly and, to his astonishment, Hugh realised that she could actually read.

Rowena handed the document back.

'Your Duke cannot give away what he does not own. The true lord of Wynburgh is dead, but Edenwald is mine,' she repeated.

Her cool insistence aroused a flicker of reluctant admiration in Hugh. She had courage, he'd give her that. But she was mistaken.

He shook his dark head. 'All England belongs to the Duke. The land of those Saxons who fought against him at Hastings has been confiscated. In his mercy, the Duke is prepared to restore property, on payment of a suitable fine, to those who swear loyalty to him, but this leniency cannot apply in your father's case.' Hugh paused fractionally. 'He did fall in battle, didn't he?'

Bitter laughter answered him.

'My father died fighting the Norse at Stamford Bridge. He was never at Hastings.'

'But I was told——' Angrily, Hugh bit off the rest of his reply.

Rowena regarded him with a mocking smile.

'I warn you, don't try to trick me. You will regret it,' Hugh snapped.

'I'll leave such underhand behaviour to you Normans,' she retorted.

Hugh's black brows drew together. 'Keep a more civil tongue in your head if you wish to preserve it intact, wench!'

'Go ahead, Hugh de Lacy. Use torture like your master. It will be even easier than Alençon — there are only old men, women and children to conquer here!'

The scorn in her voice acted on him like a lash.

'Be silent!'

Sure that he was about to strike her, Rowena recoiled involuntarily, fright blanching the colour out of her thin cheeks.

Hugh lowered his raised arm.

'Get back to your loom, girl,' he said with a sigh of wry exasperation. 'And do not meddle in matters beyond your understanding. I shall deal with one of the village elders.'

'You cannot dismiss me so easily!' Rowena glared at him, forgetting her fear. He thought she was a child! 'My people will not listen to you unless I tell them to.'

'Then get it into your thick Saxon skull that I am master here!' Hugh roared. 'You will obey me!'

'Never!' Rowena screamed back at him.

Greatly tempted to haul her over his knee and beat some sense into her, Hugh swung away, breathing hard.

Rowena regarded his mailed back with trepidation. Oh, God, what would he do to her? Her whole body was aching with tension and the effort needed to stop her teeth from chattering. The aura of power that this man radiated was frightening. He scared her. He didn't even look like any of the men she knew. His strange short hair and clean-shaven face were unnatural. If she didn't get away from him soon, she might sink to her knees and start babbling for mercy!

Hugh was thinking rapidly. William had told him that he wanted to create a new integrated society in this land. He had warned his knights to conduct themselves as befitted Christians. They were to uphold the good name of Normandy. Already he had prohibited brawling and looting and ordered that women were not to be molested.

This policy was partly dictated by the Duke's genuine piety—he was generous to the church and he frowned upon excessive drinking and brothels—but it also showed good sense. Treat the natives harshly and you risked rebellion. It would not help his position as Edenwald's new lord if he strung up its erstwhile mistress as she so richly deserved!

He turned back to face her, his expression impassive.

'Give me your word that you won't try to cause trouble, and I will allow you your liberty while I decide what to do with you.'

Rowena stared at him suspiciously. 'And if I refuse?'

'Then I will confine you until you see reason.'

Rowena clenched her fists impotently. 'And my people?' she asked in a tight voice.

'Don't worry. I won't inflict unnecessary suffering on *my* villeins. I intend to see to it that this place is run properly.'

Goaded by his mocking tone, Rowena snapped, 'Edenwald doesn't need Norman interference.'

'No?' Hugh leant towards her with a suddenness that made Rowena jump. 'You little fool, you don't realise how lucky you have been! That forest out there is full of outlaws and brigands just itching to get their hands on a fat plum like this. An old dotard to watch your gates and not one man guarding the palisade; is that your idea of good government? Anyone could have walked in here.'

'Better if it had been outlaws. At least they would have been English!' Rowena flung back at him.

Hugh growled a French curse.

'You need to learn better manners, wench!' he said, and shouted for his lieutenant.

Odo de Nevil came lumbering into the hall at a run.

God's teeth, but what had the girl said to put that black look on Hugh's face?

He wasn't given a chance to ask.

'Confine her in her usual sleeping-quarters. Set a guard and see to it that no one enters without my permission,' Hugh barked.

Odo nodded and reached out to put a large hand on Rowena's shoulder.

She shook it off. 'Don't touch me, Norman pig!' she spat and with her chin held high swept past him, heading for the doors.

Odo shot a startled look at Hugh. 'God's teeth!' he muttered and hurried after her.

Alone, Hugh wiped a hand across his brow.

'What the devil am I to do with that little hellcat?' he exclaimed in exasperation. She would have the place about his ears if he wasn't careful!

Shrugging irritably, he thrust the problem aside for the moment. He'd deal with her later. For now, he wished to acquaint himself with his prize.

His gaze roamed the hall. It was a splendid building, strongly constructed from massive log-posts with timber planking between and an impressive sixty feet long and thirty wide by his reckoning. The floor was strewn with rushes, recently sweetened, to judge by their fresh smell, and a good fire burnt on the large central hearth.

Hugh smiled in approval.

One day he would raise a castle here, but for now there was nothing to complain of. . .except that obstinate wench!

The frown returned to his lean face. It was foolish of him, but something about her had snared his attention. God knew what! She was no beauty. Her eyes were lovely, but she was too thin and, anyway, she was only a child.

But her hostility was not childish.

Hugh found he was staring at several lighter patches discolouring the walls. Once weapons must have hung there. Weapons that had vanished along with their owners.

A faint sigh escaped him. No wonder she hated them and yet hadn't she declared that her father had died at Stamford Bridge? That claim might bear investigation.

Slowly Hugh walked to the end of the hall and lifted the deerskin curtain. The rich furnishings confirmed his guess that here were the private living-quarters of the lord of the manor.

Very well, he would make them his own. This was his property and he'd be damned if he'd let that skinny little creature interfere with his enjoyment of it or his plans for the future.

'Oh, my lady, are you all right? I've been worried sick!'

Elgiva's cry greeted Rowena as she was thrust inside the bower and the door slammed shut.

Rowena managed a weak smile and sank down thankfully on to a stool.

Elgiva stared at her anxiously. 'What did that brute say, my lady? What are they going to do to us?'

Rowena shook her head wearily. 'I don't know,

Elgiva. He claims that Duke William has given our land to him.'

'His men are counting every pig and sack of grain,' Elgiva informed her.

'What shall I do?' Rowena put out an imploring hand to her nurse. 'If I counsel resistance, our people will be killed!'

Elgiva patted her shoulder comfortingly. 'You'll think of something, my lady,' she said stoutly. 'Everyone knows how clever you are.'

Rowena struggled to quell her panic. Clever! She didn't feel in the least bit clever. Her head felt empty and she was sick to her stomach. That dreadful man had meant every frightening word he'd said!

'Shall I bring you some ale, my lady? You look as if you could do with it.'

Rowena nodded, curbing the urge to give way to hysterics. She couldn't afford such luxury right now.

'De Lacy wants me to promise obedience,' she told Elgiva, taking the beaker from her. 'If I don't, he'll keep me shut away.'

'The cheek of the man!'

Elgiva's loyal indignation warmed Rowena's bruised feelings. She began to relax and immediately an idea stirred in her head. 'Perhaps Father Wilfrid might know of a way.'

A doubtful sniff greeted her suggestion.

'The good father lives up in the clouds, my lady, you know that.'

'Then Oswald?'

'I swear your father only kept him on as reeve out of pity, my lady. When there were plenty of young backs to do the work, his mistakes were less obvious, but now. . .' Elgiva's voice trailed off miserably.

Reluctantly, Rowena conceded that her nurse was right.

There was no one to turn to, no one she could rely on.

'How I wish Godric were here! With a few trained warriors, we could have made that arrogant swine eat his insults.' Tears sparkled in Rowena's eyes, but she refused to let them fall and after a moment she'd recovered enough to add, 'I wonder if we could poison their food?'

Elgiva gasped. Dear God, the child would imperil her immortal soul! 'I reckon it wouldn't work, my lady,' she said carefully. 'That Norman looks a sharp one. I'll wager he'd sniff out such trickery.'

'Perhaps you are right,' Rowena sighed. 'But I've got to think of something, and soon.'

A sudden knock at the door made them twitch in alarm.

'Open it,' Rowena ordered, rising to her feet.

'Father Wilfrid.' Rowena glanced anxiously at the soldier guarding the door, but the priest smiled at her reassuringly.

'De Lacy has given his permission for me to speak to you for a few minutes,' he said, closing the door behind him and coming into the room. 'He said it might help you to a proper womanly submissiveness.'

Rowena snorted and then, remembering her manners, invited the priest to sit down.

'Well, Father, have you any idea how we are going to get rid of these accursed Normans?' she asked.

'My child, I don't think we can.'

A mutinous glower greeted his reply and Father Wilfrid restrained a weary sigh. Could he persuade her to face the unpleasant facts?

'If you submit to his authority, de Lacy swears he will

treat you well. Not that he would dare do otherwise; it would cause too much unrest.'

Rowena ignored this shrewd comment. 'I won't swear loyalty to save my own neck,' she replied through clenched teeth. 'I'd rather raze Edenwald to the ground than hand it over to that man!'

Father Wilfrid shuddered. He was of good birth and had travelled widely in his youth but, unlike other more worldly clerics, he was a gentle, scholarly man. Given to fasting and penance rather than the pursuit of power, violence was abhorrent to him.

'You are bitter, my child, and no wonder, but violence never solves anything,' he said softly. 'How would your people manage without their home?'

Rowena shrugged, avoiding his gaze. She hadn't really meant that threat, but her tone was resentful as she exclaimed, 'You think I should submit, don't you?'

He nodded. 'I know it is hard, but sometimes God requires great sacrifices of us. If you do not acknowledge de Lacy, it will cause hardship to all at Edenwald. The village will follow your lead and de Lacy will punish them for their disobedience.'

A look of doubt passed over her troubled face and Father Wilfrid knew he was reaching her. 'Don't let stubbornness tempt you into the sin of pride, my child,' he continued with all the persuasion he could muster.

Rowena stared at him uncertainly. De Lacy had treated her like a child and she had detested it. Was hurt pride affecting her judgement?

'Remember your promise to your father. He left Edenwald in your care. Do you want the Norman to destroy us?'

'He wouldn't dare.' Rowena's mouth trembled.

'He might, if you provoke him! Oh, Rowena, listen to

me,' Father Wilfrid pleaded. 'He has the power of life
and death over all of us, the power to do anything he
wants without fear of reprisal. Only the Duke himself
could countermand his orders.'

'Then I shall appeal to Duke William.' A shaky laugh
escaped Rowena's lips. 'You told me yourself that he is
reputed to be a fair man. If he really intends to deal
justly with the people of England, then he will have to
uphold my claim to my inheritance.'

Father Wilfrid goggled at her in horror.

'Are you mad, child? I know I said that the Duke was
a good ruler, but he won't favour you above one of his
own knights!' The priest gazed in despair at the stubborn expression on her face. 'And besides, how do you
propose to put your case before him when he is in
London and you are confined to your bower?'

'I shall persuade my lord de Lacy to release me,'
Rowena retorted with a determination that silenced his
objections.

'Then you'd best attend supper in the Great Hall
tonight,' Father Wilfrid murmured helplessly. 'De Lacy
asked me to tell you that he wanted you present.'

Rowena grinned suddenly. 'You see? He's already
begun to realise that he can't afford to keep me locked
up. Threats will only work so far; he needs my co-
operation to run Edenwald.' Triumph coloured her
tone. 'Don't fret; I shall inveigle him into letting me go.
He's only a Norman; he won't suspect what I'm up to.'

Father Wilfrid exchanged a worried look with Elgiva.
For Rowena's own sake, he could only hope she was
right in her low estimation of Hugh de Lacy's intelligence but privately he doubted it!

* * *

The warmth inside the Great Hall was almost over-whelming. A log fire roared on the stone hearth, shedding light and scorching heat while torches flared with smoky brilliance all round the walls.

Rowena paused for a moment to catch her breath. Crossing the courtyard she'd shivered even in her squirrel-furred mantle for the ground was hard with frost and she wouldn't be surprised if it snowed soon.

'Come, Lady Rowena. Join me.'

The command rang out from the dais where Hugh de Lacy sat at his ease in the high carved chair that had been her father's.

The surge of anger that shot through her gave Rowena the courage to ignore the curious glances cast her way by the soldiers seated at the long trestle-tables set up along the sides of the hall. She marched past them, her chin held high, and Elgiva panted at her heels, struggling to keep up.

Hugh could read the thoughts snapping in her eyes and his mouth twisted, amusement mingling with a sudden stab of sympathy.

He had half expected that she would fling his invitation in his teeth, but she had come and taken the trouble to dress in something better than the plain gown she'd had on earlier.

He rose to his feet to welcome her, his keen gaze flicking assessingly over her bright blue overtunic. The finest spun wool and, unless he was mistaken, the jewelled circlet that confined her delicately embroid-ered veil was made of gold, as was the heavy, ornately enamelled brooch pinning her mantle.

She no longer looked like a peasant wench, but her eyes still smouldered with hostility.

Rowena returned his appraising look with a pretence

of haughty indifference, but she was very aware of it. . .and of him. He had shed his armour and was wearing a simple knee-length red tunic over a yellow linen shirt and ankle-tied braies, but he still radiated that sense of raw power.

'Sit here on my left, Lady Rowena,' Hugh said pleasantly.

Rowena hesitated. In any well-conducted Saxon household it was normal for the ladies to dine at a separate table, but perhaps Normans did things differently. In any event, since she did not want to offend him, she had better agree to sit next to him.

She moved to take her place and Hugh motioned dismissal to the plump maid that hovered so protectively at her side. Elgiva returned his glance solidly and remained where she was until Rowena nodded.

Hugh's mouth tightened.

Rowena hid her satisfaction and turned her attention to scanning the hall. There were no Saxons present, apart from the serving-thralls and Father Wilfrid, who was also seated at the high table, next to the man called de Nevil.

Another younger knight sat at the high table. Rowena couldn't remember having seen him before. He affected the strange cropped hairstyle and clean-shaven face of the other Normans, but his colouring was almost Saxon-fair.

At that moment he glanced up and noticed her regard. A wide grin split his smooth, boyish face.

Involuntarily, Rowena returned his smile.

'Will you try some of our wine?'

Hugh's abrupt question recalled Rowena to her senses and she flushed as she realised what she was doing.

'No, thank you. I have no taste for French imports.'

Hugh waved away the serving-maid. 'I'm glad to hear it,' he answered with distinct irony.

Rowena stared at him indignantly. Did he think she was trying to flirt with his young lieutenant? She wouldn't demean herself!

Hugh observed the play of expressions flickering over her face. Good, she understood him, but all the same he'd have that warning word with young de Beaumont. The last thing he needed was for Gerard to seduce the wretched girl!

One of the thralls came up to heap roasted meat on to Rowena's plate. Her hands were shaking with nerves and Rowena smiled reassuringly at her.

'You eat well here,' Hugh observed. He eyed the fine silver plate and the precious glass goblets that came from the East, items normally hoarded for feast-days. 'Better than I expected.'

Rowena inclined her head in gracious acceptance of his compliment. She had raided the best of the winter stores for this feast, which was to have been a thanksgiving marking a new beginning for Edenwald, but she wasn't going to tell him that.

They ate in silence for a while, but Rowena was too worried to have much appetite and she soon pushed her plate aside.

'Not hungry, my lady?' Hugh enquired. 'Or do you fear I might poison you?'

Rowena smiled at him sweetly. 'This meal was prepared by my own cooks.'

'And served under the supervision of my guards,' he agreed smoothly. 'An arrangement which will stand until I give the order otherwise.'

The flicker in her lovely eyes confirmed his suspicion

that she had considered ridding Edenwald of their presence by such means.

He raised his goblet. 'To our mutual good health, Lady Rowena. Long may it continue.'

Rowena met Father Wilfrid's worried gaze. He too had understood that dulcet warning. Should any of his men fall prey to sudden sickness, de Lacy would blame her.

She took a nervous swallow at her mead. Had she underestimated this man? He seemed to have an uncanny ability to guess what she was thinking.

'With regard to provisions, I have been questioning your steward,' Hugh remarked. 'He seems strangely lacking in knowledge. Or did you somehow manage to tell him to flout my orders?'

Rowena wanted to say that she wished she had but she confined herself to a cautious shake of her head.

'In that case the fellow is an incompetent fool.'

'Oswald has served this household since before you were born!'

'Then it's time he retired.' Hugh's voice was hard. 'I'll not keep men in my hall who are too old or too lazy to work.'

Rowena's goblet trembled in her clasp.

'You'll. . .you'll not harm him?'

Hugh stared at her impassively, but triumph sang in his veins. Here was this proud little hellcat's weak spot! She truly cared for these peasants.

'My lord, may I be permitted to speak?' Father Wilfrid's gentle voice broke the silence. At Hugh's nod, he continued, 'It would be a grievous thing to turn such an old man out. Homeless and masterless, he would never survive, but he gave many years of devoted service until the burden grew too great for him.'

Hugh considered the matter for a moment.

'Loyalty always deserves a reward. Very well. He may stay if there is someone to take him in.'

'Oh, there is plenty of room to spare at Edenwald these days,' Rowena announced with a bitterness she couldn't conceal.

Father Wilfrid shot her an imploring look and she fell silent, fighting down the urge to hurl the contents of her cup into that arrogant Norman face.

'Oswald has a married daughter living in the village. I am sure she will welcome her father into her home,' the elderly priest continued.

'Then I'll see that she does not lose by it,' Hugh said unexpectedly.

A small purse was in order, he decided. He would not have these folk think him niggardly. But he hadn't changed his mind.

'However, he is dismissed from my service from this day forth.'

Rowena gritted her teeth against the protest she longed to make. *His* service! She had vowed to keep her tongue sweet, but how much more of this could she endure?

The meal seemed endless but at last it was concluded and Hugh waved the serving-wenches away.

Watching the men not on duty eyeing them as they left the hall, Rowena said abruptly, 'I trust you will keep your housecarls in order, my lord. My thralls are used to decent men.'

Hugh raised his dark eyebrows at her. 'Do gently born Saxon maidens normally discuss fornication at the dinner-table?'

Rowena flushed at the sarcasm in his deep voice but

she stuck doggedly to her request. 'I do not want them abused.'

'Then it should relieve your mind that I have already given orders that none of the women is to be molested, free-born or slave.'

'Thank you.' The words stuck in her throat and almost choked her.

'I'll hang any man who commits rape,' Hugh continued as if she hadn't spoken, 'but don't blame me if a lusty crop sprouts nine months hence. Your Saxons have been gone a long time and some of those wenches look more than willing.'

Rowena bounced to her feet. Oh, how dared he make such a vile claim? 'Goodnight, my lord.'

'Wait!'

His sharp command halted Rowena's precipitate exit.

'I wish to talk to you.' Hugh descended from the dais and moved to the deerskin curtain. 'In here.'

Rowena hesitated and then, gathering her courage, nodded consent. 'And my maid?'

'She can wait with the priest. You don't need a chaperon. I practise what I preach and anyway you are too young to appeal to me.' There was a grim amusement in his voice.

He stood waiting, holding the curtain aside, and, fuming with the rage she dared not utter, Rowena walked towards him. She had to pass close to enter the private chamber and with a flicker of surprise realised that he was taller than she had thought. She had compared him to Godric and her father and found him wanting but in truth he must stand nigh on six feet high.

Covertly, Rowena studied him as he moved briskly to check that the iron brazier which heated the room was burning properly.

Now that she had grown more used to it, his clean-shaven face no longer seemed so shocking. Naturally, any right-thinking woman would prefer a man with a good beard and moustache but perhaps some might find him attractive, lacking though he was.

He didn't have Godric's regular, clear features but there was strength of character in his wide brow and that strong chin, so firm that it made his well-shaped mouth seem almost sensual in contrast. His nose had been broken at some time and it had healed slightly crooked but he had excellent teeth, very white in his weather-burnt face.

He's got the sort of olive skin which takes the sun easily, Rowena decided, and wondered how old he was. There were a few lines about his strange-coloured eyes but his thick, springing hair was free of grey threads. It was as black as midnight.

Could he be as old as thirty? He had all the authority of a mature man — his men jumped to obey his lightest word — but his tall body moved with a lithe grace that spoke of youth. Or maybe that was the result of hard exercise? He hadn't got those muscles in his arms and broad shoulders by wielding a pen! They proclaimed him a warrior and she had the instinctive feeling that he was a very good one.

Rowena gave up. That indefinable aura of power, which hung over him like a cloak, made it hard to judge his age. It didn't really matter. Like his master, the Wolf of Normandy, Hugh de Lacy was a ruthless, dangerous man.

'Be seated.' Hugh remained standing but he waited courteously until she was settled before continuing. 'Have you thought over what I said, my lady? Will you give me your word not to cause trouble?'

Rowena shifted awkwardly in her chair and glared at him. She had planned to promise him anything he asked so long as she could win her freedom but, now it came to it, the words stuck in her throat.

'Your hostility cannot stem from your father's death.' Hugh regarded her through narrowed eyes. 'If what you told me was true, of course.'

'Is your presence here not enough to explain it?' Rowena countered.

His mouth thinned at her sarcasm but he did not lose his temper.

The silence stretched out between them and Rowena was uncomfortably reminded of the patience shown by a cat playing with a mouse.

'The man I was to have married was slain at Hastings. Does that satisfy your curiosity?' she snapped, provoked at last into answering him.

'Who was he?' Hugh enquired, displaying no sign of embarrassment.

'What does his name matter to you?' Rowena shrugged angrily. 'He is dead.'

Hugh inclined his dark head. 'As you say, it is none of my concern.' There was no need to pursue the issue. He had the information he wanted. She bore them a personal grudge.

Had she loved her slain warrior? Or had the match been arranged to suit the thegn's convenience? For all her vehemence, somehow she didn't seem grief-stricken in the manner of a woman who had lost her lover. Perhaps she was too young for such emotions.

How old was she, anyway? Fourteen? Fifteen?

Hugh regarded her with fresh interest. Her thin features were immature but her eyes were the bluest he had ever seen, and he'd encountered plenty of blue-eyed maidens in this new land. Was she blonde-haired too beneath that concealing veil? Although her eyelashes and brows were a pleasing brown, surely her hair must be fair or it would show through the delicate material.

'Are you a rich man?'

Rowena's abrupt question cut through his idle musing like a knife but Hugh managed to hide his surprise.

'Why do you ask, my lady?'

Rowena coloured, realising how forward she must sound. Saints defend me, but my mother must be weeping from shame! she chided herself.

'Is it an English custom perhaps?'

'I wish you would take me seriously and stop treating me like a child.' Rowena's eyes acquired a dangerous sparkle at his amused tone. 'My reason for asking is sound.'

'Then let me hear it.' Hugh sat down, his air expectant.

Rowena moistened her dry lips. 'Would you accept silver instead of Edenwald?'

He raised his dark brows. 'Don't you think it a little unwise to dangle that carrot in front of my nose? What is to stop me discovering your hidden store and keeping both?'

Rowena flushed, cursing her own stupidity. 'I thought you might be a man of honour,' she flung at him angrily.

His mouth tightened. '*If* I gave you my word, I would keep it,' he growled in retort. 'But I'm not a fool, lady. I don't need to promise you anything. Everything here at Edenwald already belongs to me. It is mine by right of conquest!'

The vehemence in his tone shook Rowena to the core.

'Why? Why do you want Edenwald so much?' she gasped. 'You must have other homes.'

Hugh stood up abruptly. 'Enough of your chatter, wench. Will you promise to behave yourself or do you remain a prisoner in your bower?'

Rowena stared at him. She had failed. He wasn't going to take the silver and go.

However, there was more than one way to skin a rabbit!

She rose gracefully to her feet. 'I promise I won't cause trouble here at Edenwald,' she said sweetly.

'See that you don't.' He glared at her. 'And I'll have the keys to the storerooms off you. Oswald claimed you held them.'

Rowena curbed the desire to scream. 'I'll send them to you in the morning, my lord,' she said meekly, sweeping him a deferential curtsy. 'Now, may I have your leave to retire?'

Hugh nodded. He watched her go, wondering why she smiled.

CHAPTER THREE

'MY LADY, don't go. It is madness!'

'Your protests won't change my mind, Elgiva. All you are doing is delaying me and increasing the risk that I might get caught,' Rowena answered firmly, pulling on the stoutest pair of boots she owned.

'What if Ethelwine Alfredsdaughter won't give you an escort?' Elgiva wailed.

'Then I'll ride to London alone!' Rowena snapped, and then relented at the expression of horror on her nurse's face. 'Oh, Elgiva, do you think I want to plead my case before Duke William?' she sighed. 'I know my chance of succeeding is slight but I've got to try. How else can I keep Edenwald safe?'

'At least let me come with you.'

Rowena shook her head and moved to the door.

'No, I won't involve you. It is too dangerous if things go wrong. I have my rank to protect me. De Lacy is ruthless but he isn't a complete barbarian. I doubt if he will harm me.' Rowena tried to sound more confident than she felt.

She cracked open the door of her bower and peered out. It was later than she'd thought. The sky was already streaked with dawn but at least de Lacy had removed the guard outside her door as he had promised. For the moment, she was free.

Elgiva crept up beside her.

'Take care, my lamb,' she whispered. 'And God go with you!'

59

Rowena smiled at her gratefully. 'Remember, I was gone before you awoke. You know nothing.'

Elgiva nodded and Rowena slipped out of the bower like a wraith.

Dressed in a dark grey mantle borrowed from her nurse, she merged into the shadows as she crept towards the dark safety of the hall entrance porch. Blending into the furthest corner, she watched the gates and waited.

As she had feared, the gates were guarded but soon they would open to permit the busy life of the community to go on. Thralls would leave their sleeping-mats in the hall and bustle about drawing water and tending the beasts and the village folk would enter, bringing in produce for the household and their own loaves of bread for baking in the communal bake-house at the rear of the kitchens.

It was her intention to mingle with the crowd. In her shabby clothes the Normans would not recognise her. She would just be another peasant returning to the fields.

To her relief, she didn't have to wait long. The guard was plainly anxious to break his fast. He opened the gate and stood impatiently, ready to hand over to the next man.

'Shush!' Rowena laid a finger to her lips in a swift gesture to stifle the exclamations of surprise from a group of thralls, who emerged yawning and blinking into the grey daylight. 'You haven't seen me,' she ordered in a fierce whisper.

They nodded, quickly understanding that their mistress was hiding from the hated Normans.

Rowena merged into their midst and they all moved off across the courtyard. As they neared the gates, a group of villagers entered, one of them struggling with a plump goose, destined for the Norman high table.

Rowena drew level with the gate and, as if in answer to her silent prayers, the goose broke loose. It flapped across the courtyard with a frantic honking and its owner and his friends gave chase.

It was the perfect moment. The guard was distracted, all his attention focused on the opposite direction and Rowena slipped away to freedom.

'Lady Rowena? What are ye doing here? Have ye no escort?'

The old manservant stared at her, shock written on his lined face.

Rowena had come by the forest tracks that led to Wynburgh. She was breathless and red-faced with exertion, her appearance equally dishevelled, but she ignored his scandalised mutterings. 'Is Lady Ethelwine in the hall?' she demanded.

'Nay, she's in her bower.' Rowena whirled and he added hastily, 'She's busy, my lady. No one is allowed in.'

Rowena shrugged away his protests and hurried towards the snug dwelling where Godric's mother lived with her two daughters.

Leoba, Godric's younger sister, answered her impatient knock.

'Rowena?' Her pleasant round face mirrored the servant's astonishment but she recovered quickly. 'We have a guest, Mother,' she called.

Ushered into the hot, stuffy room, Rowena braced herself. If only Godric's mother didn't dislike her, it would make this difficult task easier!

'Why have you come?' Ethelwine's greeting was stark.

A retort burned on Rowena's lips but she curbed it.

Ethelwine was seated in the only chair in the room. She was a tall, statuesque woman, richly gowned and hung with jewellery, her expression disdainful.

She doesn't want me here, Rowena thought, acutely aware of the dislike that glittered in the older woman's eyes. She never approved of Godric's wish to marry me.

Deliberately, she forced her resentment down. Soon she would have to tell them the bad news that William had given Wynburgh to the Normans but first she needed to secure Ethelwine's assistance, so she made her tone polite as she replied, 'I'm here to seek your help.'

'Why?' Ethelwine regarded her with suspicion.

'Mother, I think we ought to ask Rowena to sit down. She looks exhausted,' Leoba said with quiet insistence.

Recalled to her duties as hostess, Ethelwine nodded ungraciously. 'Have you broken your fast? No? Then you must eat.'

Thankfully, Rowena collapsed on to a wide, fur-covered stool and Wulfhild, the younger girl, brought ale. 'Shall I fetch you something from the kitchens?'

Rowena refused. She was too tense to feel hunger but the ale was cool to her dry throat and she drank it thirstily. Setting her beaker aside, she noticed the disordered state of the room for the first time.

'We are packing.' Unbidden, Wulfhild supplied the answer to the puzzlement in their guest's face. It earned her a dark look of reproof from her mother.

'You are leaving Wynburgh?' Rowena's eyes widened.

'Aye, we are going north. To my brother's hall,'

Ethelwine said harshly. Her beringed hands clenched on her skirts. 'My son is dead but my daughters need husbands. I am taking them north to find them. North, where I've kin to protect us and where we can live free of the accursed Norman.'

For a brief moment, grief ravaged her stern face and sympathy flared in Rowena but she was given no opportunity to express it.

'So, if you have come seeking my aid to help you run Edenwald, Rowena Edwinsdaughter, you are too late. God's blood, I haven't even the manpower to till my own fields!' She flung out an angry hand. 'What will happen to my girls if I stay? Who is there left to marry them? Without sons-in-law, who will look after the land?'

She sighed and shook her head, her anger collapsing. 'Think me weak if you wish but I see no point in staying. It is better we leave now, taking all that we can. Otherwise, in the end, the Normans will dispossess us or we will be reduced to living like churls amid the ruin.'

The despair in her voice stilled Rowena's tongue.

Godric's mother was running away. She would take as many of her people as she could but the rest would have to fend for themselves. She was abandoning Wynburgh but she hated the necessity.

A faint unworthy relief filled Rowena. If Ethelwine was leaving, then there was no need to add to her misery by telling her that the Norman usurper she feared was already here. Let her depart with her pride intact. With any luck, she would be gone before de Lacy had time to turn his attention to Wynburgh.

'You misunderstand my errand,' Rowena said gently. 'I need only a horse and perhaps a couple of reliable men.'

'Have all the horses at Edenwald gone lame?' Ethelwine demanded with a return to her usual asperity. 'Explain yourself, girl!'

Rowena did so, and a gleam of approval lit up Ethewine's hard eyes.

'I doubt if your scheme will work,' she said frankly, 'but for the first time I begin to understand what my son saw in you.'

Rowena winced at this two-edged compliment but quickly pressed home her advantage.

'Then you'll lend me what I require for my journey to London?'

'Aye. Wynburgh is not what it was but we can manage this much at least,' Ethelwine affirmed. 'I have a man who knows the road to London and you shall have one of our best ponies.'

Rowena understood. Ethelwine was a proud woman and it galled her to leave her home, even though she had convinced herself it was the right decision. Helping Rowena was balm to her pride.

'Thank you!'

'Don't thank me. I think your quest is doomed but I owe it to Godric's memory to help you.' Suddenly Ethelwine smiled. 'And you are not the book-stuffed little lackwit I thought. God aid you to defeat your usurper, Rowena Edwinsdaughter. You deserve to if only for your courage in trying!'

Relief washed over Rowena in such a giddy wave that for a moment she couldn't speak.

'Does your offer of breakfast still stand?' she asked at last with a catch in her voice. 'Suddenly I feel quite famished!'

'Wulfhild will bring you something while your escort

is made ready.' Ethelwine chuckled. 'Now, tell me more about how you escaped from Edenwald.'

Rowena obliged.

She would never be friends with the woman who should have been her mother-in-law but at least they would part on good terms and somehow she felt that somewhere in heaven Godric would be pleased.

'You will tell me where she has gone, old woman.'

Hugh de Lacy's voice was quiet but Elgiva shivered.

'I don't know, my lord,' she muttered. 'My mistress disappeared before I awoke.'

'You are lying.'

Hugh surveyed her with narrowed eyes and the hall fell quiet, awaiting the explosion of his wrath.

It was mid-morning. When the keys she had promised him had failed to appear, Hugh had sent a messenger to summon Lady Rowena to the hall. Unable to fulfil this task, the man had dragged Elgiva into Hugh's presence instead but Elgiva had stuck stubbornly to her story.

'Shall I beat the truth out of her, my lord?' enquired Odo de Nevil, who was seated on the dais at Hugh's side.

Hugh was tempted.

'No.' He shook his head. 'Not yet.' The woman's obstinacy was infuriating but he did not enjoy making war on the defenceless.

His gaze sought out a familiar face in the crowd of frightened Saxons, herded into the hall by his soldiers. 'You. Priest. Come here.'

Father Wilfrid took a deep breath to steady his nerves and obeyed.

'Do you know aught of this?'

'No, my lord.'

Hugh nodded, convinced. 'Very well. Now tell me, where do you suppose Lady Rowena has gone?'

Father Wilfrid hesitated. It went against the grain to lie but how could he put this man on to Rowena's scent?

'Answer me!' Hugh banged the palm of his hand down flat on to the table and the little priest jumped.

'I cannot, my lord,' he whispered miserably.

'If you do not, I shall hang the old woman.'

Elgiva screamed.

'My lord, you. . .you cannot!' Father Wilfrid began to sweat. 'It would be unjust.'

'Unjust?' Hugh trained a gimlet eye upon him. 'Do you think you can play at words with me, priest? Know this; I am the justice here. I can burn down this hall and hang every man, woman and child if I've a mind.'

Father Wilfrid gulped. He had warned Rowena of the danger of tangling with this man. Oh, why had she not listened?

'Well? Which is it to be?' Hugh demanded inexorably.

'She. . .she may be at Wynburgh,' the priest mumbled, unhappily aware of Elgiva's reproachful gaze.

Hugh rose swiftly. 'You shall be our guide,' he ordered and, ignoring Elgiva's venomous glances, he strode from the hall, snapping instructions as he went.

'Odo, come with me. Between us we should be able to take care of any escort she may have obtained. Gerard, you are in command here. See that everyone returns to their proper business. And confine that woman securely. I don't want her disappearing too.'

A few minutes later, they were mounted and riding through the gates.

'She has a good start on us, Hugh,' Odo observed. 'And the weather is milder today.'

'Aye, but she was on foot. She probably obtained a mount at Wynburgh but it would have taken time. I doubt if she can be far ahead,' Hugh replied.

Turning in the saddle, he addressed Father Wilfrid. 'Is there any way we can cut her off?'

The priest hesitated. 'If I tell you, what will you do to her?' he blurted.

'Set your mind at ease. I am not in the habit of hanging children.' Hugh's tone was dry. 'She is in more danger attempting such a hare-brained journey than she is from me.'

Odo snorted. 'The little hellcat deserves a thrashing,' he muttered. 'Wasting our time like this.'

Hugh shrugged. They could devise a suitable punishment later. What concerned him now, oddly enough, was Rowena's safety. Without a strong escort travel was always risky and a strange sense of urgency filled him. He had to find her before she ran into trouble!

They rode hard and soon reached the place Father Wilfrid had suggested. Dismounting, Hugh examined the ground. After yesterday's rain, there had been frost overnight but it had thawed in the pale sunshine and the track was soft. It bore no trace of recent travellers.

'I think we are in luck.' Hugh straightened and remounted.

He was scarcely settled in the saddle before they heard the sound of approaching hoofbeats.

'Quickly!' Hugh motioned them to take cover behind some trees.

A few moments later their quarry came into sight. Hugh's brows drew together in a frown. Curse it, but they were ambling along, laughing and talking, easy prey for any outlaw!

Rowena was feeling amazingly content. At last she was doing something positive instead of being forced to wait tamely upon events. She had escaped that dreadful man and her fate was in her own hands. In her present optimistic mood, it was actually possible to believe that her quest might succeed. Even the weather favoured her this morning!

'Lady Rowena.' Hugh urged his stallion forward, blocking the track.

At the sound of that hated voice Rowena's heart turned over. Damn! Damn! Damn! How had he found her so quickly?

One glance was all it took to show that there was no way to pass him so she sprang from her saddle. The woods were thick. On foot, she might shake off pursuit.

'Guard that man!' Hugh leapt after her.

Rowena accounted herself fleet-footed but to her terror she could hear him close behind. The breath sobbed in her throat as she dodged between the trees, weaving an erratic path through the undergrowth.

It was no use! He was catching up on her!

Suddenly, her skirts snagged on a briar.

'Stand still! You'll rip your hands to shreds.'

Rowena renewed her frantic struggles to free herself and Hugh swore colourfully as he knocked her hands aside and disentangled the clinging thorns.

He was in the act of straightening from this task when Rowena gave him a hard shove in the ribs. Taken by surprise, he went sprawling.

'Why, you little——' Hugh regained his feet and ran after her.

This time he caught her with ease.

'I ought to beat you,' he growled at her, holding her by the shoulders in a fierce grip.

Rowena's chin tilted and she met his angry gaze with a defiant stare. 'Do so. It won't make any difference to the way I despise you,' she replied breathlessly.

He shook her, hard. 'If you were a man, my lady, you'd regret those words.'

'If I were a man, I'd kill you!'

The fury in her eyes startled him. By the Rood, she meant it!

Reluctant admiration overcame Hugh's anger. What a spirit the wench had! 'I dare say you would at that,' he agreed drily, releasing her.

Thinking he mocked her, Rowena exploded and all the frustration and rage of the last twenty-four hours boiled forth.

'I hate you, Hugh de Lacy,' she cried at him bitterly. 'You claim to be a man of honour but you would steal my lands without the least shred of justification. My father never fought against Duke William and you have no right to Edenwald.'

She paused, gulping for breath. 'If you truly believe in honour, let go to London to plead my case before the Duke.'

Hugh stared at her in astonishment. 'Is that where you were heading?'

Rowena nodded. 'I only promised you that I would not foment trouble at Edenwald. I didn't promise not to escape.' Balling her hands on to her slim hips, she flung out a challenge. 'Well? Will you let me go to London?'

Hugh began to laugh.

'You little hellcat, I should wring your neck for your impudence!'

'Or are you afraid I might win my case?'

Abruptly, Hugh's amusement ceased.

'I agree. On one condition,' he snapped.

'Name it.'

'You must abide by the Duke's decision. Remember, if he finds in my favour, and I expect him to, you will have to cede all authority to me and cease from rebellion.'

Fear raced up Rowena's spine. She was agonisingly conscious that her chance of success was remote. Yet it was the only hope she had.

'I agree,' she said firmly, forcing aside her panic.

'Then come.'

Obediently, Rowena followed him back to where they had left the others.

She saw relief dawn on Father Wilfrid's face but before she could greet him Hugh said sharply, 'Wait here.'

She watched him stride towards the priest. He said something and she saw her chaplain hand over the simple wooden cross he wore.

'Now, I will have your oath, my lady,' Hugh announced, and before Rowena could protest he pulled her to him, capturing her right hand and enclosing her fingers within his so that they both gripped the cross.

'Swear that you will abide by the Duke's decision.'

Rowena tried to squirm free but his other arm shot about her waist and held her fast. Trapped against the broad wall of his chest, she could not move.

They were so close, she could feel the heat of him, smell the clean masculine scent of him, see the steady pulse beating at the base of his strong throat. . .

The blood pounded in her ears. In a daze, she lifted her gaze to meet his and surprised a fleeting expression of confusion in his ice-grey eyes.

'How do I know you will keep your side of the bargain?' she panted angrily, furious with herself for being affected by his nearness.

'I, Hugh de Lacy, swear to uphold the decision of my liege lord, William of Normandy.'

Hugh's voice was steady, giving no clue to the sudden inner turmoil he was experiencing.

Why had he never realised how soft and full her lips were until now? By the Rood, she wasn't as much of a child as he'd thought! In fact, one day, when she had grown out of this awkward, coltish stage, it wouldn't surprise him if she turned into a very beautiful woman indeed.

Fighting off the crazy impulse to lower his head and capture that delectable pink mouth with his own, Hugh said sternly, 'It is your turn, my lady.'

Submitting to the inevitable, Rowena gave the required oath and he immediately released her.

'We shall leave for London as soon as the arrangements for the journey can be completed,' he informed her.

Rowena stared at him, her bruised fingers forgotten.

'Do *you* intend to accompany me?'

'How else would you accomplish your scheme?' Hugh glanced scornfully at the escort she had borrowed. 'Without my help, I doubt if you'd get within a mile of William.'

Rowena longed to contradict him but she had the depressing feeling that he was right. However, she couldn't bring herself to thank him.

Correctly guessing her thoughts, Hugh's mouth twisted wryly. 'Mount up, my lady. We must return to Edenwald.' He paused and added, 'Where you will remain under guard until we leave.'

'There is no need to continue holding me a prisoner!'

'No? I have no fancy for a dagger-thrust between my ribs. I do not trust you, my little Saxon,' Hugh replied softly.

He gestured towards the horses and there was nothing left to do but turn and walk away with all the remaining dignity at her command.

They set out two days later on a freezing-cold morning. The iron-grey sky held the threat of snow but Hugh declared that since the road was open the journey would go ahead.

Elgiva was to accompany her but, at Rowena's request, Father Wilfrid had agreed to stay behind. He was concerned for Rowena's safety but since he was the only person who spoke French he was needed at Edenwald to act as an interpreter for Odo de Nevil, who was to oversee the estate in Hugh de Lacy's absence.

In spite of the early hour, the whole village turned out to wish her Godspeed and Rowena's eyes smarted with tears she was too proud to shed as she waved farewell.

'Your people love you, my lady.'

Rowena glanced at him quickly but Hugh de Lacy's dark face wore an enigmatic expression.

'I have ordered them to obey de Nevil,' she replied curtly. 'There will be no trouble while I am gone.'

'I hope not.' Hugh's tone was dry.

Unable to think of a cutting answer, Rowena urged her horse forward and soon Edenwald was left behind.

Moonlight, her little mare, was fresh and her friskiness taxed Rowena's skill. An hour into the journey and her wrists were aching. Even worse, the road was frozen into a thousand ruts, slowing their pace and spine-joltingly uncomfortable.

Rowena flicked a glance back to where Elgiva sat reluctantly on a shaggy pony. Her round face wore a scowl and Rowena had to restrain a giggle.

It was the only amusement she found all morning.

To her disappointment, this venture into the world beyond Edenwald didn't match up to her dreams. The freezing weather had kept other travellers at home and there was little to see except the vast expanse of forest they were skirting. The tall trees were certainly impressive but their stark branches swayed in the wind with a little moaning sound that was depressing.

The noise also made Moonlight nervous, making her skittish and hard to handle. Enviously, Rowena noted how easily Hugh de Lacy controlled his big black stallion. She had heard her father speak of the Normans' skill with horses and de Lacy seemed to bear those rumours out.

He rides as if he were one with that beast. No wonder the Wolf of Normandy uses cavalry in battle if all his riders are as good as him! she mused.

The thought brought her predicament surging into the forefront of her mind. She had tried to convey a ray of hope to her Saxons but in her heart Rowena knew that she needed a miracle. What would she do if the Duke said no?

By midday, Rowena was so cold and cramped that even this anxiety had taken second place to sheer physical discomfort. Huddling within her mantle, she tried to blow a little warmth on to her frozen fingers but her breath merely steamed in the icy air before being whisked away by the bitter wind. Even her thick wolfskin outer cloak and the soft leather leggings she wore beneath her skirts to prevent her skin from chafing were no protection against its penetrating gusts. She had forgotten her feet had ever existed!

Would they never stop and rest? She longed to request a halt, and her gaze sought out Hugh de Lacy, who was riding on slightly ahead. To her dismay, he was whistling a cheerful tune, seemingly oblivious of the weather.

Rowena gritted her teeth and attempted to pull her hood closer about her face. She would not display any weakness before that hateful man!

A few miles further on Hugh espied a sheltered spot where the road dipped down into a hollow, which was fringed by a coppice of oaks. They would screen out the worst of the wind, he decided, signalling for the small party to halt.

'We will stop here and eat,' he announced.

Ordering Gerard de Beaumont and the other men to collect wood to build a fire, he dismounted and came over to Rowena. 'Let me help you down,' he offered, noting how pinched and pale her face seemed.

'I prefer to manage by myself,' she replied haughtily.

Hugh shrugged and went to assist his men.

Rowena scrambled stiffly from the saddle, her joints protesting.

'Are you all right, my lady?' Elgiva came hurrying up.

Rowena stamped her feet to bring them back to life.

'Apart from being almost frozen solid, I am well enough. And you? Is that pony giving you trouble?'

Elgiva scowled. 'It is a stupid beast.' Her expression lightened. 'At least I am well-cushioned, my lady,' she said, patting her plump buttocks. 'You must be black and blue from bouncing over these misbegotten tracks!'

Rowena grinned but her smile faded when Hugh de Lacy beckoned her to join him. Her chin jerked up at his imperious summons but the crackling fire was too tempting a lure to resist.

A large flat rock made a handy seat and Rowena perched upon it gingerly. Elgiva sat next to her. When they were settled Hugh de Lacy said a brief grace and the food was handed round.

To her surprise, Rowena discovered that she was hungry.

'Thank you.' She took a hunk of bread from Gerard de Beaumont and tried not to think that it had been freshly baked at Edenwald only hours earlier.

There was cold meat and a ripe cheese to accompany the bread and Rowena's weariness faded as she ate.

'Strange, but this tastes even better than it does at home,' she remarked quietly to Elgiva.

'The fresh air has given you an appetite, my lady,' Hugh answered.

Rowena glared at him. 'I was speaking to my maid,' she said pointedly.

'Am I to assume you have no wish for my conversation?' Hugh's tone was innocent but his light eyes sparkled with malicious amusement.

Rowena blushed. He was making a mock of her again! Refusing to answer, she turned her attention to her meal.

Swallowing the last crumb of cheese, Rowena dusted off her hands and held them out to the fire, relishing its warmth. A sense of well-being crept over her. For the first time today she felt warm and relaxed. She stretched contentedly and strove to conceal her yawns.

Hugh watched her. She reminded him of a kitten basking in a patch of sunlight. How blue her eyes were!

Rowena suddenly became aware of his regard. She

sat up straighter, feeling ridiculously self-conscious, and said hastily, 'When do you expect us to arrive, my lord?'

'Before sundown, I hope.'

A leather bottle of ale was circling. Hugh took a swallow and handed it to Rowena.

Too thirsty to refuse, Rowena looked him in the eye and made a great show of wiping the top before raising it to her lips. At her side, Elgiva sucked in her breath.

Hugh felt himself redden but he would not give her the satisfaction of seeing that she had scored a hit.

'We have tarried long enough,' he said calmly, rising to his feet. He walked off towards the tethered horses, leaving Rowena with the uncomfortable feeling that she had been foolish to try and pay him out for his staring with such a childish trick.

The going was easier once they joined the old Roman road but it began to snow before they reached the outskirts of London. They entered the city by the Bishopsgate just as darkness was descending and the wind whipped the wet flakes into their faces with a persistence that made the last few miles seem like a hundred.

Rowena felt like crying with relief when they halted, her bad temper long forgotten in the wearying struggle against the elements. In the gloom it was difficult to pick out much of her new surroundings but she spotted an ivy bough hung up over the lintel of the doorway and realised that it must be a tavern.

Dismounting with difficulty, she followed the two Norman knights into the large building. A smell of roasting meat immediately titillated her nostrils.

'Go and sit by the fire.' Hugh de Lacy threw the order at her and turned away to shout for the landlord before Rowena could glare at him.

The landlord, a stout middle-aged Saxon who spoke mangled French, appeared to recognise his new guests.

'My lord de Lacy.' He bowed low and scurried to bring them mulled wine.

The taste prickled Rowena's tongue but she drank it, too grateful for its reviving warmth to insist on mead. She flung back her hood and rubbed her cold hands together, trying to listen to what Hugh was saying to the landlord.

After a few moments the landlord bowed himself away and Hugh turned to her.

'I've ordered him to prepare a chamber for you and your maid,' he said. 'We shall be sleeping near by but remember to bolt your door. This is a respectable inn, we have used it before, but knavery can happen anywhere.'

'Of course I shall bolt it! I am not a half-wit!'

Hugh's eyebrows quirked. 'Supper will be served in half an hour,' he murmured, the tiniest quiver in his voice.

Rowena glowered at him suspiciously but the advent of a serving-wench come to escort them to their room prevented her from demanding to know if he was laughing at her.

The tavern boasted an upper storey, allowing the landlord to provide the rare facility of private chambers, and it appeared that de Lacy's influence had secured a whole room for just the two of them. Thankful to be spared the ordeal of sharing with strangers, Rowena exchanged a relieved look with Elgiva.

The chamber into which they were ushered was small but well-appointed and their guide efficiently lit the dish-shaped lamp and checked that the brazier was working properly before saying, 'I'll bring you some hot washing-water in a minute, my lady.'

'Well, it's passably clean, I suppose,' Elgiva commented, once the girl had gone. She ran a finger for dust over the stools and inspected a blanket from one of the pallets. 'I reckon we could have fared worse.'

Rowena nodded, recognising from her nurse's tone that Elgiva was impressed but unwilling to admit that Hugh de Lacy had done them proud.

'Do you think I should change into a finer gown?' she asked uncertainly.

'You need to get out of those damp clothes at any rate.' Elgiva opened the small wicker hamper that had been slung over the back of one of the ponies. 'It's a pity we didn't have time to sew a new outfit for you. You are growing out of everything, my lamb.'

She fished out a green roc. 'Wear this over your tawny kirtle tonight and save your crimson for your meeting with the Duke. You'll want to look your best then.'

Rowena winced. The less she thought about *that* the better!

The maid returned with the promised hot water and Elgiva helped Rowena change and tidy herself.

'Faugh, this fish-oil stinks!' Rowena laughed, picking up the little coarse pottery lamp to light their way.

The stairs were dark and she held the lamp aloft as she descended with Elgiva at her heels. Warmth and good cooking smells wafted up to greet her and Rowena paused, scanning the main room from her vantage point.

It was mostly empty. In the far corner an elderly man, a Saxon merchant to judge by his dress, huddled over a cup of wine but Rowena's attention was drawn to the pair of younger men sitting close to the fire.

Both Normans had discarded their heavy travelling clothes and were wearing good linen. Gerard de Beaumont was peacock-fine in a short orange tunic and yellow hose but Rowena scarcely spared him a glance.

Hugh de Lacy was laughing! How utterly different he looked with a smile softening his austere features! Until this moment it hadn't occurred to her that she had never seen him smile.

Rowena stood rooted to the spot, unable to drag her eyes away.

His senses prickling, Hugh looked up. She was standing in the shadows but the lamp she held lit her thin features with a soft glow, highlighting their fine-boned delicacy and making her eyes appear enormous. She looked desperately young and vulnerable. . .and unexpectedly enchanting!

'My lady.' Hugh bowed, his smile abruptly vanishing.

At his curt greeting, Rowena rediscovered the use of her limbs. Angry at her own stupidity, she descended the final few steps and walked briskly towards the fire.

'Allow me, my lady.' Gerard rushed to set a stool for her and Rowena thanked him with a smile.

In so far as it was possible to like any Norman, Rowena liked Gerard de Beaumont. His hazel eyes and fair hair, in sharp contrast to his commander's alien darkness, seemed comfortingly familiar and he had pleasing manners.

Supper was served at their table by the fire. The food was excellent and Rowena believed Gerard when he declared that this was the best tavern in London.

'No doubt you have tried them all, my lord,' she told him pertly but her smile robbed the words of any sting.

Gerard chuckled. 'Not yet, my lady.'

His merry laugh rang out frequently as the meal

progressed and he tried ever harder to converse with her in his execrable English.

'Forgive me, my lady,' he sighed. 'Your beauty. . .*alors*. . .it. . .hinders my tongue!'

Rowena blushed.

'Gerard, you will oblige me by going to check on the men and horses.' Hugh decided it was time to put a stop to his young lieutenant's nonsense.

Gerard rose to his feet with fluid grace and, kissing his fingers to Rowena, went whistling out of the room.

Elgiva snorted with approval and bestowed a kind glance on Hugh de Lacy for the first time in their acquaintance.

Rowena bridled at this betrayal. She frowned at Elgiva and then swung back to face Hugh with a black scowl.

'I'm sorry if his departure displeases you, my lady, but I didn't bring my lieutenant to London for the purpose of dancing attendance on you.' Hugh's tone was dry.

'Indeed. I thought you both were supposed to be my escorts,' she retorted.

How dared he sit there meanly begrudging her a little pleasant conversation when he had sat virtually silent throughout the meal, a dour look on his swarthy face?

'You mistake the matter.' Hugh's brows drew together in a frown and he abruptly waved Elgiva away.

Rowena moved to leave the table but subsided again when he snapped, 'Sit down and listen. It is time I made a few things clear, my lady.'

'Really? All I am interested in is in seeing the Duke as soon as possible,' Rowena drawled back at him.

His light eyes darkened at her insulting tone but Hugh kept his voice calm. 'Tomorrow when I go to court I shall enquire if my lord will receive your petition but you must steel yourself for delay.'

'Why?' Rowena snapped the word at him, abandoning her worldly pose.

'The coronation ceremony will be held in two days. Naturally, he is extremely busy.'

Rowena gaped at him, her mouth falling open in consternation.

'Didn't you know that my lord was to be crowned at the West Minster on Christmas Day?' Hugh enquired sweetly.

'Then you planned to return to London all along.' A haze of red fury swam before Rowena's eyes.

'Of course. Why else would I leave my new estates and undertake a journey in such vile weather?' He smiled at her, a cool mocking smile that made her long to hit him. 'Did you imagine you had swayed me with your pleading?'

'You are a liar and a cheat!' she spat at him. 'You tricked me into that oath of obedience!'

'Oh, no, my lady.' Hugh shook his dark head. 'I promised I would escort you to the Duke and I shall do so.' He paused, enjoying the wild rose colour that bloomed in her cheeks. 'Eventually.'

Beneath the cover of the table Rowena's fingernails dug into her palms as she struggled to contain her temper.

'How long must I wait?'

Hugh shrugged. 'A few days perhaps.'

'It cannot come soon enough for me.' Rowena's voice shook with passion and she leapt to her feet. She would throw something at him if she stayed here an instant longer!

'Are you so certain of victory, then?'

His softly spoken question halted her flight and she whirled back to face him.

'No, of course I am not, but at least I will have tried!' she declared proudly.

Hugh saw the shine of tears in her lovely eyes and his conscience pricked him. Her insults had irritated him but she didn't deserve his scorn. She was too brave for that.

He held out his hand in a gesture of reconciliation.

'Forgive me,' he said awkwardly, glad that none of his men was present to hear him. They would think he had run mad! 'It was unfair of me to mock you.'

He smiled at her, the warm engaging smile that transformed his dark face, making him seem younger and strangely attractive, and Rowena felt her knees begin to tremble. Absurdly, she wanted to cross the floor that separated them and take the hand he held out to her.

'Save your apologies, Hugh de Lacy, for I want none of them,' she spat, her voice quivering in spite of all her efforts. 'You are my enemy and there can be nothing but hatred between us.'

Hugh's hand dropped back to his side.

'So be it,' he replied, but their eyes met and held and Rowena's heart began to hammer.

Was she imagining it? Was there regret in his gaze? Did he too wish those hasty words had been left unsaid?

Sternly, Rowena curbed her wayward thoughts and turned to leave.

She had spoken nothing but the truth. They *were* enemies and she would do well to remember it!

CHAPTER FOUR

'MY LADY, he has forbidden you to go.'

'Why should I not see the Wolf of Normandy crowned king?' Rowena tossed her braids. 'I am tired of sitting cooped up in this inn.'

'We went out this morning,' Elgiva reminded her mistress.

'Only to hear Mass.' Rowena's brows drew together in a truculent scowl.

It was Christmas Day and Hugh de Lacy had left for Thorney Island and the great new church built by the late King Edward. The Abbey of St Peter's, already becoming known as the West Minster as opposed to St Paul's in the city itself, had seen the coronation of Harold Godwinson a little less than a year ago. Today it would witness William of Normandy receiving the crown from Bishop Aldred.

But Rowena had been warned to stay indoors.

'The Duke will see you the day after the Feast of St Stephen,' Hugh de Lacy had told her. 'Until then you will remain here.'

'But I am weary of being mewed up like a caged bird,' Rowena had protested. She had recovered from their journey and she was bored by the lack of activity. It wasn't in her nature to remain idle. 'I want to explore the city.'

He had frowned. 'The streets are not safe. Feelings are running high,' he'd said shortly. 'And I cannot spare my men to escort you on a pleasure jaunt.'

'The Londoners have no love for your Duke,' Rowena had retorted with a savage satisfaction.

'He does not require their affection, only their obedience.' Hugh had fixed her with a fierce stare. 'Obedience, my lady, which I will have from you! Stay indoors!'

And he had gone, in a swirl of fur-trimmed dark mantle, leaving the inn seeming quieter than ever.

Rowena couldn't bear it. The contrast to last year's Yule when Edenwald had rung to the sound of feasting and her father's hearty laughter was too cruel.

Flinging a veil over her loose braids, she jumped to her feet.

'Fetch me my mantle, Elgiva. I have decided. I am going to have a look at this famous Abbey.'

'My lady, do you think it wise to provoke de Lacy at every turn?' Elgiva wrung her hands in concern.

'I owe him nothing! Why should I obey him?' Rowena's eyes flashed militant fire.

Nothing Elgiva could say would dissuade her and, recognising that stubborn expression of old, Elgiva went to see if the landlord could find a man to guide them.

Thorney Island lay two miles up the river from the city. It was surrounded by the marshes of Tyburn Brook and the muddy bank of the tidal Thames and Rowena eyed it dubiously.

'Why did King Edward choose such a dismal spot? It is full of nothing but bramble bushes!'

Rolf, their guide, gazed at her reproachfully.

''Tis a place of holy reputation, my lady. In the past, hermits dwelt here.'

Rowena viewed the low-lying site with fresh respect.

It still had something of a wild, lonely air but this

faded when they got closer to the open square about the Minster. A dense crowd had formed but Rowena's attention was caught by the soaring pinnacles of pale stone.

'I've never seen anything like it!' Elgiva exclaimed and Rowena nodded in agreement, impressed in spite of herself.

King Edward had ordered his church to be built in the Norman style, to the disapproval of many members of his Witan. Rowena could remember her father complaining that the King was too much influenced by the years he had spent in his youth at the court of Duke Robert the Magnificent, William's father.

'I know his mother was a Norman but must Edward ram their foreign customs down our throats?' the thegn of Edenwald had grumbled. 'He appoints Norman priests to hold Canterbury and Norman favourites take precedence at court. Even this new church of his must be a tribute in stone to his beloved Normandy.'

Rowena had come prepared to dislike it but the beauty of St Peter's took her breath away. She gazed entranced at its graceful lines until someone trod heavily on her toes and she became uncomfortably aware that the crowd had grown even bigger.

'At least the wind doesn't feel so sharp this way,' she said to Elgiva.

'Aye, but it's going to snow any minute.' Elgiva eyed the press of bodies around them uneasily. 'This square is too narrow; there's hardly room to breathe now, my lady. You've seen what you came to see. Let's leave before we become hemmed in.'

'In a moment.' Rowena was barely listening. The restless excitement stirring all around them had seized her in its grip.

It was bitterly cold, slivers of ice hung from the beautiful stone carvings, but Rowena didn't care. Even when the snow started to fall her attention remained fixed on the Norman soldiers standing on guard outside the church. They were shifting from foot to foot, casting worried glances at the crowd, and she experienced a malicious satisfaction at their obvious uneasiness.

Suddenly, there was a great sound of shouting.

The crowd began to mill in confusion and Rowena was swept half off her feet as the mass surged forward. To her horror, the guards began to wield their long swords to beat back the tide threatening to engulf them.

Trapped within the narrow confines of the square, there was no room to escape. Bodies surged and eddied in mindless panic, the noise indescribable as men swore, women shrieked and children wailed.

'Elgiva!' Rowena tried to grab at her nurse's arm but someone came between them and she found herself being swept further away.

A gap in the crowd opened for an instant and she saw a soldier holding a torch to one of the surrounding houses. The timber and thatch dwelling burst into flame. Streaks of fire shot up into the dark winter sky, showering sparks and clouds of choking smoke on to the people near by.

'Stop it, you stupid fools!' Rowena screamed in futile protest as another house was fired. Did they think it was a riot? If so, their method of trying to quell it was the worst they could have chosen, for the crowd was going mad with fear!

Men came running out of the Abbey but then her view was blocked as the press around her convulsed in threshing terror. A sharp tug at her veil warned her that a loose end had caught on something, probably a

brooch, and an instant later it was ripped from her head
with a force that made her cry out.

A wave of panic rose in Rowena's throat as she
struggled to keep her footing. She had lost Elgiva and
Rolf completely!

A thud between her shoulder-blades almost sent her
sprawling and she recovered her balance only to find
herself trapped against the wall of a house. Bodies
pressed on her, crushing her into the timbers with their
weight. Rowena screamed, striving to fend them off
with her hands.

I am going to die, she thought in dull shock, scarcely
able to believe what was happening to her.

Suddenly, the pressure eased as the crowd melted and
broke. Gasping and winded, Rowena was too weak to
move. She slumped against the wall, too dazed to
recognise the tall knight who had cleared a path to free
her.

'Rowena! God's blood, what are you doing here?'

Hugh de Lacy's angry roar barely penetrated
Rowena's stupor. Her ears were ringing and unwitting
tears began to pour down her white face.

She felt him sweep her up from the snow-covered
ground into his strong arms and clung to him wordlessly.
Her loosened hair rippled free to cover them both like a
golden cloak as he carried her to safety.

'Shall I bring up some hot broth, my lord?'

'Aye, and the strongest wine you have,' Hugh replied
without taking his anxious gaze from the slight figure
lying on the bed.

She hadn't moved since he had brought her back to
the tavern. Her eyes were closed, the long, thick lashes
like dark strips of silk against her pale skin, and her

breathing was swift and shallow. Hugh thought she was conscious. It was her dreadful experience that had left her dazed and unable to answer him.

Suddenly she shivered and he swirled the heavy cloak from his shoulders, adding it to the pile of coverlets he had already heaped upon her. Then, somewhat hesitantly, he took her cold hands between his own and tried to chafe warmth into them.

Rowena's eyes fluttered open.

'Elgiva?'

Hugh understood. 'Was she with you at the Abbey?'

Rowena nodded. Her throat felt sore from the smoke she had inhaled but she managed to whisper, 'We had a guide. A man named Rolf. The landlord knows him.'

'I'll send Gerard to look for them. Don't worry. He'll find them safe.'

Hugh spoke with a confidence he did not feel. The scene at St Peter's had been a bloody one. The guards on duty had mistaken the shouts of acclaim within the church when William was presented to the nobility for the noise of a budding riot. Their attempts to quell it had caused havoc.

Inside the Minster, the screams followed by the sight of flames lighting up the precious glass windows had in turn created panic. Men and women of all ranks had fled in superstitious terror. Only a few had remained to witness the end of the ceremony.

William himself had trembled violently at this apparent omen as the new-made crown with its rare imported gems hovered above his brow.

It was the first time Hugh had even seen his liege lord show fear. Was William wondering if God had turned against him at this supreme moment of his life?

The doubt which had surfaced once before when they

were preparing for the invasion rose again in Hugh's mind as he stared down into Rowena of Edenwald's white face.

Was their cause just? Did they really have the right to take over English lands?

'How did you find me?'

Rowena's whisper interrupted his thoughts.

'By accident,' he replied harshly, angry at his own folly. William had been confirmed by God as Edward's rightful heir. *They*, not the Saxons, had won the trial by battle! England needed a strong hand and so did the rich acres of Edenwald!

'I saw a woman in danger of being crushed and went to her aid.'

He hadn't known her identity at first. It was that amazing golden hair which had attracted his attention, a bright beacon drawing his eye as he had emerged from the church.

Involuntarily, Hugh put out a hand to smooth back a lock which had drifted across her cheek. It felt warm and soft, living silk to the touch. . .

She had been as light and fragile as thistledown in his arms. The strangeness of it was with him still. . .

A tap at the door heralded the return of the maid.

'Tell Gerard de Beaumont to attend me,' he ordered, taking the steaming bowl.

When his lieutenant arrived a few moments later, he gaped at the astonishing sight that met his eyes.

'Don't stand there grinning like a lack-wit,' Hugh snapped, abruptly laying down the broth he had been spooning into Rowena's reluctant mouth. 'Get out and search for the woman Elgiva. She was at the Abbey. The landlord can give you a description of the man with her.'

His words had the desired effect. Gerard departed in haste.

The sound of his boots clattering down the stairs faded.

'Thank you.'

'Hush and finish drinking this,' Hugh ordered gruffly.

Rowena obeyed but she refused the wine he offered once the broth was done. 'I am feeling better now,' she murmured. The hot soup seemed to have cured the huskiness in her throat.

She watched him lift a goblet to his own lips. He hadn't even reproached her for disobeying him.

'I am sorry for causing you trouble,' she said abruptly. 'I should have heeded your orders and stayed indoors.'

'It does not matter now.' Hugh set his wine down. He smiled at her faintly. 'You are safe. That is more important.'

Colour rushed into her pale cheeks. 'I should not blame you if you wished me dead,' she whispered. He was being kind, far kinder than she had any right to expect!

Hugh shook his dark head at her. 'I have no desire to win Edenwald at such a cost.'

To his astonishment, Hugh meant it. Oh, it would be far more convenient if the nuisance that was Rowena of Edenwald ceased to exist but he could not find it in him to wish for such a drastic solution!

The sincerity in his deep voice convinced her. Strange as it seemed, this Norman appeared to want nothing but her good. She didn't understand it but the knowledge sent an unexpectedly warm glow coursing through her veins.

'I hope I may repay you one day, my lord.' Rowena gazed up at him, a shy smile trembling on her lips.

Hugh caught his breath. Slowly, without conscious volition, he leant forward and his dark head dipped until he found her soft mouth with his own.

Astonishment held Rowena motionless.

Lips gentle and warm, softly brushing hers in a tender caress. . .a kiss lasting no longer than a breath.

Hugh straightened and Rowena's fingers fluttered to her mouth. They stared at one another in dream-like silence.

'Oh, my lady! Oh, my lady, I was frantic with worry! Are you all right?'

Elgiva erupted into the room and abruptly the spell was broken. The world swung back into focus.

Hugh saw the hostility return to Rowena's eyes but before she could say a word he rose swiftly to his feet.

'Try to sleep, my lady, and recover your health,' he instructed coolly. 'The King will not be pleased if you fail to attend the audience he has granted.'

And, with a curt bow, he quit the chamber.

Rowena straightened from her obeisance. Her heart hammering, she lifted her gaze to meet the hard, dark eyes of her new King.

William of Normandy had a strong-featured face with a hawk-like nose and a determined mouth. Rowena felt her innards quake and swallowed nervously. Thank the blessed saints that de Lacy's influence had secured them a virtually private interview! She could not have borne to endure this torture under the curious eyes of all those loud-voiced, confident foreigners out there in the hall.

'So this is your Saxon heiress, Hugh.'

William spoke in French, he knew little English, but Rowena understood his meaning. Her glance flicked to the man at her side. Hugh de Lacy's swarthy face was impassive.

'Aye, my lord,' Hugh replied with cool indifference and Rowena's chin came up. She would not let them know she was afraid!

The Duke stared at Rowena, his interest aroused by Hugh's story.

A girl verging on womanhood, he decided, slender as a willow in her crimson gown. He noted the heavy gold bracelets encircling her thin wrists, the long rope of pearl beads and the enormous disc-shaped brooch of brilliantly enamelled workmanship that pinned her mantle.

So, she wanted him to know she was of noble blood and not to be trifled with.

William smiled. He liked the way her eyes met his with unwavering steadiness. Pride was to be admired — providing it did not lead to disobedience and folly.

However. . .

'I have heard your claim, lady,' William said. 'But you misunderstand the situation. Edenwald belongs to *me*. *All* England is mine to do with as I please. And it is my wish that the gift I granted to Hugh de Lacy should stand.'

Rowena paled. She did not need Hugh's translation to realise that she had lost.

'Is this your idea of justice, William of Normandy? Will you deprive me of my rights without letting me speak for myself?' she shouted in desperation.

There was a sudden deathly hush in the chamber and William's heavy eyebrows met in a frown.

'*Your* rights, lady? By the splendour of God, you have only the rights I choose to grant you,' he snapped.

Rowena was acutely aware of his angry stare and she

began to tremble. But Hugh's hand pressed hers fleetingly and she took courage. Perhaps he only meant to warn her to stay silent but she found his warm touch reassuring in a way she didn't want to examine.

The silence lengthened.

'Tell me, would your father have fought against me at Hastings if he had lived?' Abruptly, the Duke flung the question at her.

Rowena bit her lip. She dared not deny it.

'And you, Lady Rowena, where does your loyalty lie? Would you be willing to place your hands between mine and swear an oath of fealty?'

The blood drained from Rowena's face. She stared at him in dismay. She had thought he would demand her assurance that Edenwald would not rise in rebellion but she hadn't dreamt that he might require her personal oath of loyalty.

'Your silence speaks for itself.' William's tone was harsh. He shook his cropped head. 'I will not grant land to those I cannot trust.'

Involuntarily, a little groan of despair escaped from Rowena's clenched lips. What had she done? Her stubborn pride had brought ruin down on her people!

'Perhaps the Lady Rowena needs more time to consider, my lord. She is very young and girls of her years are apt to be foolish.'

Rowena turned to stare at Hugh de Lacy, too amazed at his unexpected championship to feel insulted by his unflattering remark.

His knight's intervention brought a look of puzzlement to the Duke's face.

'Do you realise what you are saying, Hugh?' He began to frown. 'Or do you rate my gift so low that you would toss it aside unwanted?'

'My lord, nothing could be further from the truth!'

By the Rood, what witchcraft did this skinny little wench possess to make him jeopardise his position so carelessly? William had a highly developed sense of his own worth. It was dangerously easy to insult him!

The dark eyes surveyed him thoughtfully.

'You have always served me well, Hugh de Lacy. At Hastings you offered me your own horse when mine collapsed beneath me,' William announced at last. 'Therefore, I accept you intend no slight.' His stern expression eased. 'In fact, to appease your tender conscience, I am willing to consider your request.'

He turned and spoke in a low voice to one of the men standing by his chair.

Hugh contained a sigh of relief. Glancing at Rowena, he saw from her anxious expression that she had not understood his exchange with the King but before he could whisper a translation William's companion beckoned her forward.

Geoffery de Mowbray, Bishop of Coutances, was one of the Duke's earliest supporters. A worldly churchman, he was a patron of the arts and possessor of a clever mind, which rendered his advice valuable.

'How old are you, Lady Rowena?' There was an appreciative gleam in his connoisseur's eye as he noted her budding beauty.

Rowena disliked his smooth voice but she curtsied low and answered politely, 'I am sixteen, my lord Bishop.'

'And you are an orphan?'

Rowena nodded.

'Is there a possibility of other heirs to Edenwald coming forward?'

Hugh translated and Rowena denied it. 'My mother

bore three sons but they all died in infancy. I am her last-born and the sole surviving member of my family.'

She strove to mask her unease as the Bishop turned to say something to the Duke but she couldn't help shivering when William's hard black gaze swivelled to fix on her once more.

'The Bishop suggests that you be placed in the care of his cousin, who is Lady Abbess at the nunnery of St Etheldreda, in Sussex. You will remain there until I send for you. Until that time, the revenues of Edenwald go to the Crown.'

His smile of satisfaction indicated William's approval of the Bishop's scheme.

Hugh noted it with wry amusement. His liege lord was a practical man and careful with his money; a new source of income would not go amiss.

Rowena's eyes began to blaze as the meaning of the decree sank in but Hugh hastily thanked the Duke on her behalf and asked for permission to withdraw.

It was given and he firmly steered her from the royal presence, not stopping until they had reached the courtyard. Thanks to the bitter weather, it was virtually deserted and Hugh finally permitted Rowena to shake off his restraining hand.

'I'll not do it. I'll not be shut away in some convent to suit Norman greed!'

'Not so loud!' Hugh glared at her. 'Do you want everyone in there to hear you?'

'I don't care if they do!' Rowena spat. 'And you needn't go on pretending concern for my welfare, Hugh de Lacy! It has all worked out very conveniently for you. I am to be locked away and forgotten while you are free to return to Edenwald.'

A harsh exclamation escaped Hugh. Mastering his

temper, he said shortly, 'I was as surprised as you by the outcome.' He shrugged. 'Furthermore, I doubt if I will see much of Edenwald in the months to come. William wants me to remain at court.'

Rowena bit down savagely on her lip. She owed him an apology. He had fulfilled his promise but she couldn't bear to thank him. Tears stung her eyes and her chest was tight from the effort of holding them in. Banishment! She was being banished from Edenwald!

'My lady, there is nothing you can do. You must obey the Duke.' Hugh's voice was gentle.

A tiny sigh escaped her clenched lips. Unfortunately, he was right!

'I'm sorry. It is unfair of me to criticise you,' she managed. Blinking hard, she added, 'Do you think they will let me visit Edenwald before I am sent away?'

It hurt to quench the desperate hope in those speedwell eyes but Hugh shook his head firmly. 'William expects his orders to be obeyed promptly.'

She looked so very young and woebegotten that he longed to sweep her into his arms and comfort her but he resisted the temptation. She would probably spit in his face if he tried! What was more, he couldn't afford such ridiculous weakness. It was a lunacy which had already come close to losing him favour in William's eyes.

Fortunately, for Hugh's peace of mind, a page emerged into the courtyard at that moment.

Snapping his fingers, he summoned the boy. 'Escort this lady to the stables, where you will find Gerard de Beaumont,' he instructed.

His deep voice carefully impersonal, he continued, 'My lieutenant will take you back to the tavern, Lady Rowena.'

Hugh half expected that she would protest but she merely nodded in a dejected fashion. Quickly, he turned away and, hardening his heart, did not look back.

'Here we are at last, my lady.'

Rowena glowered at the middle-aged knight escorting her and he subsided into silence. She returned her gaze to the prospect before them.

Lying in a sheltered dip in the downs, the nunnery of St Etheldreda was built in the old Saxon manner with a cluster of thatched timber huts surrounding a square-towered church. From their vantage point she could see the neat kitchen garden, a small orchard and a tiny vineyard. Beyond lay a few bare fields and everything was enclosed by a great thorn hedge.

In the fading January daylight the place looked desolate and Rowena wanted to turn her mare's head around and flee.

'We must go on, my lady.'

Reluctantly, Rowena urged Moonlight forward and they rode towards the gate. The Norman knight escorting her, one of William's personal servitors, ordered a man-at-arms to ring the bell. It jangled loudly, grating on Rowena's sensitive nerves, but the portress appeared instantly.

'I will accompany Lady Rowena and her maid inside. Wait here,' the knight told his men. 'I won't be long.'

Instinctively, Rowena straightened her shoulders and her chin tilted up as they were admitted to the Abbess's parlour.

'Thank you, my lord.' The elderly woman seated by the brazier rose at their entrance and accepted the letter handed to her. 'Will you stay and take some refreshment?'

Hastily, Rowena's escort shook his head. It was growing dark and he wanted to find shelter for himself and his men well away from the atmosphere of female sanctity!

The door thudded shut behind him and Rowena started nervously. She glanced at Elgiva and saw that her nurse was looking uneasy too.

'Please be seated.' The Abbess had a surprisingly musical voice.

They obeyed and waited in silence while she read the letter.

Pretending a calm she did not feel, Rowena surveyed Abbess Mildred. She was small with a spare figure and a somewhat sharp-featured face. Her hair was completely hidden by the immaculate white coif she wore but her sallow complexion hinted that it might be as dark as her eyes.

When she looked up again Rowena saw that her gaze was curious.

'So you are to be our new boarder. My cousin writes that you may have a religious vocation. Is this so? Do you wish to become a novice?'

Bright colour flared into Rowena's cheeks. 'No!'

To her surprise, the Abbess gave a dry little chuckle.

'Don't look so alarmed, child. No matter what Geoffery may hint, or the King may wish, I will not accept anyone who does not offer herself freely to God's service.'

Rowena's taut muscles relaxed.

'I am glad to hear it,' she said frankly. 'For I must tell you, madam, that I have no wish to be here.'

Elgiva winced but this lack of tact only produced another chuckle.

'You are honest, child, and since we must live

together that is a good beginning,' the nun announced, rising from her stool. 'Now come. I will conduct you to the guest-house and then you may join us for supper.'

Obediently, Rowena followed her to the door.

'This is not a rich house. You will find we lead a simple life here,' Abbess Mildred informed her as she led the way across the frozen grass. 'If you wish, you may join us in our daily tasks but you are under no obligation to do so. The King has arranged a sum of money for your keep.'

'Out of my own revenues!'

The Abbess paused at this indignant outburst and gave Rowena a considering stare. 'You shall tell me the whole, child, but not now. It is growing late and supper will not wait. There will be time enough tomorrow.'

Rowena soon learnt that there was always time enough at St Etheldreda's. It was a well-ordered, peaceful place.

At first she was sullen but as the weeks passed her mood slowly brightened in response to the cheerful friendliness shown to her by all the nuns. Her small cell in the guest-house was cold and bare but the warmth of her welcome made up for the lack of comforts.

The nuns worked hard and Rowena was glad to use up her energy in helping them. It made it easier not to think of Edenwald or grieve for her dead when she was exhausted from a day spent milking cows and working in the fields or pounding dough for bread.

To her annoyance, Hugh de Lacy was often in her thoughts. Mixing potions in the infirmary under the supervision of little Sister Elfgift, she would find herself remembering the deep quality of his voice or the way his rare smile transformed his austere face. His memory

even intruded on her prayers as she knelt in the incense-
filled chapel.

Each time it happened, Rowena swore it would be
the last. That wretched man was at the root of her
imprisonment but, even as she tried to fan the flames of
her hatred by recalling every slighting word and insult
he had thrown at her, Rowena was aware that her
feelings had subtly changed.

Then, one day in the middle of February, the Abbess
sent for her and Rowena felt her pulse begin to race as
she knocked on the parlour door and the musical voice
bade her enter.

'I'm sorry, child, but there is no news for you,' the
Abbess said quickly.

Rowena's eager expression faded but she schooled
herself to listen attentively as the nun continued.

'I asked you here for another reason. You have shown
yourself a willing worker and I would like to do
something for you in return. There is nothing I can
teach you in the arts of embroidery and weaving — your
skill exceeds that of most of my nuns — but perhaps you
would like to learn to speak French?'

Rowena's eyes widened and Abbess Mildred smiled.

'I heard you mention to Sister Frideswide in the
rectory last night that you had once studied the language
but were forced to abandon your lessons. I could help
you polish your skill.'

Rowena looked doubtful and the nun laughed
merrily.

'I see you have forgotten that I am related by blood to
the Bishop of Coutances. I may live isolated from the
world but I have not allowed my French to grow rusty.'
She eyed Rowena thoughtfully. 'I suppose you are
wondering how the connection came about?'

Rowena admitted it.

'The Bishop's grandmother and mine were sisters. My grandmother came to England in the train of the Lady Emma, our late King Edward's mother. Eventually, she married an Englishman but insisted that all her family learn to speak good French and keep in touch with her kin in Normandy.' A little sigh escaped Abbess Mildred. 'It has been a great sadness to me that we had to fight each other. So much blood has been spilt on both sides! I pray daily that now we may grow together in peace and harmony.'

Rowena glanced down at her hands lying in her lap. They were so tightly clenched that the knuckles showed white.

'Do you disagree with me, my dear?'

Rowena sucked air into her tight chest.

'I don't know!' she cried wildly and promptly burst into tears, the first she had shed since the day she had heard of her father's death.

Wisely, the nun allowed her to cry her fill and then said gently, 'It is fitting that you should mourn, Rowena, but there comes a time to put away your tears and get on with life. We have a duty to the living as well as the dead.'

'But nothing is the same any more,' Rowena muttered. 'My life is ruined! I might as well have died too! Sometimes I wish I had!'

'My dear! You must not speak in such a sinful way.' Abbess Mildred shook her head in disapproval. 'You are young. You have your health and strength and, God willing, one day you will leave here and take your rightful place in the world again.'

'And what is my rightful place?' Rowena dried her

face with the edge of her veil and, recovering her poise, met the Abbess's gaze with a challenging stare.

The Abbess coughed awkwardly. She knew Rowena's history. 'No doubt the King will soon decide that thorny question. Only remember that there is right on both sides, my dear.'

Could it be true? Troubled, Rowena allowed her thoughts to drift as the Abbess continued to speak comforting words.

Looking back, she could see that Hugh de Lacy had treated her with more kindness than her behaviour had warranted. The nuns, who seemed to hear everything, had several tales to tell of outrages committed by Normans aggressively eager to display their power.

Hugh had permitted neither rape nor brutality. In fact, he had behaved with scrupulous fairness. He had even saved her life. Was it his fault that William had chosen to give him Edenwald or banish her into exile?

And yet he was a Norman. They had invaded her country and she could not forgive them for the death of Godric.

Rowena shook her head, trying to clear it. Her temples were beginning to throb from the effort of trying to disentangle her emotions.

'You look tired, child. Shall we speak of this matter of learning French another day?'

The question dragged Rowena from her disturbing reflections.

'I should like to learn,' she said quickly. 'It will give my brain some exercise.'

The Abbess smiled. 'Then we shall begin tomorrow.'

Rowena thanked her. She would enjoy stretching her mental capacities again but, even more important,

learning to speak their language properly would help
arm her in the struggle to come.

The Abbess was right. It was foolish to despair and
she must put aside such weakness. Hugh de Lacy hadn't
won Edenwald yet!

Rowena hung on to her resolve as Lent came and went.

She studied hard in the evenings after days spent
pruning vines in the little vineyard or tending the
fishpond, which provided the nunnery's food during the
fast before Easter. When that great Holy day arrived an
altar cloth she had helped embroider was chosen for use
at the High Mass and she felt a glow of satisfaction, but
still no word came from the King.

In June they cut their hay and the hard labouring in
the fields diverted Rowena's anxiety and then, suddenly, it was August and her birthday.

It was a golden day and she was seventeen. Surely the
King would send for her soon and she would see
Edenwald again!

A tiny voice on the fringes of her mind whispered that
she would also encounter Hugh de Lacy but she thrust
the thought from her, quelling the strange excitement
that made her stomach quiver.

A few days later she was in the kitchen garden
weeding between a row of beans when Elgiva came
running out.

'Quick, my lady. The Abbess wants you.' Elgiva
shrieked, catching sight of Rowena's flushed face and
dirt-streaked hands. 'Dear saints, look at you!'

Rowena began to laugh. 'The Abbess has seen me
dirty before now.'

'No, you don't understand.' Impatiently, Elgiva

tugged her away from the garden. 'There's someone come to see you. From France.'

Her heart pounding, Rowena allowed herself to be hurried indoors. In a feverish daze, she ripped off her soiled gown and rinsed her hands and face clean.

'I can't wear that!' she wailed as Elgiva produced her crimson roc. 'It's too tight!'

'You've grown, my lady. Too much in some places for my peace of mind, if you were to ask me!'

Rowena ignored this muttered comment and snatched up the white linen tunic she had sewn for the Easter feast. It was plain but at least it was clean and it fitted her better than any of the gowns she had brought with her from Edenwald.

'You must hurry, my lady. They are waiting for you,' Elgiva clucked.

There was no time to rearrange her hair so she left her braids loose and threw a fine veil over them.

'I'm ready,' she said breathlessly.

The man awaiting her in the visitors' parlour bowed low at her entrance.

'Do you remember me, my lady?'

Rowena fought against the surge of bewildering, sickening disappointment. 'How could I forget?'

Gerard de Beaumont's confident smile of greeting dissolved into an expression of astonishment. 'You have learnt our language!' he exclaimed, choosing to ignore the barb hidden in her perfect French.

'It seemed. . .prudent,' Rowena murmured.

Gerard nodded. 'Of course.'

Rowena invited him to be seated.

'One of the nuns will bring refreshments in a

moment,' she explained. 'But first, won't you tell me
what brings you here?'

Gerard launched into a prepared speech while admiring Rowena's graceful deportment as she moved across
the room and sat down.

Who would have thought it? The skinny little Saxon
hoyden had turned into a ravishing creature! He hadn't
relished the task of journeying to England but the
tedious duty had suddenly acquired unexpected
compensations.

'So you see, my lady, it was to bring you this gift that I
came,' he concluded, taking a small canvas-wrapped
bundle from his gipsere pouch.

Rowena stared hard at him. 'Hugh de Lacy has sent
me a present?'

'For your birthday.' Gerard held it out to her. 'I am to
tell you that he regrets he could not deliver it in person
but the King requires his presence in Normandy.'

Rowena allowed her eyebrows to soar. 'It occurs to
me that your Duke may as well have never bothered to
invade if he intends to spend so much time out of
England,' she retorted with poisonous sweetness. 'Or
am I to wait until my hair turns grey before he summons
me to court?'

She made no move to accept the parcel and Gerard
coughed awkwardly.

'I am afraid I have no knowledge of the Duke's plans,
my lady,' he muttered, feeling uncomfortable. 'However, it is rumoured that he will return in the autumn.'

'Autumn!' Rowena's eyes began to blaze. 'Do we
matter so little to him?'

Gerard shifted uncomfortably in his seat. He couldn't
help but feel sympathy for her plight and he knew that
Hugh de Lacy felt the same.

'The Duke should return to England. The longer he stays away, the more trouble there will be,' Hugh had prophesied bluntly, and it seemed that he was right for Gerard had already heard of disturbances in the West Country.

'The Saxons lack a leader to match William but that won't prevent bloodshed,' Hugh had told him and, looking into Rowena of Edenwald's angry eyes, Gerard realised it was true. Instead of relying on the important hostages he had taken back with him to Normandy the Duke ought to heed Hugh's advice!

Uneasily, he shrugged this disloyal thought away and changed the subject.

'Won't you open your gift?' All the force of his considerable charm went into this request. 'Please!'

The admiration in his eyes was as flattering as it was unexpected and, somewhat flustered, Rowena allowed her anger to be diverted.

What could Hugh de Lacy have sent her?

'Oh!' The exclamation escaped her before Rowena could prevent it.

'Do you like it? My lord wanted most particularly to know.'

With trembling hands Rowena unwound the length of silk and held it up. The rich soft folds caught the light and gleamed with sapphire fire.

'It is beautiful,' she murmured shakily.

Rowena had never seen such a wonderful fabric before. Of course, silk was fabulously expensive. In all her married life, her mother had possessed only one silken gown but nothing as fine as this!

'From Byzantium, my lady.' Gerard could hardly keep a grin from his face. 'Shall I tell my lord you are pleased?'

For an instant, Rowena was tempted to hurl the silk at him but of their own volition her fingers clenched shut and would not let go.

The entrance of Abbess Mildred, who arrived with one of the nuns bearing a tray of refreshments, saved her from having to find a reply. Gerard had brought letters for the Abbess from her kin and by the time greetings had been exchanged and Gerard had consumed a honey-cake or two Rowena had recovered her composure.

'Since my lord de Lacy has been in attendance upon the Duke all these months, who has been looking after Edenwald and Wynburgh?' she asked.

'Odo de Nevil,' Gerard answered. He paused fractionally and then added, 'It may interest you to learn that my lord has decreed that both manors shall be run as one to be known simply as Edenwald. Wynburgh no longer exists.'

A little pang of sorrow shot through Rowena. How glad she was that Ethelwine and her daughters had left before this situation had come about. They would have been humiliated beyond bearing!

'I am to visit Edenwald and carry back Odo's report to Normandy.'

Gerard's remark snatched Rowena from her reflections. 'Let me ride with you!' The words tumbled eagerly from her lips.

'Child, you know it is forbidden for you to leave the convent without the King's permission!'

Rowena flushed and the Abbess gave her a sympathetic look. 'I understand how you feel but your safety is my responsibility. Even if I allowed you to disobey the King, journeys are never without risk. No, let me finish,' the nun continued firmly, waving away

Rowena's attempt to interrupt. 'There is unrest stirring in the land. You might run into danger.'

'My lord de Beaumont here could protect me,' Rowena argued.

Gerard changed colour. She had no right to involve him in her crazy plans! De Lacy would have his head!

Before he could frame a protest the Abbess shook her head. 'It is out of the question. I cannot permit you to leave.'

Angrily Rowena rose to her feet.

'Then I can only pray that the Duke returns soon,' she snapped and, sweeping them a curtsy, marched from the room.

The year turned slowly, bringing autumn at last.

The falling leaves brought sharp memories of the previous October and Rowena grieved afresh for her father and Godric. Her despondent mood was not improved by the fact that William was still in Normandy.

'We shall remain here as prisoners until we are dead!' she cried in despair to Elgiva.

Then, just before Christmas, they heard that the Duke was back in London.

'Oh, at last!' Rowena exclaimed, her black depression lifting as she hurried to pen a letter asking William to receive her at court.

No reply came.

The disappointment was crushing and when she finally learnt the reason why Rowena's hatred of the Normans exploded into new life.

'He has not answered because he is too busy killing Englishmen. He has gone to besiege Exeter,' she explained bitterly to Elgiva. 'The citizens there are still defying him.'

'Sister Frideswide told me that it is the sons of our late King Harold who are behind this rebellion.'

'Then I hope he treats them better than that unfortunate hostage. Did you know that he actually had the man blinded before the city gates when they refused him entry?' Rowena shuddered. 'He is a monster!'

Elgiva nodded unhappily. 'Aye, but you think he will win, don't you, my lady?'

Rowena sighed. 'I wish it were otherwise.' Tears gleamed in her lovely eyes. 'But they are killing machines, these Normans. We will never be rid of them!'

To her intense annoyance, a sudden image of Hugh de Lacy's austere features flashed into her mind. She had not managed to obliterate his memory but she refused to think of him now. He was probably in the West Country with William, hacking innocent citizens to death!

Sure enough, on a blustery day in March, Rowena's fears were confirmed.

'It says here that Exeter has surrendered and the King intends to hold Easter at Winchester,' announced Abbess Mildred, waving her letter at Rowena. She laid the parchment down and surveyed her young charge thoughtfully. 'I think you may expect to hear of your release very soon.'

Rowena coloured at her choice of phrase. 'Please don't think me ungrateful. You have been very kind.'

'But you have not been happy here.' The Abbess gave her a faint smile. 'I understand, my dear. May God grant you better peace in the future.'

Rowena knelt for her blessing.

'Now go and put your belongings in order. You must be ready when the escort comes to conduct you to Winchester.'

'I will be,' Rowena replied grimly.

The time of waiting was over.

CHAPTER FIVE

'CHEER up, lad. Anyone would think this was a funeral and not a feast to judge from your expression,' said Odo de Nevil, giving his liege lord a jovial nudge.

Hugh de Lacy smiled thinly.

'Seek fresh company, Odo. You'll find others more entertaining tonight.'

'What you need is a drink.'

Odo summoned a page and instructed the boy to refill Hugh's winecup.

'There, a good red Bordeaux. Get that down you, Hugh, and you'll feel better.' He grinned. 'If you'd had to drink as much Saxon ale as I've done recently you'd appreciate the luxury of a little civilisation.'

Hugh nodded politely but his eyes roamed with restless boredom over the long chamber.

Odo sighed.

No expense had been spared in making this Easter festival a dazzling occasion. Determined to celebrate his recent victory in the West Country, the King had sanctioned every lavish proposal.

In a blaze of light and colour, knights and their ladies circulated to background music provided by a dozen minstrels, their leather-shod feet crushing flower-petals strewn amid the sweet rushes. A great fire roared at one end of the room, sending out waves of heat to increase the thirst of the courtiers who cried out merrily for more wine.

But it appeared that Hugh de Lacy took no pleasure in the scene.

From what I've heard, he's been in a dismal mood since he went back to Normandy, Odo thought, wondering if the question mark hanging over Edenwald's future could be the cause. Hugh hadn't said much but he knew that the lad had been delighted to be granted such a fine manor. God rot that little Saxon vixen!

'Come and join us, de Lacy!'

'Thank you but no,' Hugh refused, rejecting the invitation from a group of revellers.

Almost, he wished they were back on campaign. The turmoil in the West Country had been bitter and yet he would willingly endure the danger and discomfort all over again for the oblivion fighting brought. He'd had no time then to indulge in black brooding!

'I detest these stupid affairs,' he muttered abruptly.

'Can't think why when the wenches spend all their time ogling you,' Odo retorted.

Hugh had been ignoring several bright-eyed glances cast hopefully in his direction but even as Odo spoke one young woman, bolder than the rest, strolled across to where they stood.

'I give you greeting, my lords,' she said, dropping them a graceful curtsy.

A violet gown spun of the finest wool clung closely to her ripe, curving figure and her hair was as black as ebony beneath her thin silken veil.

'Lady Judith. I did not know you were in England,' Hugh said slowly.

The Countess de Montfort responded with a husky little laugh. 'We arrived a few days ago but the journey was too much for my lord. He is still resting.'

She raised her long amber eyes to Hugh's face.

'My cousin escorted me here tonight but he has deserted me. Won't you keep me company, Hugh?'

Odo coughed and looked uncomfortable. 'With your permission, my lord?' he murmured.

Hugh glanced at him and nodded.

Odo walked away, a frown furrowing his weather-beaten brow.

'Your friend still disapproves of me, I see.' Laughter bubbled in the Countess's low and alluring tones. 'A worthy man, de Nevil, but something of a bore,' she added wickedly.

'Judith, I won't hear you slander my friends ——'

'Oh, come, don't frown at me,' she interrupted him with a prettily winning smile. 'Not now, just when we have found one another again.'

She laid one white, heavily beringed hand upon his sleeve. 'Aren't you at least a little bit pleased to see me?' she breathed.

Hugh swallowed hard, wondering how to answer. He had very mixed feelings about the beautiful Countess de Montfort!

His silence did not deter her. Moving closer, she smiled at him with seductive warmth. 'Sit with me at the banquet tonight, Hugh, and we can renew our acquaintance.'

Hugh stared down into her upturned face, skilfully painted to enhance her natural beauty. Her lips were berry-red and parted in blatant invitation.

Repressing a quick surge of desire, he shook his head. 'You have a husband, Judith.'

Her almond-shaped eyes narrowed at his reply.

'It did not worry you before,' she observed with a shrug of her shapely shoulders.

Hugh was forced to acknowledge it. 'But that was ten

years ago, my lady, when I was new to court and friendless.'

It hardly seemed polite to add that she had chased him shamelessly.

Attracted by her beauty, Hugh had eventually abandoned his scruples and succumbed to the promise of warmth she had held out only to discover too late that beneath the charming façade she was selfish and calculating.

'What does it matter if I am married?' the husky voice demanded. 'You know they wed me to Roger when I was barely fifteen and he almost fifty. I gave him the son he desired and two daughters besides before I was twenty.'

She shrugged. 'I never wanted to marry him and now he is no longer capable of being a true husband to me. All he cares for is the nostrums the doctors brew to ease his aches and pains.'

Her long eyelashes fluttered and she heaved a plaintive sigh. 'I have done my duty, Hugh. Would you confine me to the sick-room? Surely I am entitled to a little happiness now?'

Hugh stared at her thoughtfully, wondering if he could believe her claims. Not that it really mattered. Adultery was still adultery whatever the excuse!

When he had been nineteen, his heart had been touched by her plight and in a way he still felt somewhat sorry for her. It could not have been pleasant to be forced into marriage with a man more than twice her age but the Count de Montfort was no ogre.

'Roger is an indulgent husband, Judith. He has forgiven you your sins against him.' Hugh gently removed her hand from his arm. 'He even forgave me.'

'There was no need for you to confess. No one suspected us of having an affair,' she said hotly.

'There was every need. I had injured his honour.' Hugh's tone was stiff. He had bitterly regretted hurting the older man.

'Honour! Your stupid notions led to Roger insisting we retire to his estates.' The amber eyes flashed with remembered annoyance. 'It was months before I could persuade him to return to court and by that time you had disappeared off on some task for William.'

Judith sighed and shook her head. 'In all the years since, we have never had a chance to talk alone until now.' Her expression brightened. 'Oh, Hugh, don't let us quarrel! I have never forgotten you, you know. You were such a wonderful lover!' She bestowed a caressing smile upon him, passing her tongue over her lips reminiscently.

Hugh gave a reluctant laugh. He had forgotten what a deliciously, shockingly sensual creature she was.

His amusement brought a sparkle into her eyes.

'You see! I could always make you smile! You were looking so gloomy earlier.'

Hugh admitted it. 'But that doesn't mean that I want us to become lovers again,' he added bluntly. 'I won't betray Roger a second time.'

'Then I shall settle for your friendship.' She smiled at him with limpid innocence.

Hugh eyed her sceptically. Over the years several tales of the Countess of Montfort's scandalous behaviour had reached his ears. He doubted if he'd been her first lover and he certainly hadn't been her last!

Maybe he ought to feel flattered but he suspected it was the thrill of conquest that made her want to renew their relationship. He had rejected her and she wanted to bring him to heel.

'Tell me, do you still have that marvellous falconer of yours?' he asked blandly. 'Drogo. Wasn't that his name? A marvellous fellow with hawks.'

Conceding a temporary defeat, she allowed him to change the subject.

The sound of the clarions announcing the arrival of new guests interrupted their amicable discussion on hunting.

A ripple of interest stirred in the enormous chamber. Judith de Montfort felt the man at her side tense and her gaze travelled curiously to follow his.

A young girl stood alone on the threshold, a tall, slender figure gowned in silk that matched the colour of her speedwell-blue eyes. Her style of dress and the golden hair blazing beneath a transparent veil announced her Saxon origins.

She advanced gracefully into the room, her head held high. The delicate colour that suffused her smooth complexion revealed that she heard the whispers which attended her progress but her manner remained serene.

'Rowena? Rowena of Edenwald!'

Hugh moved to intercept her, his expression filled with wondering disbelief.

Forced to halt, Rowena looked up at him coldly.

'You are blocking my way. I must pay my respects to the Duke.'

Rowena spoke in English, her voice tightly controlled but her pulse began to race. She had forgotten how tall he was and how overwhelmingly virile.

'You are angry with me still?'

'Need you ask?' Rowena glared at him. 'I have had many months to rue the day you crossed my path.'

'So you blame me for William's tardiness?'

Rowena nodded curtly, not trusting herself to answer. In spite of the fine gift he had sent, which she had not been able to resist making into a gown for her appearance tonight, he was still her rival for Edenwald.

'I had nothing to do with it.' A frown tugged Hugh's black eyebrows together.

'So you say.' Rowena snorted. 'How convenient it would have been if I had wearied of the struggle and given up my claim!' Her eyes flashed angrily. 'That's what you wanted, isn't it? For me to become a nun?'

To her astonishment his well-cut mouth curved into a slow smile.

'Nay, my lady. That would have been a waste.'

Rowena was so taken aback that she could think of absolutely nothing to say in reply.

'Let me escort you to the King.'

Seizing advantage of her silence, Hugh firmly took her by the elbow and steered her towards the royal dais.

'Lady Rowena. So we meet again.' William greeted her with a nod as she rose from her obeisance. 'I bid you welcome to our court.'

Rowena thanked him, switching into French so perfect that it startled Hugh de Lacy.

Now he came to think on it, Gerard had made some mention of the fact that she had learnt their language but he hadn't led Hugh to expect such fluency or such a cultured accent!

Hugh reminded himself to have a word with his young lieutenant. The wretch had also failed to tell him what a change the last fifteen months or so had wrought in Rowena's appearance!

Gone was the skinny little hoyden. She had grown several inches taller and acquired the most tantalising curves. Moreoever, her thin features had matured into a delicate loveliness.

She has grown into her face, Hugh decided. He had suspected that she might blossom into a beauty and tonight he was proved right. She was the loveliest woman in the room!

Desire rose in him with devastating swiftness. He wanted her!

'May I beg the favour of a private word, my lord?'

Rowena turned to glare at Hugh. He would ask now when she had just nerved herself to enquire if William had made his mind up yet about Edenwald!

The Duke nodded. He had been watching the pair closely and he was interested to hear what Hugh would say. Had the obvious solution to this dilemma occurred at last to his faithful knight?

'You may retire, Lady Rowena.'

The King crooked a finger to summon one of his courtiers.

'Attend this lady and find her a cup of wine,' he ordered and, having no choice, Rowena curtsied gracefully and allowed the lavishly dressed gentleman to lead her away.

Itching to know what was being said on the royal dais, Rowena paid scant attention to the compliments paid to her. His attempt to make polite conversation receiving little encouragement, it was with some relief that her escort saw the signal to return his awkward charge to the King.

'Are you ready to swear fealty, Lady Rowena?'

The abrupt demand made Rowena swallow nervously.

'I am ready, my lord.'

She had pondered this question time and time again

before finally coming to the decision that her personal
feelings could not be put above the duty she owed to
those in her care. She had promised her father that she
would look after Edenwald and this was her only chance
to keep it.

'I am glad to hear it. Your sojourn at St Etheldreda's
was not in vain if it taught you the value of obedience.'
William smiled thinly. 'However, another solution has
occurred to me. One that will satisfy both claims.'

Rowena paled. 'My lord?'

'What say you, lady, to a Norman husband?' William
glanced across at Hugh, his smile broadening.

'Marry?' Rowena croaked in amazement. 'You want
me to marry *him*?'

'Aye.' William laughed in satisfaction. 'Then it is
settled. You will be wed here at Winchester as soon as it
can be arranged.'

Rowena recovered from her stupefaction. 'No! I
won't do it!'

A heavy frown descended on the Duke's face and
Rowena remembered how he hated to be crossed.
'Thank you for your kind concern, my lord,' she
continued quickly, 'but I would prefer the nunnery to
marrying this man.'

'You have no vocation.' William waved this objection
aside.

'But I *cannot* marry him!'

'By the splendour of God, you will do as you are bid,
girl, and be grateful for the honour,' he growled, losing
patience. 'Now, the banquet is about to begin. Take her
away, Hugh.'

William dismissed them both with an abrupt wave.

'Let me go,' Rowena spat, trying to shake off the
iron grip.

'Be silent, you little fool!' Hugh pushed her down into an empty place on one of the dining-benches and sat beside her.

Becoming aware that every eye down the long length of the table was upon them, Rowena subsided, her colour dangerously high.

The banquet commenced.

Rare and strange delicacies appeared. A swan roasted in honey, its beak and feet gilded with real gold, dishes of spiced quail and fowl, venison and boar, and eels stewed in cinnnamon.

Rowena refused them all.

'You ought to eat something,' Hugh said.

'It would choke me,' she retorted savagely.

Her heart was hammering as if it must burst. She wanted to scream and shout and overturn the table so that all the expensive dishes were flung to the floor and ruined.

'Then at least have some wine,' Hugh insisted.

He had been drinking steadily, trying to drown his unease. Had he done the right thing? Dared he confess? But if he told her the truth, she might never forgive him!

Hugh raised a hand to summon one of the scurrying pages to fill her goblet but Rowena shook her head, refusing his suggestion.

'Why should I?' she answered with poisonous sweetness, her gaze scornful. 'You are drinking enough for both of us.'

'Don't try my patience too far, wench!'

Hugh's voice was harsh but he spoke in English, mindful of listening ears.

'Then tell your Duke you'll not marry me,' she countered in the same tongue, her eyes glittering with fury.

'You little lack-wit, it would do no good. William would just give you to another.' There was a rough sympathy in his tone as he shook his dark head at her. 'You will never regain Edenwald in your own right.'

His prophecy sent a shiver through Rowena.

'You. . .you are lying,' she said weakly.

'You know I'm not.' He banged his winecup down on to the oaken board. 'Stop behaving like a child, Rowena, and listen to me. You are a ward of the King like any other fatherless heiress. It is his right to bestow you and your lands in marriage. You cannot refuse. . . unless you take the veil.'

Rowena shuddered. She had told William she wanted to be a nun but at heart she knew that she could not bear to live so sterile a life. She wanted a home and babies of her own to love!

And a husband? What would it be like to be wed to Hugh de Lacy?

Rowena tried to ignore the treacherous stirring of excitement in the pit of her stomach.

'Why you? Why do I have to marry you of all men?' she asked angrily, hating herself for her weakness.

Hugh steeled himself against the sudden hurt caused by her bitter words.

'Because it is William's wish,' he replied calmly. 'Surely by now you have realised that he always gets what he wants in the end?'

The colour drained from Rowena's face.

'Unless you marry me you will lose Edenwald.' Hugh spoke softly but the words hit her like a blow.

Struggling to maintain her composure, Rowena stared blindly down at her clenched hands. Much as she hated to admit it, she knew that Hugh de Lacy was right. The best she could hope for if she defied William was banishment to some nunnery like St Etheldreda's. But if he chose, he could strip her of every possession, including her life, and there was nothing she could do to prevent it.

Except marry a man she loathed.

The Minster was cold. Rowena could feel the chill striking up from the old stones through the soles of her dainty bridal slippers. By sheer determination, she controlled her shivers. She would not let them think she was afraid.

He gown was of heavy white samite encrusted with silver embroideries and her hair flowed loose beneath a virgin's crown of spring violets. Rowena heard the appreciative murmuring which followed her down the nave but the admiration of the wedding guests left her unmoved.

She felt numb.

All through the lengthy toilette to prepare her for the ceremony, she had been desperately hoping that something, anything, would happen to stop it going ahead. The giggling comments of the high-born damsels sent to attend her by the King had flowed over her unheard. William himself had paid for the bride-clothes and ordered that she be treated with all honour.

Rowena had endured their ministrations, allowing them to do as they wished with her, but, hope fading, she had had no interest in the mirror they had produced when at last they had declared her ready.

'Take it away,' she'd ordered and, giving the weeping Elgiva one last kiss, she'd walked out of the room, her head held high.

Pride was all she had left to sustain her and Rowena's will-power didn't falter even when she caught sight of

William in his place of honour near the altar. But it was more than she could endure to meet Hugh de Lacy's grey eyes as she came to a halt by his side.

Carefully, she averted her gaze from her bridegroom and stared instead at the magnificent candlesticks adorning the altar.

The rich tones of the Bishop of Coutances filled the old church and Rowena supposed she should feel flattered. All the Saxon kings since the Great Alfred had been crowned here at Winchester and William no doubt meant to honour her by his choice of place and priest, but it meant nothing to her.

'I, Rowena Edwinsdaughter, take thee, Hugh de Lacy. . .'

Rowena spoke the vows in a cool voice, her expression remote as the heavy gold ring was slipped on to her finger.

Thankfully, it was soon over.

They emerged into the thin April sunshine and an errant breeze snatched up a lock of her hair and blew it across Hugh de Lacy's broad chest.

'My lady.' He untangled it from the silver pin that fastened his blue mantle and smoothed it back into place.

With a curt gesture of thanks, Rowena reluctantly met his gaze at last.

A tide of hot colour flooded her cheeks and she turned away from him quickly.

All through the long and elaborate wedding-feast which followed the look of desire which she had surprised in her new husband's eyes haunted her.

I thought he found the idea of marrying me distasteful. Perhaps I was wrong? she mused.

A queer excitement set her stomach rolling. Did he actually find her attractive?

Hastily, Rowena took a gulp of wine and almost choked.

'May I assist you in any way?' her bridegroom enquired courteously as she coughed and spluttered.

Recovering, Rowena swiftly shook her head and he turned his attention back to the jugglers who were performing for their amusement.

Covertly, Rowena studied his profile from beneath her lowered lashes. What was he thinking? His expression was remote. She'd assumed that he had married her out of duty since he was William's loyal knight. Yet surely he disliked having a Saxon bride foisted on him? Perhaps she had imagined that flash of desire in his eyes.

Rowena continued to stare at him, her thoughts in turmoil.

They were seated side by side at the high table in the places of honour. Hugh was more richly dressed than she had ever seen him in an ankle-length, formal tunic. Its glowing amber hue enhanced his dark colouring and for the first time she secretly admitted to herself that he was a very handsome man, albeit in his foreign Norman way.

A memory of Godric's blond-bearded face floated to the surface of her mind and for an instant Rowena allowed herself a pang of regret. Her feelings towards Godric had been so simple and easy. . .

The banquet dragged on, a medley of noise, colour and rich, spicy aromas. Rowena's head began to ache. Would this ordeal never end?

At last the bridal attendants swarmed up to the high table and bore her away. Swept along in their laughing midst, Rowena tried to quell the sudden panic that fluttered along her nerves.

The King had announced that one of the small bowers, usually allocated as sleeping-quarters for honoured guests, should be theirs while they remained at court. When Rowena entered the small round building, she saw that someone had bedecked its single chamber with bridal greenery and her mouth twisted into a wry grimace.

An elaborate bronze brazier standing in the middle of the room emitted a sweet applewood-scented warmth.

'Not that you'll need it. You won't feel the cold tonight!' one of her attendants informed her with a giggle.

With a great deal of similar jesting, they ruthlessly divested Rowena of her bridal garments. Then someone dragged an ivory comb through her hair while another noblewoman brought rosewater and splashed it over Rowena's icy hands.

'Quickly! I can hear the bridegroom's party coming!'

Before Rowena could draw breath, she was bundled into the wide bed and a silken coverlet flung over her to conceal her nakedness.

The door was opened with a flourish and someone cried, 'Your bride awaits you, my lord!'

Hugh entered the bower accompanied by his crowd of male companions. He had exchanged his finery for a loose robe, open at the neck. Rowena could see the dark hair hazing his bare brown chest and in spite of her attempts to prevent it a blush rose to her cheeks.

It deepened as the bevy of tipsy guests came crowding around the bed, flinging lucky charms, flower-petals and herbs for fertility amid shouts of bawdy advice and raucous laughter.

Hugh said something quietly to the King and to Rowena's relief William ordered everyone else to leave.

Still laughing and joking loudly, they all trooped out.

'A word of advice before I too depart,' William announced, his expression turning serious.

Rowena composed herself to listen but behind her show of obedience she seethed with resentment.

'This marriage blends the best of Norman and Saxon blood. It will be a pattern for the future if my hopes are fulfilled. Your children will live in a new England, an England of my making. Do not fail me!'

William's grave look lightened.

'And now I will bid you joy of your wedding night. God grant it produce a son.'

Rowena stared down at the coverlet, hiding the anger in her eyes, as Hugh escorted the King to the threshold and showed him out.

The door closed with a faint click and then there was silence.

Rowena kept her gaze averted but she sensed Hugh moving towards the table near the brazier where a flagon of wine and two goblets had been placed in readiness.

'Will you join me?' Hugh poured out the rich red liquid.

Rowena shook her head silently, unwilling to look at him.

'By the Rood, have you lost your tongue?' Hugh's goblet crashed down untasted. 'You have not spoken one single word since we exchanged vows.'

Rowena's head jerked up.

'I have nothing to say to you, Hugh de Lacy. You and your King forced me into this marriage but I will not pretend it pleases me. No, not even if you beat me!' She glared at him scornfully. 'They say your Duke whipped the Princess Matilda until she agreed to marry him—a fine example of you Norman wooing, I suppose. You may do as you will with me but my thoughts shall remain my own.'

'Harsh words, my lady.' Hugh controlled his temper with difficulty. 'But without cause. You are my wife and I will honour you.'

She cast him a disbelieving look. 'Are you trying to tell me you wanted to marry a Saxon?'

Her challenge made him hesitate for an instant and then he said smoothly, 'I mean you to understand that I have no intention of treating you harshly.' He paused significantly. 'Unless you drive me to it.'

Rowena sniffed disdainfully. 'Your threats don't impress me. I expect nothing but violence from a Norman!'

Hugh stifled an urge to curse and waved a hand to encompass the room about them. 'Does it look as if I intend you harm?' he said between clenched teeth. 'What more could you ask for?'

Rowena's glance travelled over the rich furnishings. There were costly tapestries upon the walls and a bearskin to warm the floor. Even the bed on which she lay had a goose-feather mattress and silken coverlets.

The Duchess of Normandy couldn't have asked for better!

Briefly, Rowena wondered whence he had obtained such luxuries but her voice was cold as she replied, 'It is still a prison.'

Hugh expelled a deep, angry breath. So much for his attempts to please her! He might as well have thrown the purse William had handed him as a wedding-gift into the palace midden!

The silence deepened.

Rowena sat rigid, bolt upright in the middle of the bed. Oh, Holy Mother, would this nightmare never end?

Hugh watched her. The torchlight made her hair gleam like burnished gold, casting faint shadows on her averted face and, unconsciously, his gaze softened as he absorbed her delicate beauty.

He decided to muzzle his pride and try again.

'I know this marriage was not of your choice but it is done now,' he said quietly. 'And William was right about one thing at least: we have to learn to live together. So tell me, what is it that you want?'

His gruff question startled Rowena into blurting out the truth. 'I want my freedom!'

A faint grimace twisted his well-cut mouth.

'You ask for the one thing I cannot grant.'

Rowena laughed but the sound had no mirth in it. 'Then it's as well I didn't believe you,' she retorted with a shrug.

She had intended her gesture to convey her indifference to anything else he might offer but to her dismay the sudden movement sent the coverlet sliding down from her shoulders. She snatched at it hastily, her mouth drying in sudden alarm as she saw his gaze come to rest on the rounded outline of her breasts.

Her skin had the glow of polished ivory. It looked warm and soft to touch. . .

'I think we have wasted enough time in talking, my lady,' Hugh said softly.

Rowena froze as he strode purposefully towards the bed. Unwillingly, her mind registered how he moved with a lithe and easy grace and her pulse began to quicken.

Without taking his eyes off her, Hugh stripped off the single garment he wore.

Broad of shoulder and narrow of hip, he had the superbly sculptured body of a warrior. Crisp dark hair hazed his muscular chest, descending in a narrowing spiral to the flat abdomen. . .and beyond. . .

Rowena barely managed to stifle a gasp of embarrassment. She longed to avert her gaze but was frightened that he would laugh at her. Trying desperately to appear calm, she sat very still as he slid into the bed but she was achingly aware of his nearness.

'Have you never seen a man naked before?' Hugh asked with a hint of amusement in his tone.

Rowena shook her head. 'I had no brothers,' she answered him stiffly.

Hugh nodded. 'Your priest, Father Wilfrid, told me that you were promised in marriage ——' he began, but she interrupted him.

'If you are trying to discover whether I am still a virgin, then the answer is yes!'

Rowena could feel the angry colour flooding into her cheeks. How dared he question her like this?

'I did not mean to doubt you. I noticed that you wore a maiden's crown. I am merely endeavouring to find out if you know what happens in a marriage-bed.'

His mild reply threw her. 'Oh. . .oh, I see,' she mumbled in confusion.

'Well? Do you, Rowena?' he asked softly. There was a laughing tenderness in his tone as he spoke.

'I know my duty,' she whispered hoarsely.

To Rowena's utter consternation, he didn't answer but began to trace her collarbone with one long forefinger.

'I will give you sons, if God grants it,' she managed to

add, unable to understand why such a feather-light caress was burning her to the bone.

'And will you take pleasure in the begetting of them, I wonder?'

His teasing tone bewildered her. Totally at a loss how to answer him, Rowena took refuge in silence but her blush deepened.

She had promised herself that she would stay calm and unafraid no matter what happened! Anticipating that he would pounce on her the minute they were alone, she had vowed that she would not beg for mercy. She would endure his lusts and pray that a child in her belly would soon release her from his unwanted attentions.

But nothing was happening as she had expected!

'Rowena, I don't want us to spend all out time together fighting.' Hugh's voice was quietly persuasive. 'There are better things we could be doing.'

The warmth from his naked body and the faintly musky, masculine odour of him was all around her, swamping her senses.

Fighting for composure, Rowena groped for a reply.

'You—you are my enemy,' she stuttered, her breathing swift and shallow. 'I could never find pleasure in your arms.'

Hugh smiled, the rare engaging smile she found so devastatingly attractive.

'Allow me to prove you wrong, my lady,' he murmured, and drew her into his embrace.

Instinctively, Rowena stiffened. 'Let me go,' she whispered.

Hugh shook his dark head. 'Not yet.'

She began to tremble, hating herself for her weakness, but all he did was to gently stroke the curve of her back. It was strangely soothing and gradually her shaking ceased.

'You have such beautiful hair,' he murmured, taking one long golden lock between his fingers. 'It is a crime to hide it away.' He raised the strand to his lips and kissed it.

Rowena watched him in wide-eyed silence and Hugh was reminded of a wary doe, ready to take flight at the slightest alarm.

'Don't look so afraid. I won't hurt you,' he whispered and his lips swiftly stifled her automatic protest.

His mouth was warm and gentle, evoking a strange yearning that left Rowena confused and shaken. Instead of pushing him away as she had intended, she allowed his weight to bear her back against the pillows.

'You are so lovely,' he breathed, lifting his dark head and staring down at her.

Rowena gazed into his grey eyes, no longer ice-cold but burning with passion and, like someone in a dream, raised her hand to touch his cheek with timid fingers.

A tiny sigh of satisfaction escaped him and he kissed her again.

'There, you see. This isn't so bad, is it, sweeting?' he said softly.

Unable to frame a coherent word, Rowena nodded silently. He smiled at her and slid both hands across her silken skin to find the rounded warmth of her full breasts.

'No, no, you mustn't!' Rowena shook her head, trying to draw away, as he caressed her with a skilful expertise that sent a slow, insidious pleasure unfurling in the pit of her stomach.

Hugh gave her another reassuring smile. 'We are man

and wife, sweeting. There can be no wrong in what we do together.'

He had misunderstood her hesitation but Rowena had no intention of revealing the truth.

She had never dreamt that a man's caresses could be so exciting! Godric's occasional kisses had never aroused her like this! They had made her feel happily content but Hugh's touch evoked a feverish desire to twine her limbs around him and kiss him back with all the passion that was burning in her.

It feels as if the blood in my veins has turned to liquid fire, she thought in terror and she shivered uncontrollably as he started to stroke her nipples.

They hardened instantly into tight, aching crests and Hugh's breathing quickened.

'Rowena!' The way he said her name it was almost a groan and his eyes blazed with desire as he kissed her again, this time more passionately so that his lips parted hers.

Their breath mingled. An exquisite delight shot through Rowena as his tongue slipped past her teeth and caressed hers. Her head swimming, she kissed him back.

Lost in the sea of strange new sensations overwhelming her, she almost cried out in disappointment when his mouth left hers but her anguish changed into a gasp of excitement as he took her nipple into his mouth and began to suck on it.

Someone. . .somewhere. . .was making queer little cries of mindless bliss. . .

To her horror, Rowena suddenly realised that the incoherent moans were coming from her and she caught her breath in sudden shame. What on earth was she doing? He was her enemy!

Desperately, she tried to recall her hatred, willing herself to resist, but her body seemed to have acquired a volition of its own. Of their own accord, her hands slid over his smooth olive shoulders, tracing the strong muscles in his upper back. An overpowering longing to feel every inch of his skin against her own swept over her and she pressed herself against him.

'Kiss me!' she demanded in a hoarse voice she didn't recognise as her own and, burying her hands in his thick black hair, she tugged his head back up to hers.

Triumph sang in Hugh's veins. His kisses deepened and became more demanding. 'I want you, my little Saxon,' he murmured thickly.

In answer, Rowena twisted her arms around his neck, drawing him even closer and kissing him back with a matching fervour before lifting her mouth an inch away from his and whispering in a voice so low he could barely hear it, 'Then take me.'

Hugh stared down into her speedwell eyes. They were hungry with passion and he laughed a little wildly, elated by her abandoned response. His skilful fingers slid down over her stomach and found the tender core of her womanhood, beginning to weave a new magic. Rowena gasped and writhed against him, tormented by a need she could not name. She could hardly believe what was happening to her. The pleasurable sensations flooding over her were so intense, she thought she might faint.

'Now, sweeting, now!'

Hugh's voice was hoarse in her ear as he cupped her buttocks and raised her hips to meet his entry.

Rowena buried her hot face into his shoulder. A tremor of fear shook her before her instincts took over, bidding her open to him like flower-petals unfurling in the warm sun.

For an instant, there was a sharp, brief pain and then he was inside her. The feeling was indescribably strange and yet, somehow, it was as if her body had always known this joy was meant to be.

Restraining his own desire for fear of hurting her, Hugh slowly deepened his possession and Rowena's eyes opened wide at the growing waves of sensuous rapture that started to build within her with each thrust of his manhood.

Breathless with amazement, she finally abandoned the last barrier of mental self-control. She was no longer Saxon nor he a Norman. They were just a man and a woman, caught up in an experience as old as time. Only the senses ruled in this enchanted world; all else was forgotten. Hugh quickened his erotic rhythm and the breath caught in his throat at her passionate response. 'You. . .are. . .a. . .marvellous pupil, my lady,' he rasped as they began to move together in perfect harmony.

'Oh, Hugh!'

He silenced her cry of pleasure with a burning kiss that seemed to sear her very soul.

Eyes tightly closed, her heart thundering, Rowena clung to him. He was her rock in the storm of sensations crashing all around her.

The the waves of pleasure intensified, sweeping her up to a new peak until she was carried beyond the boundaries of self to drown in a sea of ecstasy. . .

'Well, my lady?'

Reborn safe in his arms on another shore, Rowena

opened her heavy eyelids and saw him smiling down at her.

'Was I right?' There was a teasing note in Hugh's deep voice.

Unable to summon the energy to speak, Rowena nodded sleepily, wondering what on earth he was talking about. Her brain felt as if it was made of straw.

Hugh chuckled softly as he took in the extent of her exhaustion.

'Poor sweeting!' he murmured. 'Did I tire you out?' he asked, rising from the bed. 'Then let me make recompense.'

Rowena blushed as she suddenly realised his meaning. She had found pleasure in his arms in spite of all her denials!

When he returned a moment later, he brought the bowl of rosewater abandoned by her attendants and a towel and, in spite of Rowena's embarrassed protests, set about making her more comfortable.

'When you are on campaign, you have to learn to be handy at all sorts of tasks,' he joked, handing her a goblet of wine and turning away to smooth the bedclothes.

His kindness surprised Rowena. He was trying to ease her embarrassment by making fun of himself.

'You are full of surprises, my lord,' she murmured demurely, recovering her composure.

Hugh eyed her, wondering precisely what she meant, but decided against disturbing the fragile harmony of the moment. Behind her serene expression, he sensed that she was wary. Did she regret her sensuous abandonment?

In fact, Rowena was trying very hard not to think at all. She felt so wondrously content that she couldn't bear to examine her feelings. I am too tired to make any sense of what has happened tonight, she told herself, sipping her wine.

But she knew she was lying.

When Hugh had finished, only the stain on the coverlet remained as evidence of her lost virginity. Rowena surveyed it proudly. There, let any of those high-born Norman ladies make sneering comments about her virtue now!

The short time it had taken to arrange the wedding hadn't been an easy one for Rowena. Thanks to the King's protection, no one dared to act in an overtly hostile fashion but she was aware that many people didn't want her at court. They made it very plain that they despised anyone of Saxon blood and thought themselves superior in every way.

Watching Hugh remove the soiled towel, Rowena remembered how one of them in particular, a raven-haired woman of outstanding beauty, had seemed to take an especial pleasure in baiting her. Rowena hadn't learnt her name but her sharp remarks had hurt.

However, she forgot all about her adversary as Hugh slid back into bed.

'Come here, wife.'

Feeling suddenly shy, she hesitated as he held out his arms to her but Hugh wasn't having any nonsense.

'For tonight, at least, let's have a truce, my lady,' he said firmly, pulling her into his embrace.

The spell he had woven earlier began to exert its compelling magic and Rowena nodded helplessly.

'Do you think we ought to try again and see if it was just by luck that my embraces were not distasteful to you?' Hugh gave her a wicked grin as he posed the question and Rowena caught her breath in surprise. She had never seen him look so carefree before. Could she have actually made him happy?

Distracted by this strange thought, she forgot to answer and, taking her silence for consent, Hugh started to kiss her.

And suddenly Rowena realised she wasn't tired at all. . . .

CHAPTER SIX

ROWENA awoke to find herself alone. Bright daylight filtered in through the stretched membrane covering the narrow window and for an instant a nameless feeling of deep contentment filled her.

Memory returning, she sat up abruptly, her stomach churning.

She had behaved like a shameless trull! In spite of all her fine avowals, she hadn't been able to resist Hugh de Lacy's blandishments.

Pressing her palms against her hot cheeks, Rowena wondered what on earth had possessed her. She had betrayed her father and Godric for the sake of her own gratification!

A tap at the door announced the arrival of Elgiva.

'Oh, my lady!' she exclaimed anxiously, catching sight of the tears in Rowena's eyes. 'Did that brute hurt you?'

Rowena denied it but she was glad to rest her head against her nurse's plump bosom when Elgiva hurried over to the bed to give her a comforting hug.

'Oh, Elgiva, I have been such a fool!' she sighed.

Little by little, Elgiva managed to prize the truth out of her.

'Well, to my way of thinking, you ought to be glad you didn't find his embraces distasteful, my lamb,' Elgiva asserted, her tone robust.

Rowena blinked at her.

'You are young and healthy. Naturally, your body is ripe for love. De Lacy might be a Norman but he's an

attractive man.' Elgiva's eyes held a knowing twinkle.
'Why shouldn't you make the best of things since you'll
have to submit to his demands anyway?

'I thought you hated all Normans!' Rowena
exclaimed.

Elgiva shook her coiffed head. 'I did at first but hate
doesn't change things. All it does it take up too much
energy.'

She fixed Rowena with an encouraging look. 'For one
of *them*, he's behaved well. He acted fairly over
Edenwald and he's treated you kindly. That's good
enough for me to acknowledge him as master.'

Rowena's confusion showed on her face and Elgiva
gave her a sympathetic smile.

'Let it be, child. You've done your best to save
Edenwald and now the outcome is in God's hands.
Enjoy this new life and forget the past.'

A frown creased Rowena's smooth brow.

'I don't know if I can,' she said slowly.

'I'm sure your sainted mother would give you the
same advice if she were here,' Elgiva insisted. 'It's a
man's world and we women have to learn the art of
submission to survive. De Lacy is your husband. There's
no going back. You'll only make it harder on yourself if
you kick against his authority all the time.'

She winked at Rowena broadly. 'Mind you, there are
plenty of other methods of getting your own way.'

'My father never treated me like an inferior,' Rowena
muttered rebelliously.

'Your father over-indulged you,' Elgiva retorted
sharply. 'I've always said so. Most men want their
women to be submissive. De Lacy won't like it if you
argue and air your learning.'

Rowena bit her lip, wondering if her nurse was right. Did Hugh want a docile wife?

'Come, my lamb, let me help you get dressed,' Elgiva urged, her tone softening. 'When you have breakfasted you'll feel better.'

In addition to her bridal finery, King William had also paid for several other gowns to be made for Rowena, saying that she was his ward and must have clothes to suit her new station. Rowena had barely glanced at them but now, as Elgiva brought them forth from the storage chest, her natural curiosity was aroused.

Elgiva cunningly encouraged her to examine each one and by the time they had selected a pale rose-coloured kirtle to wear with the green embroidered over-tunic excitement had banished the guilt and misery lingering in Rowena's eyes.

Satisfied, Elgiva carefully braided the thick golden hair and arranged Rowena's veil. 'There, my lady, you look lovely, just as a new bride should. These Norman fashions suit you.'

Unlike her Saxon rocs which were closely fitted to the body, this tunic was cut loose and meant to be worn with a girdle. It was also somewhat longer in length and the sleeves were tight, not full. Instead of falling loosely to the elbow they reached the wrist, where they were gathered into an embroidered band so that the sleeves of the under-kirtle didn't show at all.

It felt a little strange but Rowena decided that Elgiva was right. The effect was quite pleasing, even though the embroidery was not up to the standard she was used to. English women, it seemed, were still superior in that art!

'Shall I go in search of some food?' Elgiva enquired. 'Or would you prefer me to set this room to rights first?'

'As you wish,' Rowena replied absently, fingering the elaborate girdle of silver cord tied low on her waist. The ends hung almost to the ground and were finished with fancy tassels which swung against her legs in a way which felt odd.

'I'll replenish the brazier and you can sit by it,' Elgiva said. 'It's a cold morning and I don't want you catching a chill.'

She quickly accomplished this task and then remade the bed, carefully removing the stained sheet. It would be held back from the laundry until everyone with the right to do so had satisfied themselves as to Rowena's virginity.

'Thank you, Elgiva. It is not your place to perform such menial tasks.'

Elgiva laughed, secretly pleased by Rowena's concern. 'Don't fret, I'm hale enough for any work, my lady. Now, what would you fancy for your breakfast?'

When she had disappeared off to the kitchens the small chamber seemed very quiet. Rowena wandered round examining the furnishings before finally sitting down again.

Finally, she allowed her thoughts to turn to her new husband. She hated to admit it but she was piqued that he had disappeared without a word. Where could he have gone?

'Perhaps he is attending Mass?' she murmured to herself, trying not to wish that he had asked for her company.

Suddenly the door opened. 'Good morrow, my lady.'

Rowena jumped. 'I. . .I thought you were Elgiva returning with breakfast,' she stammered, trying to recover her composure.

'You need a page to run such errands,' Hugh

announced cheerfully, kicking the door shut behind him and coming into the room. 'I'll find a suitable boy and you can train him to your liking.'

Rowena nodded, aware of a ridiculous feeling of shyness. Last night they had come together in the most intimate way possible but in all other respects she barely knew this man! What on earth were they going to find to talk about?

To cover her nervousness, she said brightly, 'What have you got there?'

'Mead, my lady,' Hugh replied, setting down the leather bottle he carried. 'I'm sorry it took me so long. I hoped to get back before you woke. Still, I think you prefer it to our Norman wine.'

Rowena coloured a little. 'I dare say I shall grow accustomed to wine in time,' she said primly.

Hugh flashed a grin at her. 'No doubt.'

Rowena's eyes widened when he produced two curved ox-horns bound with silver from the oak cupboard under the window and proceeded to fill one with the mead. 'Where did you get those?'

'I bought them a week ago,' Hugh answered, handing the full horn to her. 'It is your Saxon custom to serve mead to a bride and groom, is it not?'

Rowena nodded, watching him fill the second horn.

'I was told it brought good luck,' Hugh added, his gaze warm as it rested on her.

She looked as fresh and lovely as a spring flower in her new gown and Hugh had to curb a longing to snatch her into his arms but his instincts warned him to tread carefully.

His patience was rewarded when Rowena tentatively announced that it was the custom to drain the contents of the horn in one gulp. 'Otherwise, the charm doesn't work.'

Did he know that mead was supposed to encourage successful bedding? Rowena wondered as she raised the horn to her lips and swallowed down the sweet fiery liquid.

'I meant to use these yesterday,' Hugh said, putting down his empty horn. 'But the palace steward couldn't lay his hands on enough good mead to serve at our wedding feast. So, let's hope the charm works even if it's a day late.'

From the gleam in his eye, Rowena guessed he knew precisely what the drink was supposed to do!

All the same, he had gone to a lot of trouble to try and please her. . .

To her surprise, Rowena found herself saying in a reassuring tone, 'No harm done. We didn't need its help,' and then, aghast at her boldness, she blushed hotly.

Hugh chuckled, delighted by her frankness.

To Rowena's alarm, he pulled up a stool and sat down next to her.

'Have I told you yet how lovely you look this morning, wife?' he said softly.

Rowena's fingers curled into her palm. His nearness was having a strange effect on her breathing!

In self-defence, she dropped her gaze into her lap and took refuge in silence.

Hugh surveyed her averted profile and restrained a sigh. She was as wary as a half-starved cat!

To Rowena's relief, the tension was broken by the arrival of Elgiva with a tray of food.

'Have you broken your fast, my lord?' Rowena asked.

He shook his dark head and she politely invited him to share her meal.

'You have little appetite, sweeting. Is this fare not to your liking?'

Rowena stopped crumbling a piece of bread and tried to smile. 'I'm not very hungry,' she prevaricated.

Half an hour ago she had been ravenous. How could she admit to him of all people that it was his nearness which had destroyed her appetite?

Elgiva cleared away the dirty dishes and departed.

A strained silence fell once more.

'We are too late to attend Mass but perhaps you would like to take a walk instead? The grounds here are pleasant.' Hugh put the suggestions forward with more confidence than he was feeling. When would she begin to trust him enough to talk to him?

Rowena accepted and hurried to don her mantle.

'Change your shoes for a stouter pair,' Hugh advised.

'Is it so cold out? It looks a bright day.'

'Aye, but the grass is wet.' He smiled at her suddenly. 'And I shouldn't want you to spoil your new finery. Not after William spent so much of your revenues on it.'

Rowena couldn't help laughing at his wry grimace. '*My* revenues, my lord?' she enquired pertly. 'Don't you mean *our* revenues? Or am I to understand that you have given up your claim to Edenwald?'

Hugh's grin broadened. 'What I have I hold, wench!' he said, reminding her of the motto on his banner.

For the first time, the thought that she was no longer in sole charge of Edenwald didn't sear her soul.

Hugh had half expected her to fly at him, and, encouraged by her silence, he went on earnestly, 'I want your help in running Edenwald, Rowena. You know the manor much better than I do. Your opinions will be valuable to me.'

She smiled at him cautiously; a fresh optimism began to bubble up inside her, dissolving her anxious tension.

Perhaps he really means it, she thought as she hurried to change her shoes, excitement stirring in the pit of her stomach. I'd be a fool to reject a chance to start afresh, she told herself, discreetly eyeing her good-looking husband from beneath her lashes as she pulled on a pair of ankle-length boots. After all, as everyone keeps reminding me, we are married. Nothing but death can separate our lives now!

My father wouldn't have wanted me to marry a Norman but perhaps, in the circumstances, he might have approved of this one, she decided, moving to join Hugh at the door.

'My lady.' Hugh offered her his arm, wishing he knew what thoughts lay behind her sudden smile.

The royal pleasance was an attractive place with its sweep of flower-starred greensward. Several fruit trees, bedecked in new spring foliage, were cunningly placed to offer shade and there were even rose-bushes. Rowena had never seen anything like it.

'This is beautiful, Hugh!' she exclaimed, much impressed.

The idea of having a garden that served no function but to please was one that she could rapidly grow accustomed to, Rowena decided. At home, they'd simply grown food or herbs.

'Do you think we might create something like this at Edenwald?' she asked, her earlier feeling of constraint vanishing.

'If you desire it, I'm sure it could be arranged,' Hugh answered, secretly delighted by her enthusiasm.

Rowena felt a spurt of relief. He hadn't made fun of her suggestion. Perhaps he no longer thought of her as a child.

A sudden blush coloured her cheeks. After last night, surely she needn't doubt it!

Luckily, Hugh didn't seem to notice her rosy flush but announced thoughtfully, 'I expect there are other changes we will need to make too.'

'We will need more servants,' Rowena agreed.

'A good cook would not come amiss.'

'Are you saying you don't like our Saxon dishes?' Rowena enquired innocently but her eyes danced with mischief.

Hugh grinned and avoided the trap by murmuring that she might like to choose some ladies-in-waiting to attend her.

Rowena nodded. Most married women of rank had several attendants. 'My father made me the same offer after my mother died,' she said shyly. 'It didn't seem necessary at the time. I had Elgiva for company and in any case I rarely ventured beyond our boundaries but I suppose things are different now.'

They walked on, discussing other changes they might make.

'And eventually I shall undertake a programme of building,' Hugh concluded.

'Building?' Rowena echoed in surprise.

'For defence purposes,' Hugh murmured vaguely.

Rowena stared at him but his expression was bland.

'If you wish, you may hire new servants now,' Hugh remarked, hoping to divert her.

He was tempted to tell her the truth but he had the feeling it was too soon. One day he would have to confess that he intended to build a castle at Edenwald, but not yet. He would wait until she trusted him better and could understand his plans for the future.

'Elgiva does need some help,' Rowena answered. 'But I should like to find a Saxon lad to be my page.'

'Of course.' Hugh nodded briskly. 'And we can take them back with us to Edenwald if they prove satisfactory.'

Rowena's eyes flew to his face, sudden hope brightening their sapphire depths. 'Does that mean we are leaving soon?'

'Not yet awhile, I'm afraid,' Hugh replied, wishing he'd had the sense to keep his mouth shut. 'William wants me to remain at court.'

Striving to keep the disappointment from showing on her face, Rowena inclined her head in understanding.

'But we will return there before the summer is out, I promise you.'

There was a reassuring note in his deep voice and a tiny shoot of hope blossomed in Rowena's heart. He *did* want to please her!

Perhaps Elgiva was right. Maybe Hugh would prove a good husband. At least he understood how homesick she felt. Only time would tell, but if they were both willing, then they might be able to make this strange marriage work.

Rowena was changing her gown for supper that evening when Hugh asked Elgiva to leave them.

'But we will be late!' Rowena protested as the door closed behind her maid.

'My question won't take long,' Hugh said with one of his rare smiles.

Rowena's heart began to race as he walked over to where she sat, her golden hair still in loose disarray.

Taking her gently by the shoulders, Hugh raised her to her feet.

'Tonight William will ask you if you are content with this marriage,' he said softly. 'How will you answer him, my lady?'

His touch was beginning to make her head spin.

'Well, Rowena?' Hugh urged.

'I . . . I don't know,' she replied shakily.

Hugh restrained a groan of disappointment. By the Rood, but he was a fool!

'Don't frown, sweeting,' he murmured, releasing her. 'William will think what he likes, no matter what you say. It is a habit of his.'

Rowena nodded stiffly and, sitting down again, picked up her comb. In that case, why had he asked her?

'Let me.'

Hugh took the comb and, taking up a position behind her, began to draw it gently through the long gleaming strands.

Rowena's breathing became ragged. 'I think you had better let Elgiva do the rest,' she gasped.

Hugh let the comb fall to the floor. His hands gripped her shoulders. 'By all the saints, but you are beautiful!'

Rowena swayed, leaning back against his strong thighs, feeling suddenly boneless and weak with desire. She could feel the heat from his body against her neck and it was turning her blood to fire.

His hands slid down to cup her breasts and her nipples hardened through the thin silk.

'If we are late, we will offend the King,' Rowena whispered, catching her breath as his long fingers stroked her aching nipples.

'Damn the King!' Hugh muttered, swiftly bending to kiss her. Rowena's lips parted eagerly beneath his.

The kiss went on and on until at last Hugh broke away, murmuring, 'You little Saxon witch. How could any man resist you?'

Rowena smiled at him with deliberate provocation and with a groan Hugh cast aside the last of his control and swept her up in his arms. Carrying her over to the bed, he paused only to bar the door.

'We will have to be quick,' Rowena laughed, giggling helplessly as he struggled impatiently with her gown. 'Or we'll both be in disgrace!'

Hugh stifled her laughter with another burning kiss and her amusement fled. Desire rose in a dizzying spiral as he caressed her naked body and when he entered her she sighed with exquisite satisfaction.

'Oh, yes, yes, Hugh, yes!'

The cry of pleasure was wrung from her as the whirlwind of sensation racking every inch of her being reached its height.

An instant later, she felt his strong body convulse in satisfaction and, without stopping to think, flung her arms around him and hugged him affectionately until he became still.

Hugh eased himself from her and, propping himself up on one elbow, regarded her with a lazy smile.

'I'm sorry. I'm afraid I've creased your gown,' he apologised but his tone was triumphant.

'I can wear something else.' Rowena dismissed the problem and stretched languidly, feeling as sleepily content as a cream-fed cat.

'Up with you, my lady!' Hugh laughed and bent to kiss away the tiny beads of perspiration that pearled her brow. 'It's time we got dressed.'

A blush stained Rowena's cheeks as she scrambled from the bed. Splashing rosewater over her heated skin, she wondered if she could have a brain fever. How could she behave in this wanton manner?

'Shall I go and find Elgiva?' Hugh asked after she had hastily pulled on a fresh gown.

'Please.' Rowena could hardly meet his grey eyes.

What was it about this man that his slightest touch should turn her bones to water?

Hugh went out whistling and Rowena prepared herself to meet her nurse's knowing gaze but, thankfully, Elgiva maintained a tactful silence as she worked with speed to restore Rowena's appearance.

Due to her efficiency, they were only a few minutes late when they entered the hall and, luckily, the King had also been delayed.

Odo de Nevil joined them. He greeted Rowena with the wary air of a man uncertain of his welcome.

Rowena returned his greeting with a polite smile. 'I am willing to forget the past, my lord,' she announced, mindful of her resolve to make a fresh start. De Nevil was her husband's friend so she would have to try to like him.

Odo heaved a sigh of relief. 'I am glad to hear it, my lady,' he muttered gruffly.

Privately, Odo had been against this marriage. Sending the wench to a nunnery would have solved the problem equally well. However, it couldn't be denied that Hugh's black mood had vanished. In fact, surveying him, Odo couldn't ever remember seeing Hugh look so happy.

Odo suppressed a guffaw. God's teeth, so *that* was what had been the matter with the boy!

A page came up to offer them wine and Rowena

stood sipping it, listening to the two men talk. Many of
the names they discussed were unfamiliar but then Odo
mentioned someone she knew.

'Is Gerard de Beaumont coming to court?'

'Aye. I sent him to relieve Odo at Edenwald with
orders to report to us here once Easter was over,' Hugh
replied.

When she had first arrived at Winchester, Rowena
had wondered if she might encounter that charming
young knight but the anxiety and distress she had
suffered since then had sent all such trivial thoughts out
of her head.

'It will be pleasant to see him again,' she murmured
with a slight smile, remembering how Gerard had
brought her Hugh's gift of blue silk. He had been the
first man to behold her newly blossomed figure and she
treasured the memory of how his hazel eyes had glowed
with admiration. It had done wonders for her
confidence!

Hugh suppressed a pang of jealousy and said, 'I think
it is time I introduced you to a few people, Rowena.'

Concealing her nervousness, Rowena placed her
hand on his arm and they began to circulate. By the time
the King arrived and they were required to make their
obeisance, her head was reeling from trying to remember the host of new names and faces.

All of them sweetly smiling and polite, she noted
wryly to herself as she curtsied to the King. What a
difference marriage to Hugh de Lacy had made to her
despised status!

As expected, William quizzed her about her marriage
but Rowena sensed that he wasn't really listening to her
answers. She had become a wife and already she knew

that Normans did not place the same value on their women that Saxons did.

'Why do we lose importance to you after the wedding?' she asked Hugh as they took their places for supper. 'Saxon women have many rights in their own name. We could own property and land and swear legally binding oaths but as far as I can see Norman wives are mere appendages of their husbands!'

Hugh chuckled at her indignant tone but then he shook his dark head and answered in a serious voice.

'Having rights in law confers independence,' he said slowly. 'And there's the main difference, Rowena. Your society is, or rather was, a freer one.'

He fixed his light gaze on her and for an instant she saw regret in his eyes.

The astonishing thought that he might have disliked his part in the destruction of her world occurred to Rowena but there was no time to dwell on it. Hugh's voice was continuing and she wanted to give all her attention to what he was saying.

'In Normandy everything belongs to William and he insists all his landowners include knight service in repayment to him. We have to provide the required number of mounted and armed men, which is an expensive business, so we must make our lands yield profit. We cannot afford the luxury of allowing that profit to be diluted.'

Rowena nodded her understanding. 'So women and peasants become mere chattels,' she said bitterly. 'And you Normans think your culture superior!'

Hugh winced. Too many of the men he knew treated their wives and villeins too badly for him to refute her claim.

'You glorify war and chase after money,' Rowena accused. 'Where are your poets? Or your craftsmen? I haven't seen a piece of needlework of jewellery here that a Saxon couldn't improve on.'

They were speaking in English but the scorn in her tone was attracting curious glances and Hugh raised his brows in warning.

'Try a little of this quail and almond pottage, my lady,' he said firmly and Rowena bit her lip.

Now he would think she'd meant to attack him! And she hadn't.

'I'm sorry, I let myself get carried away,' she muttered after they had eaten in silence for a few moments.

Hugh regarded her exquisite profile and his annoyance softened. Most Normans thought the Saxons were an effete lot, soft and lazy and lacking the sense to make the most of their assets. Was it any surprise that his Saxon wife should have an equally low opinion of the average Norman?

But what did she think of him?

Roast suckling pig and rabbit in saffron gravy were served and finally Hugh couldn't stand it any longer.

'Tell me,' he said abruptly. 'Do you class me with the rest of my fellow countrymen?'

Startled, Rowena glanced up at him and saw the intensity burning in his light eyes but before she could reply Hugh continued in the same tight voice, 'Did it never occur to you to wonder why I took the trouble to learn English?'

Ashamed, Rowena shook her head. At Edenwald, she had been so wrapped up in hatred that she had taken his mastery of her language for granted. Until she had come to Winchester, she hadn't even realised how unusual his accomplishment was.

'You asked me once why Edenwald was so important to me,' Hugh said quietly. 'Now we are man and wife, perhaps it is time to tell you the truth. Although I am well-born, my family is poor. I hoped to gain land of my own after the invasion and my hopes came true.'

His low voice dropped to a whisper.

'Edenwald is the first thing of any real value that I have ever owned. It is the symbol of my success. I want to make a new life for myself, to put down roots here and found a family.'

'I see,' Rowena murmured, much taken aback by his unexpected confidence.

Hugh shrugged, his expression wry. She must have bewitched him or why else was he babbling like a fool?

'Oh, I knew there would be problems,' he continued in a brisker tone. 'I was prepared for that. However, it is a little disconcerting to discover that even my own wife thinks I'm an uncouth barbarian.'

'But I don't!'

Rowena's hand shook, spilling a little wine from her goblet on to the white linen tablecloth. She fussed at the stain for a moment before gathering the courage to look up at his face.

A sudden smile lit up his austere features.

'Rowena, I want you to know something else. It wasn't the King who arranged our——'

A fanfare of trumpets interrupted Hugh and he bit off the rest with an impatient exclamation as William rose to his feet.

In a loud voice the King announced that his wife, the Duchess Matilda, had agreed to join him. There was a flurry of cheering and comment which lasted until a troop of acrobats ran in to perform their tricks.

'You were saying, my lord?'

Hugh shook his dark head. 'It doesn't matter,' he replied lightly, knowing the moment was lost.

Rowena nodded, stifling her curiosity with a little pang of regret.

Later, when the entertainment was over, people began to circulate again.

Rowena stood up. A sensation of panic gripped her as she tried to focus on the swirling maze of colour surrounding her. All around, the richest garments she had ever seen glowed in a rainbow of colour set against a haze of scintillating jewels and loud, confident foreign voices.

It must be the wine I drank, she thought dizzily.

'My lady.'

Hugh placed a guiding hand under her elbow and a surge of relief suffused Rowena. The heat and smoke in this brilliantly lit hall were beginning to make her feel slightly nauseous.

'Thank you.' She bestowed a grateful smile upon him. 'That wine was stronger than I thought. I shall be more careful in future.'

'Maybe some fresh air would help clear your head.'

Discreetly, he led her through the throng out into the courtyard where Rowena thankfully gulped in several deep breaths of untainted air.

'Better?'

Rowena nodded, her giddiness receding. 'I'm sorry,' she murmured. 'Shall we go back now?'

In the light cast by one of the flambeaux, Hugh surveyed her anxiously. She had lost the fragile pallor that had alarmed him a few moments ago but he thought she looked tired.

'Would you prefer to retire?'

'Won't it seem odd? I don't want to cause you embarrassment.'

Hugh's excellent teeth gleamed for an instant in the darkness. 'You won't.'

Sensing that her reply had somehow pleased him, Rowena relaxed. 'I am a little weary,' she admitted.

'You didn't get much sleep last night,' Hugh agreed, so blandly that for a moment Rowena didn't realise what he had said.

The indignant look on her face made him chuckle.

'Come, let me escort you back to our bower,' he offered, his tone apologetic.

Rowena let him place a supporting arm around her. Somehow, as they walked, her head came to rest against his shoulder and she felt so relaxed and comfortable that it was with regret that she realised they had reached their sleeping-quarters.

'Will you come inside, my lord?'

Hugh was tempted by the unconscious invitation in her voice but regretfully he shook his head.

'I'd better get back,' he murmured.

Rowena curbed a sigh of disappointment.

'Of course. You must not offend the King.'

Thankful that she understood, Hugh raised her hand to his lips and kissed it.

'Sleep well, my lady.'

Rowena watched him walk away, a queer feeling of contentment washing over her. He would be back.

Sleep eluded Rowena. In spite of her weariness she could not settle.

'My lady? Is something wrong?' Elgiva enquired sleepily from her post by the door as Rowena got up and slipped on a loose robe.

'Shall I fetch you a posset?' Rowena's explanation had aroused her nurse's motherly instincts. 'There's bound to be someone still about in the kitchens.'

Rowena hesitated. Her mouth was parched but it was late and Elgiva's plump face looked drawn with fatigue.

'Thank you but no, Elgiva. I shall make do with some ale,' she said, indicating the jug that the maid had brought earlier that evening.

Trying to ignore the headache pounding her skull, she smiled. 'Go to bed now. There's no need to wait until my lord returns.'

Elgiva frowned. 'Are you sure, my lady?'

Curbing the impulse to snap, Rowena reassured her and eventually Elgiva went off to seek her pallet in the quarters assigned to female servants, an arrangement Hugh had insisted on in spite of the inconvenience it caused.

He hadn't told Rowena it was because he wanted her to himself.

Rowena sipped a little of the ale but it tasted strangely sour. She grimaced and rubbed her forehead, wishing her headache would go away.

'That's the last time I drink more than one cup of your Norman wine, Hugh de Lacy!' she exclaimed aloud, abandoning the ale and giving the nearest stool a kick.

It hurt her bare foot. 'Lack-wit!' She started to laugh at her own bad temper and went instead to ease open the door a little in the hope that some fresh air might cure her hangover.

Glancing out into the shadowy darkness, she espied a

tall male figure approaching and for an instant her heart
lurched with instinctive fear until she recognised him.

About to call out a greeting, she hesitated as a
second, slighter figure appeared and ran to catch up
with him.

'Hugh! Wait!'

'Judith?' Hugh de Lacy spun round to face his
pursuer.

'Why have you been avoiding me? You know I long
for your company.'

The blatant invitation in the woman's tone came as a
shock and Rowena frantically searched her memory.
She *knew* that husky voice!

'Judith, I'm married.'

'What difference need that make to us?'

This passionate reply carried clearly to Rowena's ears
and she gasped, but the voice continued relentlessly, the
words almost tumbling over themselves in haste.

'Everyone knows you wed that little barbarian for her
lands. Oh, not that I blame you! It is the way of the
world, but there is no need to pretend you wished for
the match with *me*!'

The intimate emphasis placed on this last word struck
Rowena like a blow and she scarcely registered her
husband's denial.

'Oh, Hugh, not even William could ask you to play
the devoted husband.' The husky voice dissolved into
laughter and in a sudden shaft of moonlight Rowena
saw her rival clearly.

An iron band seemed to grip her chest, squeezing all
the air from her lungs.

This brazen creature was none other than the woman
who had tormented her so cruelly before her marriage!
She had been at the banquet tonight at the side of an old

man whose rich apparel had proclaimed his high status. After that first glance, Rowena had taken care not to look their way again.

'Oh, my love, come with me now! Roger is asleep and I know a place where we can be alone.'

Rowena had heard enough. Flinging the door wide so that light spilled out into the darkness, she stalked towards them.

'Won't you introduce me, husband?' she demanded. 'We appear to have something in common.'

There was fury in every line of her taut figure but before the astonished Hugh could frame a reply Judith jumped in quickly.

'So, you have a tongue in your head after all, Saxon.' Her tone was as mockingly disdainful as the smile on her full lips. 'A pity you use it like a fishwife.'

She turned to Hugh as if expecting him to share her amusement but to her evident dismay he shook off her clinging hand.

'That is enough, Judith,' he growled. 'Go home to your husband.'

Grasping Rowena by the shoulder, he propelled her back towards their bower and slammed the door shut behind them.

Rowena pulled away from his hold. 'Who is that woman?'

'She is the Countess de Montfort.'

'She obviously knows you very well!'

'Rowena, don't meddle in matters you don't understand.' There was a coldness in his voice which warned Rowena that he did not care to discuss the beautiful Countess.

'Why? Are you afraid I might learn the truth?' The black look on his face was daunting but her hurt was too

deep to curb the bitter words that raced to her tongue.
'You needn't bother. I heard her! She is your mistress!'

'She is not!'

'Don't lie to me! Do you think I am a fool that I
cannot see what is under my nose?'

Hugh frowned at her impatiently. It was late and he
was tired. Judith and her wanton play-acting was the last
thing he had expected to find on his doorstep.

'Look, it isn't how it must have seemed ——' he began
in a curt manner but Rowena interrupted him.

'Spare me your excuses!' she exclaimed in a voice raw
with pain. 'I know you only wed me because the King
wanted it and your feared to lose Edenwald if you
disobeyed, but I did not think you would insult me by
consorting with your whore before the honeymoon was
over.'

Hugh's mouth tightened, the explanation dying on his
lips. 'You will accept my word that Judith de Montfort
means nothing to me.'

Rowena laughed without mirth. 'The word of a
Norman? What value can I place on that?'

Her scorn was a lash that flayed his pride, crushing his
impulse to tell her the real truth. If she preferred to
think him so mercenary, then let her!

'I see I was wrong to think you had grown up,
Rowena. It seems I have married a jealous child,' he
said coolly.

'I am not jealous!' Rowena glared at him. 'And I am
not a child.'

'No, you are not,' he agreed with sudden swiftness
and his eyes raked over her with a look that made her
step back in alarm.

It was no use.

'Let me go,' she demanded, struggling against the strong arms that held her in an imprisoning grip.

'Why? You are my wife.' His deep voice was mocking but Rowena saw desire flare in his eyes as he bent his dark head to hers.

Deafened by the hammering of her heart, she needed every last vestige of her will-power to force her mouth to stay clenched shut against his kiss.

Hugh released her stiff and unwilling body with a savage oath and Rowena experienced a moment of anguished triumph.

'So, you reject my embrace in spite of your wedding vows!' Hugh growled bitterly. 'They are as worthless as your sworn promise to abide by William's ruling. I won Edenwald fair and square but still you hold it against me.'

Stricken into silence, Rowena gazed at him in dismay. Did he really think she was so lacking in honour?

'I should have known. No Saxon can be wholly trusted, not even if they seem friendly.'

The grey eyes were hard and Rowena shivered.

'You sound as if you speak from personal experience,' she snapped, trying to make her tone defiant but anger was draining from her to be replaced by a cold dread that she had made a terrible mistake.

'Are you not proof enough, my lady?'

The sarcasm in his voice made her flinch and Hugh laughed with harsh satisfaction. He would rather have been flayed alive than admit it but her distrust had hurt him to the quick.

'Shall I tell you another story of Saxon treachery, my lady?' he added abruptly. 'Of how I met a man who came to Rouen and stayed for a year at our court? We campaigned together in Brittany and my lord knighted him. He taught me my first words of English and I thought him a friend.'

He stared at her bleakly. 'His name was Harold Godwinson.'

Rowena gasped but then rallied. 'William forced Harold to promise his aid. He kept him prisoner until he agreed.'

'He was an honoured guest! My lord even offered him his favourite daughter in marriage. Harold agreed and swore on the holy relics of Bayeux to uphold William's claim but the minute Edward was dead he pushed forward his own claim.' Hugh shook his head. 'As I said, you cannot trust a Saxon.'

Rowena took a deep breath, struggling to calm herself.

Perhaps Harold had not been the perfect hero of Godric's stories but he had been a staunch Englishman and she couldn't accept that he would have betrayed his country so easily.

'I don't believe you,' she said flatly. 'Harold wasn't that stupid. He was tricked into that oath.'

Hugh's mouth thinned. He knew the rumour but he didn't want to believe it. William wasn't the kind of man to relinquish what he felt was his but surely he wouldn't resort to sacrilegious trickery to achieve his ends? Would he?

'You seem to know a great deal about the subject, my lady,' he replied at last, ignoring the pull of conscience that warned him she might be right.

'I heard the true story from a far better man than you'll ever be,' she retorted, desperately hiding her anguish. How he would laugh if he knew that she had been on the verge of welcoming him as her husband!

She had been such a fool! She had actually begun to

admire and respect him! Worse still, she enjoyed his
company and had even dared hope he might have some
fondness for her, but all he really wanted from her was
her lands! Last night he had been kind but when he had
tired of her novelty he would cast her aside and ignore
her the way all Normans ignored their wives.

'My Godric was worth ten of you, Hugh de Lacy,' she
cried, her voice rising on a note of hysterical despair.
'You are nothing but a thief and I despise you.'

'Rowena!' Suddenly ashen, Hugh put out a hand to
her but Rowena ignored him, the envenomed words
continuing to pour from her lips.

'Everything I have ever known has been destroyed.
You have taken my lands and my body. I have nothing
left, nothing except my hatred, which is all you'll ever
get from me, Hugh de Lacy, no matter what fancy tricks
you employ to try and fool me!'

Panting, she stumbled to a halt and for one silent,
dreadful moment something vulnerable flickered in
Hugh's ice-grey eyes and then, even as she began to
regret her outburst, his handsome face assumed a
remote expression.

'So be it! I had hoped we might live together in
harmony but. . .' He shrugged and his silence was more
eloquent than words.

Rowena shivered, horrified by her own behaviour.
She hadn't meant to say such awful things to him.

'Hugh——' she whispered but he carried on as if he
hadn't heard.

'Cling to your Saxon pride if it comforts you but
remember this: do not flaunt that unseemly tongue of
yours beyond these walls or you will regret it.'

'Don't threaten me.' Summoning all her her strength,

Rowena forced the words through her stiff lips. 'I am not your thrall.'

'No, you are my wife.' Suddenly, Hugh smiled, a smile that chilled Rowena to her soul. 'I shall teach you the folly of insulting me, and when I am done, my lady, you will be obedient to my will.'

CHAPTER SEVEN

ROWENA walked within the pleasance, her step light upon the flower-starred grass, but she had no eye for the beauty around her. It was a perfect spring day, warm and sunny, but she was lost in the misery of her own thoughts.

Two weeks had passed since their disastrous quarrel, two long, unhappy weeks during which Hugh had scarcely spoken a word to her. In the midst of the frenzied activity of the court, Rowena ached with loneliness.

For the sake of appearances, Hugh escorted her on public occasions and they still shared the same bower but his hard grey eyes seemed to stare right through her, ignoring her so completely that she might as well not have existed.

His indifference wounded her far more than Rowena allowed anyone to see. She hid her hurt even from Elgiva but she knew that the court had begun to gossip. So far, everyone remained polite to her but she sensed it amused them to see her humiliation.

It was an effort to present a cool, uncaring face to the world when inside she felt so hurt and bewildered that she didn't know what to do. The strain of the pretence had robbed her of her appetite and the rosy bloom had fled from her cheeks.

Strangely enough, it was Odo de Nevil who tried to ease her isolation. His gruff attempts to befriend her had surprised Rowena. She was grateful but couldn't help wondering if his unexpected kindness was the result of his dislike of Judith de Montfort.

Rowena curbed a sigh. Hugh was forever in the company of the beautiful Countess. Yesterday, they had gone hunting together. William was very fond of the chase and the court went out almost daily but Hugh had made it plain that he did not want her along. He'd refused her permission to go beyond the boundaries of the town and so Rowena was forced to remain behind when the hunt rode out.

Were they lovers? The question tormented Rowena. In spite of the accusations she had hurled at him on that dreadful night, she was no longer sure she had been right. In fact, Hugh's attitude towards the Countess *hadn't* been encouraging. It was Judith who had flung herself at his head, which accorded with the gossip Rowena had heard. It seemed that the Countess de Montfort was shameless.

But. . .might not their quarrel drive Hugh into that slut's arms? He wasn't the kind of man to live the chaste life of a monk!

Biting down hard on her lower lip, Rowena suppressed the scream that rose in her throat. If only she hadn't allowed weariness and a stupid headache to cloud her judgement!

Hardly aware that she did so, Rowena paused and sank on to one of the wooden benches, her thoughts spinning in a painful spiral.

It had been unfair of her to blame Hugh. She had blamed him for everything! Yet he could not more help being Norman than she could change being Saxon and to hold him personally responsible for all the evils that had befallen since Hastings was childishly stupid.

She'd hoped that she had learnt a small measure of

tolerance, at least, living with the nuns of St Etheldreda's. Unfortunately, she hadn't learnt how to control her stubborn temper! Ever since her father's death she had felt helpless to control events. Fate had snatched Godric and Edenwald from her and she had bitterly resented it. She hadn't even been able to have any say in choosing her husband, and all these months tense anger had grown within her.

Seeing that hateful woman twine herself around Hugh had been the final straw. She had felt besmirched by his betrayal of her tentative trust and that inner anger had exploded. She had wanted to punish him for hurting her!

Too late, she now realised she had accused Hugh of not only lying but of being totally lacking in honour. No wonder he was offended!

I owe him an apology, she decided reluctantly, but no sooner had this sensible intention formed than her pride rebelled.

No! She was in the wrong but she would roast in hell before she would give him the satisfaction of seeing her crawl begging for forgiveness! On top of everything else, it was simply too much for flesh and blood to stand!

And yet. . .if she did not apologise, how much longer would this intolerable situation continue? Oh, what in God's name was she to do?

A small lap-dog ran across the greensward and its shrill barking roused her from her misery. Glancing up, she recognised it as the one belonging to Judith de Montfort and sure enough in the distance the voluptuous figure of the raven-haired Countess appeared a moment later.

Clad in rich orange brocade, she looked particularly beautiful and Rowena's heart sank when she saw that her companion was Hugh, his dark head bent attentively as he listened to her chatter.

Judith's hand was fastened possessively upon his arm and a memory of Count Roger as she had last seen him flashed into Rowena's mind. He was a sick old man, almost ready for his shroud. Soon, Judith would be free.

Rowena could feel the blood draining from her cheeks and a searing pain exploded in her chest as she watched Hugh's rare smile appear, curving his mouth into that engaging sweetness as he looked down at his beautiful companion.

Unable to bear it, Rowena jumped to her feet and fled before they noticed her.

Dashing through the courtyard, she collided with a solid form. Her eyes half blind with unshed tears, it took her a moment to recognise the handsome young man who was busy apologising, although he must have known the fault was hers alone.

'Gerard de Beaumont!' Rowena smiled with pleasure to see his friendly face.

'Lady Rowena.' The young knight bowed low. 'I had hoped to renew our acquaintance here at Winchester.'

There was a faint grin in his hazel eyes and Rowena laughed back at him.

'Though not, I'll be bound, in quite such a fashion,' she agreed, feeling suddenly as if she'd found a friend.

'May I escort you to your destination?'

Rowena hesitated. 'Don't you wish to report to my husband?'

'Of course, my lady.' Gerard's voice rang with self-confidence. 'But I'm sure he would not begrudge me a few moments of your delightful company first.'

Rowena hid a smile. He still had the same slightly swaggering manner that had always amused her.

All the way to the bower he chatted lightly, telling her of the perils of the road he had survived. Rowena's spirits began to rise. He was like a breath of fresh air, blowing away her gloom, and the admiration in his eyes was balm to her battered self-confidence.

'Will you come in and take a cup of wine?'

Gerard accepted her invitation with alacrity.

Elgiva looked up in surprise at their entrance but her expression changed to a smile of welcome as she recognised their visitor. She greeted him politely in the rough-and-ready French she had picked up while in Winchester as she came to assist Rowena remove her outdoor mantle.

Beneath it, Rowena wore a tunic of fine white wool over an undergown of blue linen. The bright colour matched the ribbons she had twined into her hair, which was arranged in a fresh style. Two fat braids swung loose beneath her veil to fall over her shoulders like thick golden ropes gleaming in the faint sunlight filtering in through the window.

Rowena knew this daring and original style suited her. Her unhappiness had not affected her looks, but she felt a small stab of uneasiness when she noted how Gerard's gaze fastened on her with an expression that went beyond polite admiration.

To cover her confusion, she called for wine and by the time it was poured the hungry look on his face had faded and she had regained her composure.

'Tell me, how are things at Edenwald?' she asked.

'Do not fret, my lady. Everything goes as you would wish.' Gerard smiled at her easily. 'Your priest, Father Wilfrid, sends his greetings and best wishes to you, of course.'

Rowena nodded, wondering if she was imagining the

slight wariness in his eyes. However, she continued to ply him with questions and he responded with courteous enthusiasm.

'Forgive me,' she cried at last, realising that he was beginning to sound hoarse. 'It is good to have news but I did not mean to weary you. Let me refill your cup. You must be thirsty after all this talking.'

'Aye, my lady, I'm as dry as an ancient bone,' Gerard laughed.

Rowena rose and gracefully moved to his side. She could feel his eyes upon her as she bent to pour the rich Gascon wine into his cup.

Gerard sucked in his breath. *Dieu*! When she leant towards him that gown clung to her like a second skin, moulding the sweet curves of her breasts in a way that brought a quick, familiar surge of desire to his loins!

The opening of the door made them both turn their heads in startled surprise.

'What are you doing here, Gerard?'

Gerard leapt to his feet, guiltily aware that he had been having lustful thoughts about his commander's wife. He was unable to prevent himself from stammering slightly as he framed a polite greeting, explaining that he had just arrived from Edenwald.

Hugh returned his somewhat defensive smile with a lift of his dark eyebrows. 'I see.'

There was a wealth of meaning in his dry tone and Gerard belatedly wished he'd had the sense to refuse Rowena's invitation until he had reported to his commander.

He began to apologise but Hugh waved his awkward explanation aside.

'Enough. We will speak later. You may leave us.'

Gerard flushed at this unusual curtness. Turning to

Rowena, he handed her his goblet and thanked her for her hospitality in a subdued voice.

When he had gone, Hugh said abruptly, 'You too, Elgiva.'

Elgiva, who had been sitting quietly in a corner, nodded and obeyed without a word.

'Why did you invite Gerard here?'

'It seemed polite to offer him refreshment.' Rowena shrugged lightly as she answered his snapped question. 'Besides, I wanted news of Edenwald.'

Hugh's hard expression softened fractionally. 'Very well. But do not entertain him alone in private again.'

'Alone?' Rowena raised her brows at him.

'You know what I mean.' Impatience roughened Hugh's tone. 'Do you hear me?'

'I'm sure half the court may hear you.'

Hugh glowered at her and with an impatient sigh flung off his mantle and moved to pour himself a drink.

'What a pity there was no hunt today to entertain you,' Rowena murmured.

Wary of her sweetly sympathetic tone, Hugh's light eyes narrowed but he replied evenly, 'The King wishes to wait since yesterday's chase was so poor. I doubt if we will ride out for a few days yet.'

Undeterred by his black expression, Rowena pursued her dangerous game. 'Then it is fortunate you have found an easy quarry here at the palace,' she said in the same sweet manner.

'Watch your tongue, wench!' Angry at her implication, Hugh glared at her and Rowena felt a flicker of fear race down her spine.

Sometimes, the temptation to try and provoke him into taking notice of her was too much for her good sense!

Prudently she fell silent and sat down but after a moment she couldn't resist asking, 'What did Gerard mean when he spoke of building at Edenwald?'

Hugh was in the act of setting aside his goblet. He paused but his hesitation was so slight that Rowena didn't notice it. 'Edenwald is to have a castle. I have hired masons to direct the work.'

'What? Without even telling me?' Annoyance flared into Rowena's face. 'You had no right!'

'I had every right.' Hugh's voice was cold. 'Edenwald is mine. Moreover, it is the King's wish that such defences be built throughout the land.'

Rowena struggled hard to bring her temper under control. 'You could have at least warned me what was planned,' she choked.

'It was to have been a surprise.' Wearily, Hugh shook his head. 'I'd hoped you might be pleased——'

'Pleased?' Rowena looked at him with an expression of incredulity. 'You thought it would please me to have Edenwald despoiled by further evidence of your brutal Norman presence?'

His face whitened. 'I should have known better,' he agreed, hiding his disappointment.

Rowena bit her lip. What she had really meant to say was that to Saxon eyes a castle would seem yet another symbol of unwelcome dominance. She hadn't intended it to sound as if she thought Hugh himself brutal but anxiety had made her hasty objection come out badly.

However, it was impossible to explain her true feelings when he was looking at her with that icy expression she found so unnerving.

'Since you find my presence so distasteful, I shall do my best to relieve you of it in future.'

'But I did not mean. . .' Unhappily, Rowena's voice

trailed away as pride dried the apology that leapt to her lips.

Hugh ignored her. 'The King has asked me to accompany him when he goes to meet Duchess Matilda.' He had mastered his anger and, forcing himself to pretend indifference, he surveyed his bride coolly. 'No doubt it will ease your mind to know I have agreed.'

Rowena nodded dully, the walls of loneliness closing around her once more. 'You must do as you wish, my lord.'

What else was there for her to say?

It was May. Scents of cherry and hawthorn, plum and apple blossom were sweet upon the warm air and all England was decked in beauty to greet the Duchess Matilda arrived at last to join her victorious husband.

Left behind at Winchester, Rowena maintained her pretence of haughty indifference to her humiliating situation. Her only consolation was the fact that Count Roger's illness had forced Judith de Montfort to remain at his side, unable to join the party which rode with the King.

Judith was plainly furious but there was nothing else she could do. William was pious at heart and placed importance upon the values of family life. Judith knew he regarded her with disfavour, tolerating her only because of the regard in which he held her elderly husband. One wrong move and she would banished and all her hopes of ensnaring Hugh de Lacy ruined.

Rowena guessed much of what was passing through her beautiful rival's mind. Whenever they met Judith would smile at her with poisonous sweetness, her words a barely veiled taunt. Rowena strove to ignore every malicious gibe but it hurt more than she had thought possible.

Then one afternoon news came that the royal cavalcade had been sighted. Rowena hurried with Elgiva to the palace gates. Her heart was hammering and she was hardly aware of the sullen mood of the crowd out in the city streets until Elgiva drew attention to it in a worried whisper.

'The King will be displeased. They say he adores his wife.'

Rowena sniffed. Lucky Matilda!

'At least he will approve of the effort made here,' she replied, indicating the palace behind them which had been hastily decorated with boughs and garlands and bright silken hangings to welcome the Duchess.

She was right. The burst of loud, hearty cheering eased the frown from William's face as the royal party rode into the courtyard.

Rowena's gaze flicked over the richly clad form of the Duchess, who was mounted on her white palfrey, and moved on to search for the silver swan banner. Once she'd found it, her husband's tall figure was easy to pick out. She experienced an unexpected thrill of pride at his handsome appearance and skilled handling of his fiery horse. He was the most impressive man in the cavalcade.

The Duchess was assisted to dismount and escorted towards the palace. The rest of the gathering began to break up but Rowena ignored Elgiva's suggestion that she follow the other ladies.

She was busy watching Hugh. She saw him hand his reins to his squire. He wore a thoughtful expression, which changed to a look of wary surprise when he spotted her. After a fractional pause, he strode to her side, stripping off his fine leather riding gloves as he walked.

Rowena's knees began to shake and she waved Elgiva aside with a quick nervous gesture. Their bitter quarrel had not been healed before he had ridden away. Would he repudiate her now?

'My lord.' She curtsied low and waited, feeling almost sick with dread.

'Rowena.' He took her hand and raised her with grave formality.

A tiny sigh of relief escaped her. He did not intend to disown her, or at least not publicly. The knowledge that he could do so or even have her banished to a nunnery if he wished had hung heavily in her mind during the endless days of his absence. He had the power of life and death over her and there was no redress she could have sought if he had decided to rid himself of her troublesome presence.

His lips were warm upon the back of her hand and, venturing to lift her meekly downcast head, Rowena was startled by the tenderness in his grey eyes.

Confusion flooded over her. She had been determined to show everyone that she was his acknowledged lady but his warm greeting was unexpected and she suddenly felt ashamed of her attempt to manipulate the situation.

'I trust I find you well?'

Hugh had himself in hand now and he posed the question with cool formality, his features becoming veiled in the remote mask he had assumed as his sole defence against her heart-breaking loveliness.

Rowena nodded, concealing her disappointment with a polite smile. For one glorious moment she had thought

he had forgiven her cruel words but apparently their
estrangement was not to be so easily mended.

But, as they walked to their own quarters, Hugh
regaled her with a description of his journey and the
reception given to the Duchess in London by the nobles
and clergy. Hope raising its cautious head once more,
Rowena sought to prolong their fragile harmony by
offering him wine and asking if William had mentioned
any plans for Matilda's coronation.

'They say Aldred of York will crown her,' she
remarked, handing him a brimming goblet.

'True enough. William has ordered a fine new crown
and jewelled cross to be made for the occasion,' Hugh
replied, sitting down and stretching out his long legs.

Rowena nodded. It was not a Saxon custom to make
much of the King's wife, who bore no other title than
The Lady. Queen Matilda! How grand it sounded! The
corners of her mouth curved up into an impish grin.

Hugh did not understand the reason for her smile but
it lifted his heart. Contentment welled up in him. He
was glad to be back though he did not think he would
risk saying so to his unpredictable bride.

'You will like the Duchess,' he remarked instead with
a show of confidence that raised Rowena's hackles.

'Am I allowed a choice?' she demanded wryly, forgetting her resolve to keep a curb on her unruly tongue.

'There is no reason for dislike,' Hugh answered, his
good spirits evaporating. 'She is a gentle, pious woman.'

'She is a Norman.'

Hugh laughed mirthlessly. 'There you are wrong.
Matilda is a Princess of Flanders, own niece to the King
of France.'

Rowena shrugged. 'She is married to William of
Normandy.'

'So, do you think of yourself as Norman now?'

The grey gaze gleamed with mockery and Rowena could feel herself flushing. She would never win any battle of words against this wily husband of hers!

Reading the desire to hurl her winecup at him in her stormy eyes, Hugh smothered a chuckle.

'Nay, forget I asked, my lady,' he murmured. 'But do not close your mind against the Duchess. She is both clever and capable. You might find much in common.'

Rowena glanced at him warily, wondering if he still mocked.

Hugh rose and stretched. 'I must change my clothes for the banquet.'

To Rowena's astonishment, he paused by her stool and bent to stroke her cheek with one long finger in a swift gesture. 'Don't look so anxious. It will not matter to Matilda that you are a Saxon.'

As usual, his perceptiveness made her uneasy.

'I am not ashamed of my birth,' she snapped, springing to her feet. 'My culture is older than yours and more than equal in excellence.'

His mouth tightened but his voice remained mild as he replied, 'I have never disputed it, my lady.'

The glint in his eyes told her that he was striving to keep his temper in check and Rowena wished she hadn't let her ingrained stubbornness get the better of her good intentions. If he could put aside their quarrel and try to behave in a civilised manner then it behoved her to do the same and live up to her boast of refinement.

'Forgive me. I should not have shouted in so unmannerly a fashion,' she said awkwardly, avoiding his gaze.

He took her chin firmly but gently between his fingers and tilted it so that she was forced to look up at him.

'If you think I am ashamed of your Saxon origins,

Rowena, you are mistaken.' He smiled faintly. 'There is no need to flaunt your pride in my face at every opportunity.'

Rowena's throat was suddenly too dry to answer. Her skin felt as if it was burning where his fingers touched her.

Hugh released her but did not step away. 'A word of warning. Take care that you do not annoy the Duchess. It could have unpleasant consequences.'

'Would you care if William had me punished?' Rowena managed to find her voice.

'Oh, yes, my little Saxon. I should care,' Hugh murmured. He clasped her by the waist and pulled her close. 'No one shall punish you, my lady, except myself,' he added.

Before she could protest, he bent to press a swift, hard kiss upon her lips and then let her go.

Whistling cheerfully, he strode off to summon his body-servant, leaving Rowena staring after him, her heart thudding.

Whitsuntide and the day of Matilda's coronation dawned bright and warm. The old Minster, where Rowena had been married, was hung with garlands of laurel and bay and decorated with a wealth of gold plate, for William was determined that the crowning of his beloved wife should be a splendid occasion, unlike his own hasty and ill-marred coronation.

Rowena walked in the procession from the palace to the nearby church, her hand resting lightly upon Hugh's arm. The fluid lines of her body were clad in ruby silk to match the stone set in the golden circlet which shone upon her brow.

Hugh had presented her with this gift last night and

his unexpected generosity had left her speechless. Glancing at him now from beneath demurely lowered lids, Rowena wondered if it meant he wanted a reconciliation and her pulse began to race.

At the head of the procession William and Matilda walked beneath a silken canopy, followed by the royal children and then the great nobles and clergy. Rowena recognised the Saxon Earl of Mercia and Waltheof of Huntingdonshire and many of the important Norman lords.

She had also spotted Judith de Montfort, but not even the sight of the voluptuous Countess, radiant in costly tawny and gold, could spoil her excitement.

Today the cheers of the crowd, which had gathered in great numbers, must be loud enough surely to satisfy even William. No matter what her countrymen thought in their hearts it was difficult to resist the glamour of such an occasion. Rowena could sense the holiday atmosphere all around her.

The coolness inside the church was welcome. To the sound of solemn chanting, William and Matilda took their places in the great gilded chairs which had been set before the high altar. The ceremony was long but Rowena observed the pride in William's face as his wife was presented to the people.

Involuntarily, her gaze flicked to Hugh's face but she could read nothing of his emotions. He claimed he was not ashamed of her but if only he might look at her like that!

Curbing a sigh, she returned her attention to the ceremony. Finally, the Te Deum was sung and it was all over and time to return to the palace.

The celebration feast was more elaborate than anything Rowena had experienced and the number and

ingenuity of the dishes paraded in front of her left her
gasping in admiration.

'I hope the fellow I've found to serve us at Edenwald
may do half as well,' Hugh remarked with a chuckle
when she commented on the excellence of the venison
and herb pastry.

'You have found a cook?' Rowena couldn't keep the
eagerness from her voice. Did it mean that they were to
leave soon?

Hugh nodded, a faint smile touching his mouth as he
wondered if she had any idea of how lovely she looked
with that happy radiance lighting up her eyes.

'I've given him into Odo's charge. He will arrange to
send him on ahead of us. No doubt Gerard will welcome
a change of fare.'

'I had thought you might summon Gerard back to
Winchester. His last visit was so brief and I remember
him saying that you wanted regular reports on how the
building work was going.'

Hugh glanced at her sharply. She had never shown
any interest in his scheme to build a castle before. In
fact, she had been opposed to the plan. Could she have
fallen victim to de Beaumont's famous charm?

The idea made his fingers tighten on the stem of his
goblet but he schooled his features to show nothing of
his perturbation as he replied, 'As a matter of fact, I
expected him to arrive a few days ago. He will be sorry
to have missed today's ceremonies.'

'It will be pleasant to have his company.'

Rowena wondered why he glowered at this innocent
remark but the entrance of a troop of tumblers, who
came swarming into the hall at that moment, prevented
her from pursuing the point.

The acrobats were followed by half a dozen jugglers

and then musicians. It became hotter and hotter as the evening wore on, until Rowena began to feel stifled. The band of gold about her brow seemed to be cutting into her temples and it was an effort to keep her smile in place.

'Come. I think it is time to leave,' Hugh said softly, and led her towards the royal dais.

Rowena marvelled that the Queen, who was with child, could look so fresh. Her purple robes of state must have been hot and heavy but she smiled at them with alert interest as they made their obeisances and were given permission to retire.

Outside, Rowena drank in the cool night air with relief.

'I felt as if I was being roasted alive,' she confessed, fanning her hot face with the edge of her silken veil.

'No one would guess,' Hugh reassured her. 'But perhaps a short stroll might refresh you?'

She smiled at him gratefully and they began to walk towards the pleasance.

'How did the Queen manage to look so cool and untouched?' Rowena asked with a perplexed air.

Hugh chuckled. 'She has had years of practice at this kind of thing.'

They walked on in the soft dusk, enjoying the scent of blossom suffusing the still air.

Rowena watched the last bee flit amid the flowers, drunk on nectar. 'It seems impossible that Matilda is the mother of seven children. Her eldest son is almost a man but she looks so young,' she murmured.

'Don't be misled by her frail appearance,' Hugh warned. 'She is one of the most determined women I have ever met.'

Rowena tilted her head to look at him, intrigued by the note of amusement in his deep voice.

'You, my lady, are her match,' he continued in response.

Rowena blushed. 'Do you think to flatter me?'

Hugh raised her hand to his lips. 'Why should I wish to do that?' he enquired softly, his sudden smile enigmatic.

Rowena's heartbeat quickened, making her feel giddy. 'I can think of no reason, my lord,' she said breathlessly.

Their eyes locked and Rowena couldn't tear her gaze away. They were standing in the shadow of an apple tree and she was suddenly aware of the silence all around them. For once, the garden was deserted and they were alone.

'Rowena, this quarrel has gone on too long.'

She could feel his breath fanning her cheek as he bent towards her and her pulse fluttered. It was too dark to read his expression but she heard the passion in his voice.

'My lord. . .I don't know. . .' She faltered to a halt, unable to think when he stood so close.

Her senses reeled as his arms came about her, melting her determination to resist like wax. Involuntarily, she swayed towards him, her eyes closing. His mouth came down on hers with a hungry abandon and Rowena shivered in his embrace. A wild yearning exploded in the pit of her stomach and she clung to him mindlessly.

Hugh lifted his dark head.

'Rowena, I. . .'

A loud cough made them both jump. Hugh's arms dropped away and he swung round with a muttered curse.

Gerard de Beaumont bowed deferentially.

'Forgive me, my lord,' he mumbled apologetically. 'I was told you might be here. I did not realise you were not alone.'

His fresh young face wore such an expression of consternation that Hugh's annoyance evaporated. 'I take it you have urgent news?'

Gerard heard the note of grim amusement in the deep voice and relaxed. 'Aye, my lord,' he nodded, with a hesitant glance in Rowena's direction.

'Come. You must make your bow to the Queen and then we will take a cup of wine together with Odo.' Hugh turned to Rowena. 'Forgive me, my lady. You will excuse us?'

Angrily, Rowena realised that there was no hint of regret in his crisp tone. 'Of course,' she replied with a graceful inclination of her head that concealed the rebellion burning in her heart. Naturally, she was of less import than his friends!

She accepted their escort to the door of her bower, trying not to look as if she longed to know what Hugh had been about to say.

'Goodnight, my lady.' Hugh bowed formally and as Rowena watched them walk away she wished Gerard de Beaumont to perdition!

During the next few days Rowena cursed the lack of privacy which was a hallmark of court life. Matilda's coronation signalled the start of a dizzy round of entertainment and the magic spell of that deserted garden was impossible to find again in the whirl of activity that kept everyone busy from dawn to dusk.

To make matters worse, Hugh seemed to have something on his mind. He withdrew again behind the mask of remote indifference she had grown to hate whenever she tried to ask him what was wrong. But her conviction that Gerard had brought bad news remained.

Her attempts to discover information from that young knight met with no success although they slipped back easily into their former friendship. She was glad to accept his escort whenever Hugh was busy elsewhere until one afternoon when Judith de Montfort barred her way.

'Dismiss your maid. I wish to speak to you.'

The arrogant demand set Rowena's teeth on edge but she halted, aware that they happened to be close to the Queen's own apartments and that Matilda was resting.

When Elgiva had moved to a discreet distance Rowena said, 'Well? What is it?' Behind her curt tone a demon of jealousy clawed at her innards as she surveyed the older woman whose lush beauty was enhanced by a vivid overgown of emerald trimmed with jasper.

'I wanted to give you a warning.'

Rowena tensed at Judith's sweet smile.

'You are new to court and, if I dare say it, not used to our Norman ways as yet.'

The tone was honey but Rowena sensed the malice behind the words and had to control an urge to slap the Countess's face.

'I want nothing from you, Madame,' she said coldly and would have turned away if Judith's beringed hand had not shot out and grabbed her by the wrist.

'Listen to me, you whey-faced little fool!' Judith snapped, abandoning her pretence and allowing her dislike free rein. 'Play your games with Gerard de Beaumont with more discretion or William will end by banishing you from court.'

Rowena wrenched her arm free. 'I don't know what you are talking about.'

Judith laughed harshly. 'Don't make any mistake. My concern is not for you. But Hugh is stupidly chivalrous enough to follow you into exile. Lack-wit, can't you see that your disgrace must bespatter him as well?'

Rowena felt sick. 'Are you trying to tell me that people are gossiping about my friendship with Gerard?'

'Friendship? Is that what you call it?' Judith sniggered.

Rowena sucked in her breath. She would not defend herself against such vile slander to this slut, but what if William believed it?

All his vassals depended on his continuing favour and Hugh was not a wealthy man, able to thumb his nose at William's displeasure. Dared she put Hugh's friendship with the King at risk?

Her mouth tightened. She was a Saxon. Was it likely that William would take her part against the gossips?

'I suppose I should thank you for the warning,' she said at last, aware of Judith's maliciously waiting gaze. She lifted her chin and smiled with deliberate insolence. 'You must be an expert in the art of avoiding disgrace. Tell me, however do you manage it?'

Judith's sensual lips compressed into a thin line of rage. 'You think to mock me, you Saxon peasant, but know this! When you lie alone at night, your husband is with me! He never wanted to marry you. If I had been free, he would be mine. Not even your famous dowry can keep him at your side!'

Goaded beyond endurance, Rowena gave a cry of rage and slapped her hard across the mouth. Judith screamed, the sound shockingly loud, and made a grab for Rowena's long golden braids.

A scandalised voice arrested their noisy struggles.

'Ladies! Cease from this unseemly brawling at once!'

Panting for breath, Rowena turned to see the horrified face of one of the Queen's ladies-in-waiting and
even as Judith began to defend herself noisily Matilda
appeared in the open doorway.

'Isabelle, escort the Countess to her chamber. I will
speak with her later.' Matilda's voice was as cool and
composed as her manner as she beckoned Rowena
forward. 'Come with me, Lady Rowena.'

Rowena followed with a sense of dismay, her fury
vanished.

A page sat on a footstool near the Queen's chair
strumming a harp. Matilda dismissed him with a smile
and took her seat with an elegant grace that belied her
condition.

'Now that we are alone, will you tell me the reason
for that disgraceful scene?'

Rowena bit her lip, feeling like a scolded child. There
could be no refusing such gentle implacability, she
decided.

'The Countess dislikes me,' she began hesitantly.

'Do you know why this should be so?'

To Rowena's own surprise, the whole story of her
unhappy marriage came tumbling out in response to
Matilda's sympathetic questioning.

'But it is not true that my friendship with Gerard is
dishonest. I would never betray my husband,' she
concluded firmly.

For a moment Matilda regarded her in silence and
then she nodded decisively. Waving Rowena to be
seated, she announced, 'I believe you. Do not worry. If
this rumour reaches the King's ear I shall speak for you.'

Rowena thanked her, aware of an overwhelming
sense of relief.

'However, it does not excuse your behaviour just now. You will oblige me by seeing to it that such unseemliness does not occur again.' Matilda's severe expression softened and she added with a mischief that surprised Rowena, 'Not that I haven't wanted to box that woman's ears many a time myself!'

Rowena grinned but her smile was wiped away by the Queen's next remark.

'I wouldn't have believed her nasty gossip anyway. I have seen how you look at your husband when you think no one is watching you.' She paused. 'You love him, don't you?'

A deep blush mantled Rowena's cheeks. 'You are mistaken, my lady.'

'You needn't look so concerned, my dear. I have no intention of interfering.'

Shaken by the kindness in her voice, Rowena said abruptly, 'We quarrel at every turn and agree on nothing. He only married me to solve the problem of what to do with Edenwald but he has no need of a wife.'

'All men have need of a wife.' The twinkle in Matilda's eyes softened her brisk tone. 'Quarrels, providing they do not become a tiresome habit, add spice to a marriage. Moreover, the fact that my lord arranged the match does not mean Hugh was unwilling.'

Rowena stared at her, puzzled.

'Take a look in your mirror, Lady Rowena,' Matilda laughed. 'I see no reason why the two of you should not make a success of your union. I know Hugh to be an intelligent, tolerant man and you seem to be a girl of sense. I am sure that you will arrive at some compromise for harmonious living in time.'

Rowena gave a little sigh. 'You are very kind, Madame, but I want more than a truce.'

'A truce makes a good beginning,' Matilda retorted.
'Maybe you dream of love, my dear, but the simple
sharing of life together can bring happiness in its wake. I
learnt that lesson myself.'

Rowena longed to asked her what she meant but
didn't quite dare and, seeing her curiosity, Matilda
laughed softly.

'I expect you have heard the story of how William
took a whip to me in my own father's palace?'

Rowena nodded cautiously.

'The tale is true. It pains me to admit it now but I
hated the very sound of William's name. I was so proud
I declared I would have none of him, and all because of
his ancestry!' Matilda shook her head at her youthful
folly. 'It wasn't until we were wed that I came to know
and admire his character but if I had remained obstinate
and unwilling to compromise in those early days I would
have driven him away from me.'

'I will not make the first move,' Rowena protested.
'Hugh would laugh at me!'

'How do you know until you have tried?' The Queen
gazed at Rowena earnestly. 'Do not let stubbornness
rob you of the chance to be happy.'

Rowena inclined her head. 'Thank you for your
advice, Madame.'

'But you will not heed it, will you, my dear?'

Rowena shook her head. 'I think not,' she whispered.

The Queen was being kind and treating her with more
favour than she had any right to expect but Matilda did
not understand. In relating her own story she had left
out the most important point. William loved her!

It was said that he had fallen in love with her at first
sight and certainly he had battled for years in the very
teeth of Papal opposition to win her for his bride. Secure

in the knowledge of that love, Matilda had never been
haunted by fear that she was wanted only for her dowry.

But I could have dealt with that, Rowena thought.
After all, it is a common enough fate for any heiress but
Hugh didn't even care enough to bother asking for me.
He took me only because the King commanded it!

Against such indifference she had no weapon. His
desire for her body did not salve the wound to her pride.
It meant little unless he also wanted her company but it
was the beautiful Judith with whom he wished to spend
his time.

Hugh hadn't wanted her and he didn't need her!

Matilda had advised her to put aside her pride, but
pride was the only thing she had left to cling to. It was
her shield against further humiliation and hurt.

She would not humble herself in the hope of a new
beginning. She could not afford the risk!

CHAPTER EIGHT

'RISE, my lord.'

William of Normandy waved Hugh to his feet. 'Your request is granted. You may leave for Edenwald as soon as you have made ready.'

Hugh thanked him and turned to go.

'Remember, nip trouble in the bud. If you deal harshly with the ringleaders the rest will fall into line. Leniency is always mistaken for weakness.' William smiled and, leaning forward in his chair, his powerful hands planted firmly on his thighs, added, 'Make use of your lady. She will almost certainly be able to find out the cause.'

Hugh nodded, his face impassive.

Leaving the King, he made for the stables, his mood thoughtful.

What would Rowena do if it came to making a choice? She had acquired a veneer of Norman manners but at heart she was stubbornly Saxon.

Luckily, she was still in ignorance. He had warned Gerard to keep any mention of unrest at Edenwald from her. A faint sigh escaped him. If his instincts were any judge, he might find he had more to worry about than a bunch of rebellious troublemakers. How was he going to ensure that his wilful bride didn't interfere in his plans? He'd wager all he owned that she would attempt to do so once she got wind of what was afoot. He might even have to confine her for her own safety, and then all hell would break loose!

Damn that Saxon stubbornness of hers! No matter how he deliberately flirted with Judith de Montfort to try and provoke her, she continued to deliberately withhold herself from him. If anything, her coldness seemed to have increased these last few days and he sensed a new determination to resist his every attempt to get close.

Driven at last to confide in someone, Hugh had been advised by Odo to beat some sense into her but he knew such an approach would never work with Rowena. She would never yield; her only weakness was her concern for her Saxons. She might beg for mercy for them but when it came to herself he could kill her before she would submit.

It was one of the things he loved about her.

In the stables he gave instructions concerning their departure but his mind was not on the business and, acknowledging it, he ordered a groom to saddle up his horse.

Face it, de Lacy, he admonished himself as he rode out of the main town gates, you don't know how to handle the little hellcat.

One responsive glance from those incredibly blue eyes and he would be her slave forever! He didn't dare let her know of his weakness. It would be a weapon in her hands, a weapon her Saxons might also be able to use.

He had almost made the mistake of confessing his feelings on that golden evening in the pleasance when all the world had seemed aswoon with desire. At the time, he could have strangled Gerard de Beaumont for interrupting them but it had been a blessing in disguise.

That lovely moment of accord might never have existed. They had scarcely exchanged a civil word since!

Hugh was puzzled. On his return, he could have sworn that her attitude had softened in his absence but now she seemed to want to keep him at a distance. In effect, they were back to the hostility that had marked the beginning of their stormy relationship.

A sardonic grimace curved Hugh's well-cut mouth.

William would never understand the state of armed truce in which he lived with Rowena. William adored his wife and family. He trusted Matilda implicitly and had appointed her his regent on more than one occasion. It would never occur to him that Hugh could not be sure of his bride's loyalty.

'Your move, my lord.' Rowena chuckled in delight.

'I think I cannot!' An expression of comical dismay appeared on Gerard de Beaumont's handsome face.

'Then the game is mine!'

'I am a sorry pupil, lady.'

'Perhaps the fault lies with your teacher,' Rowena murmured demurely.

'Never!' Gerard declared gallantly and Rowena laughed.

Supper was over and they were playing taefi, a Saxon game where carved wooden pieces were moved on a parti-coloured board. Gerard had been swift to understand the skills needed but he had yet to beat her.

Rowena began to collect the pieces and return them to their oaken box. She made a graceful figure in her gown of ruby-red silk and Gerard's eyes admired her as he asked lightly, 'Do you intend to go out hawking tomorrow, my lady?'

Rowena shook her head, causing her thin veil to flutter. 'I think not.'

Her easy smile remained in place and he did not guess

he had touched a sore wound. Hugh had rescinded his order restricting her to the palace but Judith de Montfort was to be one of the hawking party and Rowena was determined to avoid her. In spite of the Queen's warning, the raven-haired Countess still took every opportunity to taunt Rowena and she was tired of holding her tongue on a short rein.

'Will you join the party, Gerard?'

'Alas, I must depart for Edenwald in the morning.'

'So soon?' Surprise lifted Rowena's brows.

Gerard smiled. 'How can they manage without me?' he replied lightly, hoping to foil further questions. Hugh would have his head if he alarmed her!

His lord's relationship with his bride intrigued Gerard. To anyone who knew him well, it was obvious that Hugh cared deeply for his beautiful Saxon, but something was wrong. Whenever they were together there was a strange tension between them and they did not seek opportunitites to be alone in the manner of newly-weds. Moreover, Gerard, who considered himself well-versed in the ways of women, sensed that Rowena was unhappy.

Not that it was any of his business. He sympathised but he didn't dare interfere. It would be fatal!

Gerard knew his own weakness. He was easily tempted to lust. Rowena was one of the most beautiful women he had ever encountered but she was his commander's wife. No matter how attractive he found her, he wasn't fool enough to cross Hugh de Lacy!

Deliberately, Gerard removed his gaze from Rowena's tempting curves and said jovially, 'Is there any wine left in that jug, good Elgiva?'

Elgiva got up from her stool in the corner to fetch it

but a little exclamation of dismay excaped her. 'By St Etheldreda, it is empty!'

'I think there must be a hole in the bottom, don't you?' Rowena gave her maid a wry smile.

Elgiva coloured hotly. To her shame, she had developed a fondness for the sweet, rich Burgundy and this discovery of her greed embarrassed her greatly. Snatching up the jug, she cried, 'I shall fetch some more at once, my lady.' And she rushed from the room before Rowena could stop her.

An uneasy silence descended. 'I think I had better take my leave.' Gerard stood up abruptly.

'Please. There is no need to go.'

'People will talk.'

Rowena coloured. So he *had* heard those vile rumours! Impulsively, she rose and stretched out her hand. 'I don't care,' she announced, trying to reassure him. 'I value your friendship, Gerard.'

The blood drummed in Gerard's veins. She looked so lovely standing there with the torchlight shining on her golden hair. A sweet smile curved her lips and Gerard could not curb the desire rising in him.

He clasped her outstretched hand and conveyed it to his lips. 'Thank you, my lady.'

A quiver of unease ran through Rowena as he pressed a passionate kiss into her palm.

'You are so beautiful, Rowena,' he breathed, raising his head and gazing at her with unconcealed longing.

For an instant, Rowena hesitated. A wicked temptation to pay Hugh back in his own coin assailed her. He had made it clear that he preferred Judith de Montfort; why shouldn't she seek solace in Gerard's embrace? She had always found him attractive. He was kind and amusing and very handsome; what would it feel like to taste his mouth against her own?

Encouraged by her lack of resistance, Gerard slipped his arms around her. '*Ma petite*!' he whispered and bent to kiss her.

Quickly, Rowena turned her head so that his lips merely grazed her cheek. 'No!'

He was very attractive but he wasn't Hugh. In his arms she felt no stirring of desire. His touch didn't turn her blood to liquid fire. Only one man had the power to affect her so deeply even though he no longer appeared to want her.

'Rowena!' Gerard's low voice was husky with need and a pang of sympathy shot through her. She knew how it felt to long for forbidden fruit!

'I'm sorry, my friend,' she murmured, gently trying to disengage herself from his embrace.

To her dismay, he continued to hold her tight.

'I want to be much more than a friend to you.' Gerard stared down into her face with an intensity that alarmed her. 'Hugh is a fool to neglect you! Let me love you, Rowena! I would make you happy.' His hand inched up towards her breast.

Sweat prickled down Rowena's spine. By all the Saints, what demon had she foolishly let loose?

'Gerard, I am married,' she said, forcing her voice to stay calm. 'I will not betray my husband. If my behaviour has given you cause to think otherwise then I have been at fault and I apologise for it.' She took a deep breath and gazed at him steadily, willing him to release her. 'Now let me go before you force me into calling for help.'

For an instant, Rowena feared that her plea would

not reach him but then suddenly he shuddered and released her.

'Forgive me.' Sanity returned, he stepped back and gave her a rueful smile. 'I must ask your pardon for my presumption.'

Rowena expelled her breath in a ragged sigh. 'It is growing late. I think you had better go.'

'But I am forgiven?'

Anxiously, he reached out to clasp both of her hands in his, his hazel eyes imploring.

'Of course.' Rowena felt immensely tired. How close she had come to disaster! 'By the time we meet again we will have both forgotten this night and we can be friends again.'

Gerard nodded, thankful to be let off so easily.

Nothing but sorrow could have come of their coupling. Once his lust had been satisfied, he would have been angry and ashamed at having dishonoured his commander. He knew that he would have lost all respect for Rowena and blamed her for forcing him into a situation where he would have felt compelled to leave Hugh's service.

Dieu, but he was glad that he'd had the sense to draw back! She was lovely and he would always admire her but he was relieved that she had resisted his overtures. His feelings did not run so deep that he was willing to ruin his future for her sake!

'Thank you, my lady.' Gerard raised her hands to his lips and kissed each one with heartfelt gratitude.

They were still standing very close together, Rowena's hands in his, when the door opened an instant later and Hugh walked in.

Rowena could not prevent the hot blush that rose to

her cheeks. Her knees began to tremble and it was all she could do to return her husband's astonished gaze.

Gerard's hands dropped away as if he had been burnt but his voice was creditably level as he greeted his liege lord.

Hugh ignored him.

'Where is Elgiva?'

Rowena shivered at the ice in his deep voice. She could feel the waves of cold fury emanating from his taut figure. His grey eyes were murderous.

'She went to fetch more wine.' Gerard braved the silence.

'How convenient.'

His sardonic reply released Rowena from her trance.

'You have no right to imply that we deliberately sent her away,' she exploded, anger sweeping through her tense frame. 'We have never sought to betray you. Only a man guilty of adultery himself would think such a thing.'

Hugh whitened to the lips and, horrified at her own audacity, Rowena fell silent. At last she had gone too far and he would strike her as she deserved!

'Oh, my lord, you are back!' Elgiva came hurrying into the room only to halt in surprise at the stiff tableau facing her.

Hugh's swift glance took in the brimming wine-jug and the maid's innocent expression.

'Put that down, Elgiva, and leave us.' He rapped out the order in a harsh tone that caused her to obey without question.

'And you, de Beaumont; I do not wish to see your face at Winchester again. You have your orders. See to it that you leave for Edenwald at first light.'

A dull flush heated Gerard's cheeks but he bit back

his protests and with a curt inclination of his fair head
quit the bower.

The silence vibrated with tension.

'There was no need to act so harshly towards him.'
Rowena knew she had to speak before she lost her
courage.

'I am the best judge of how to handle my own men,
lady,' Hugh snapped savagely. 'I do not require your
advice.'

'Then go! Leave me!' Choking back the urge to
demand just what it was that he did require from her,
Rowena swung round, unable to endure his anger any
longer. Her nerves were jangling and she could feel the
tightness in her chest that presaged tears.

Presented with her stiff back, Hugh felt a kind of
madness seize him.

In two strides he caught her by the shoulders and
jerked her round to face him. 'Don't ever dare turn
away from me again,' he grated in a voice she barely
recognised.

The devil danced in his eyes and her breath caught in
Rowena's throat. 'Hugh, Gerard and I are friends,
nothing more!'

His expression didn't soften and Rowena shuddered,
forcing herself to continue. 'You did not appear at
supper and he offered to bear me company. I invited
him here to play a game of taefi. That's all! He was
about to leave when you came in.'

Hugh stared down into the pure oval of her lovely
face and saw the tears glistening in her eyes.

'Rowena!' A groan escaped him and he pulled her to
him, kissing her with a fierce passion.

Crushed to his broad chest by the hands of steel that
gripped her waist, Rowena was moulded against his tall

frame in an embrace that left her breathless. Half dazed
by the sudden unexpectedness of it, she clung to him,
her lips parting of their own volition beneath the
pressure of his demanding mouth.

'My tormenting Saxon witch!'

Hugh's hand cupped her breast, stroking her sensitive
nipple. A flame of desire ignited in the pit of her
stomach, rendering her limbs boneless so that she
trembled in his arms, ignoring the angry voice in her
head which screamed at her to reject him.

His tongue invaded her mouth and a honey-sweet
languor stole over her senses, making her so dizzy with
longing that she almost stumbled when he suddenly
released her.

'Swear to me that de Beaumont means nothing to
you!'

A dazzling light exploded in Rowena's brain. 'You
are jealous!'

'Answer me!' Roughly, Hugh shook her by the
shoulders, his eyes blazing with icy fire.

'I've told you! He is my friend, nothing more!'
Rowena's small hands pummelled his chest. 'Don't you
understand? I am lonely here. Gerard makes me laugh.'

Hugh winced. 'I see,' he said stiffly and released her.

Rowena's hands dropped back to her sides. Half
averting her head, she whispered, 'You have no cause
to doubt me. I will never betray you.'

'See that you don't, my lady.' Hugh stared at her
grimly. 'I want no more gossip to sully my name.'

A shiver went through Rowena. 'Did you believe
their wagging tongues?' she demanded with more boldness than she felt.

He shook his dark head. 'If I had, you would have
both regretted it before now.' There was a coldness in

his voice that warned her his words were no idle threat. 'I will not tolerate infidelity.'

Bitterness rose in Rowena's throat. So much for her hope that he was angry because she enjoyed Gerard's company! It was only his arrogant pride that had been offended.

'You are my wife. Your honour is as mine own.' Hugh spoke in a quieter tone.

'Indeed.'

He laughed with harsh abruptness. 'Aye. Fight against it as you may, we are yoked together, my wench. It is my duty to care for your reputation. Surely you do not dispute it?'

Rowena shrugged, avoiding his gaze.

Hugh bit off an impatient exclamation. Turning away, he flung off his mantle, revealing a muddied tunic and hose that told of hard riding.

Rowena surveyed him covertly as he removed his boots and, stripping off his dirty clothing, began to splash water over his muscular arms and chest.

Where had he been? He couldn't have been with the Countess all this time. She had been at her husband's side at supper. And, now Rowena came to think on it, she had looked as sulky as a damp fire!

'I went riding.'

With his usual disturbing perception her husband had guessed her thoughts.

'I felt a need of solitude,' he added gruffly, drying himself and pulling on a fresh tunic.

Rowena glanced at him in surprise and for the first time realised that he looked tired. Was that a hint of anxiety in his grey eyes?

'Something is troubling you, my lord?' In spite of her annoyance, she felt an absurd desire to comfort him.

'Nothing that won't keep.' Hugh smiled to soften his words.

Rowena's heart turned over. Oh, why did he have to possess that angel's smile?

To hide her confusion, she picked up the game-box meaning to return it to the coffer.

'What have you there?'

Rowena explained.

'Come, teach me how to play it.'

'Now?'

'Why not?' Hugh sat down on the stool so recently vacated by Gerard. 'I had best grow accustomed to your Saxon pastimes.'

Rowena sniffed. Was he mocking her? 'Very well,' she said, laying out the pieces.

Hugh showed a quick grasp of the rules and fought with hard, intelligent strategy. It took all her skill to withstand his attack. She won by a hair's breadth and sat back gasping.

'I must teach you the game of chess, my lady.' Hugh grinned at her. 'I think you are quick-witted enough to enjoy it.'

'Thank you!'

Rowena made her tone scathing but her heart beat faster at his praise.

She finished putting the game away and would have risen but his hand shot out and imprisoned her small fingers. Rowena hoped he would not notice how her pulse was fluttering.

'In a few days' time I leave for Edenwald. Do you still wish to accompany me?'

'What do you mean?' Alarm made Rowena's voice shrill.

'I mean that if you have no wish to be my wife I will grant you permission to retire to a nunnery.'

'You would threaten me with banishment?' Rowena tried to pull her hand away but Hugh held on to it.

'I'm offering an end to this quarrel between us. I need a real wife, Rowena.' He stared at her sombrely. 'A wife willing to acknowledge her duty to provide me with a son.'

Rowena shuddered.

With a faint sigh, Hugh shrugged and released her hand.

'A truce or a nunnery,' he said. 'I leave the choice to you.'

Rowena stared at him for a moment before rising abruptly and moving towards the bed where she began to strip off her garments until all she stood in was her shift. Lifting her arms, she loosed the heavy coil of her hair and unbraided it so that it fell in a golden torrent down her back.

Hugh watched her in silence, his heartbeat quickening.

'There. Is this what you want?' Rowena asked, her chin held high and her eyes glittering.

Unable to speak for fear that his voice would betray him, Hugh nodded and rose to his feet with a leisurely grace that masked his nervousness.

Rowena moistened her dry lips as she watched him come towards her. Blessed Virgin, give me the courage I need! she prayed silently.

The touch of his cool hands on her naked shoulders, drawing her to him, made her gasp aloud. There was an unwelcome sweet familiarity in the feel of his arms around her.

Now he was holding her close. His hard, firm body

pressed against her own, reminding her of that other night when she had first learnt the meaning of desire. His passion had awoken the same needs in her and even now she could not repress the trembling excitement that stirred in the pit of her stomach.

'My little Saxon, you would never make a good nun.'

Rowena shivered, dreading his uncanny ability to read her thoughts. She was much too aware of him as a man to be unaffected by his touch and the desire she could see blazing in his eyes.

'You flatter yourself, my lord.' Grimly, Rowena clung to her resolve, resisting the growing urge to give herself up to the pleasure of his caressing fingers.

'Rowena, don't fight me,' Hugh murmured, his long fingers gently stroking the delicate curve of her neck.

Alarm prickled along her spine. Did he guess what she intended? Involuntarily, her gaze flicked towards the bed.

'We have both been at fault but it's not too late to make a fresh start.'

It was all right. He hadn't noticed her slip. Rowena held in a sigh of relief. 'Why bother?' she retorted. 'I see no point. You will have to leave Judith de Montfort behind but before long you will have found another woman to replace her.'

'You think me so faithless?' Hugh's voice was perfectly steady.

'Oh, what does it matter what I think?' Rowena could feel her courage dwindling by the second. Soon she would lose her nerve completely! 'There is nothing to be gained by talking!'

'Then in that case, my lady. . .'

Abruptly, Hugh swung her off her feet and tossed her on to the bed. Winded and gasping, Rowena scrabbled desperately for the weapon she had hidden beneath her pillow but she was too late.

Hugh flung himself on top of her, straddling her body and using his weight to pinion her thrashing limbs. With a cry of rage, Rowena managed to wrench her arm free but before she could twist the dagger into a stabbing position he snatched it from her and threw it into the shadows.

Screaming with frustrated fury, Rowena exploded into a frenzy of clawing nails and teeth and Hugh had a hard job to contain her struggles without hurting her.

'God's blood, will you desist?' At length, feeling his own temper begin to fray, Hugh shook her mercilessly.

'Curse you, Norman!' With a final sob of despair, Rowena lay still.

Cautiously, Hugh slowly levered himself upright until he could sit back on his heels, letting the mattress take his weight.

'How did you guess?' Rowena said wearily, all the fight gone out of her.

'I did not trust such meek acquiescence. Not from you.'

She had closed her eyes so she did not see the compassion in his face as he gazed down at her. 'I suppose you will send me away?'

Rowena felt as if her heart was breaking. She had hidden the dagger on the day that Judith had told her the truth, vowing to use it if he ever tried to bed her by force. Pride demanded that she defend herself but she had lost and now she would pay for her failure with banishment from her beloved home!

'My offer still stands.'

Rowena's eyes snapped open. 'I tried to kill you!'

Hugh shrugged. 'You're not the first,' he answered

with a dry humour that startled an unwilling laugh from her.

To her surprise, he swung himself off the bed and, crossing to the carved coffer which held his personal belongings, extracted something from its depths.

'Here.'

Rowena sat upright and stared in utter amazement at the book he held out to her. 'I don't understand,' she gasped helplessly.

'It is yours.' Impatiently, Hugh thrust it into her hands.

For a brief moment Rowena allowed her fingers to trace the beautiful silver casing set with amethysts before she opened it. A Book of Hours, exquisitely illuminated and incredibly expensive. 'Why should you wish to give me anything, let alone such a gift?' Rowena lifted her gaze to his in confusion.

'You have a custom, I believe, whereby a husband gives his bride a special gift on the morning after their wedding night.' Hugh's tone was gruff but his eyes did not waver from her face. 'This is my *morgengyfu* to you—albeit a little late.'

Rowena could feel a trembling start in her limbs. He could not have chosen anything she would have liked better. Wordlessly, she stared up into his grey eyes.

Hugh reached out a hand and gently touched her hair. 'I was told that to give a *morgengyfu* was to show pleasure in one's new wife.'

Rowena flinched away. 'It merely implies satisfaction in a wife's skill in bed,' she retorted flatly, laying the book aside.

Oh, but she must be careful! It would be so easy to let herself believe that he felt affection for her, but she dared not fall into that trap. If she began to think that way she might forget her hatred. . .

'Is that such a terrible thing?' Undeterred, Hugh sat down on the bed and slipped an arm around her. 'You know I desire you —— '

'Do I?' Rowena glared at him. 'You have a strange way of showing it, my lord. You have deserted my bed for weeks!'

'Did you want me to make love to you?'

Rowena coloured hotly at this innocent enquiry. 'You are very clever at bandying words, Hugh de Lacy,' she choked. 'But nothing can disguise the fact that you prefer Judith de Montfort's company. The whole court is laughing at me because of that woman!'

'Then they are fools!' Hugh's voice was filled with annoyance but it was directed against himself. It seemed that he had gone too far in his scheme to make Rowena jealous. 'Judith means nothing to me.'

'She is your mistress. She told me so herself.'

'No!' Hugh's arm dropped away and as his hands clenched into fists Rowena could see the anger rising in him. 'I admit that long ago we were lovers for a brief time but all I feel for her now is pity.'

Rowena blinked. Pity? It was the last thing she had expected him to say!

'She is tied to an old man she hates and I think she takes lovers to try and hide her unhappiness from herself.' Hugh shrugged, his manner becoming calm again. 'You are younger and more beautiful. It made her spiteful.'

'Then she lied to me?' Rowena asked hesitantly, afraid to acknowledge what in her heart she already knew to be true.

'She lied.' Hugh nodded firmly.

A large weight seemed to roll away from Rowena's chest. Until this moment, she hadn't realised how much she had wanted to hear him deny it. She hadn't dared to admit, even to herself, how afraid she'd been that the Countess had ensnared him.

A tiny silence fell but just as Hugh was congratulating himself that he had cured her suspicions Rowena burst out, 'But it doesn't alter the fact that you have spent a great deal of time with her. She must think you love her!'

'I'm not responsible for what she thinks! I admit I am at fault for seeking her company but I did nothing to encourage her to believe I would cuckold Roger! God's teeth, will you blame me for her vivid imagination?'

Rowena's fingers pleated together in agitation. Judith was capable of lying. . . Oh, Blessed Virgin, but she wanted to believe him innocent!

Sensing her weakening, Hugh added softly, 'If you do, then you must also accept your own share of blame for Gerard's lust.'

Rowena blushed violently. Her gaze fell uncertainly from his, her brain spinning. She had never meant to flirt with Gerard but he had certainly mistaken her friendship for a warmer invitation!

When Rowena found the courage to face him again she saw that he was regarding her with a curious intensity.

'What is it to be? Are we to forgive each other or do we part company forever?' Hugh's rigid expression revealed nothing of his inner turmoil and his voice was deceptively calm as he added, 'I want you by my side at Edenwald, Rowena, but I'm no monk. Either we live as man and wife or our union ends here tonight.'

Rowena stared at him, her eyes enormous in her pale

face. A dozen conflicting emotions fought within her heart and she scarcely knew what to think any longer. Only the fact that in spite of everything he still wanted her seemed important.

'Well, my lady? Shall we try again?' As he finished speaking Hugh suddenly smiled and held out his arms to her.

Slowly, as if in a dream, Rowena moved into his embrace and as she lifted her face for his kiss a tide of desire swept over her, blotting out the rest of the world.

His mouth burning on hers was real and so was the delight coursing through her veins. With each kiss their quarrel seemed to recede until all that remained was this incredible pleasure building between them.

'Say that you want me!' Hugh lifted his mouth an inch from hers. 'Say it!'

'I want you, Hugh de Lacy. God help me but I do!' Rowena's voice was so low he could barely hear her but her eyes were fever-bright with desire and Hugh laughed aloud in triumph as he reached to remove her shift.

Soon she lay naked in his arms, her heart beating like a wild thing as he rained kisses upon her face and throat. Rowena felt their heat like a branding-iron in her flesh and she gasped with pleasure as his dark head descended to her breasts. His tongue scorched her nipples and delicious shudders coruscated through her.

Then his mouth moved lower, blazing a trail over the white skin of her stomach towards the triangle of silky gold that lay between her thighs.

The breath caught in Rowena's throat as he bestowed a light kiss upon this soft mound, sending a deep shock of excitement through her.

'Hugh!' Her eyes tight shut, she whispered his name

but even as her hands reached out blindly to urge him to continue this new delight he slipped away, his head dipping lower. His mouth caressed her white thighs, her slender knees and calves, down to her trim ankles. He kissed each arched instep and all of her small, neat toes until every inch of her felt aglow.

When he had finished he began to retrace his path, each kiss more sensual than the last, until he reached that golden triangle he had visited so briefly before. Rowena tensed, hardly able to breathe. Her heart was pounding with excitement. She didn't know how much she wanted him to continue until he paused as if seeking her permission.

Wordlessly, she arched towards him and his response was instant. His tongue gently parted the tender folds of soft flesh, seeking out the secret heart of her being. Each tiny darting movement sent waves of pleasure flooding over Rowena and she could not prevent herself from crying out with satisfaction when his lips found and encircled her.

'Hugh! Hugh!' Rowena sobbed his name aloud as tears of ecstasy spilled from beneath her closed eyelids and she threw her head back, giving herself up to his skill.

At last, her senses reeling, she felt him withdraw and then the next moment resume the path of kisses that brought his lips up to hers once more.

'It is the first rule of warfare to learn everything you can about your enemy.' Hugh looked down into her pleasure-dazed face and a wicked grin lit his eyes. 'I intend to know every inch of you, my little Saxon.'

Before she could think of a reply, he was sliding into her, hard and urgent. Rowena gave a tiny laugh of surrender and flung up her arms to welcome him,

clasping him tight, and as he thrust into her, filling all
the lonely emptiness of her days, she knew she never
wanted to leave him.

The waves of ecstasy began to build once more and
with a voluptuous sigh Rowena abandoned thought.
Tomorrow she might hate her weakness but tonight she
belonged to Hugh de Lacy!

'God's teeth, my lady, I think you have walked my
boots to shreds!'

'Sit down, Odo, and recover your breath,' Hugh
advised with a look of amusement as he greeted them
on their return from the market.

Eagerly, Rowena summoned Elgiva forward and
began to unpack the contents of the withy basket the
maid carried. 'Look, we got everything we needed,
including cinnamon.'

'Aye, after visiting every spice-merchant in the town,'
Odo groaned.

'Peace! Here, drink this. It will restore you.' Laughing, Hugh handed him a cup of wine. Turning to
Rowena, he added, 'Congratulations. Cook Robert will
be pleased.'

Shyly, Rowena returned his smile. Their truce had
held for two days now and her contentment was marred
only by a faint sense of guilt. Was it wrong to be happy?
It was so easy to forget that Hugh was a Norman.

'Shall I make a start on packing that big chest, my
lady?' Elgiva enquired when the wine was finished.

When Rowena nodded Odo leapt to his feet. 'With
your permission, my lord, I think I shall go and see how
the loading of the carts is progressing,' he announced
hastily.

His rapid exit brought a grin to Rowena's face and,

glancing at Hugh, she saw that he shared her amusement. Her spirits soaring, she said, 'Poor man. I think he dislikes all this bustle worse than Saxon ale!' Tilting her head to one side, she added thoughtfully, 'Perhaps we should plant vines at Edenwald. We could get some from the monks at St Albans or Waltham Abbey, if it would please you, my lord?'

'An excellent notion.' Hugh found himself smiling again as he took in the implication behind this suggestion. To grow vines took time. It was an investment in the future, a peaceful future that he was determined they would enjoy together once he had dealt with the troublemakers threatening his authority at Edenwald.

'Wear your prettiest gown this evening to say your farewells, my lady. We are almost ready for departure and should be able to make an early start tomorrow,' he announced cheerfully, his expression carefully devoid of any misgivings.

Rowena's eyes brightened. She was going home at last.

CHAPTER NINE

'I HAD expected those walls to be higher.'

Hugh's expression darkened and Rowena had the uneasy feeling that her impulsive remark had angered him.

Ahead, fringed by forest, green and gold fields unfurled under the hot sun. Edenwald. At first glance she had thought nothing had changed but as their cavalcade had ridden closer she had realised that work had begun on the castle.

Hugh had informed her that it was to be built in impregnable stone rather than a simple earthwork and timber structure. The site was cleverly chosen but, whatever it was she had been expecting to see, it wasn't this scene of disordered confusion!

The frown on Hugh's face mirrored his thoughts. It was worse than Gerard had described!

The boundaries of the bailey had been marked and the enormous earthen mound of the motte was well-advanced but there was no sign that any other work had even begun. Instead, untidy heaps of stone and supplies lay all over the site, an open invitation to petty thieving and bad management.

Hugh's gaze searched for the tall, thin figure of Alain, the master stonemason he had hired, and found him in the furthest corner of the site. It looked as if he was engaged in berating a pair of workmen. By the splendour of God, to borrow William's favourite oath, what was going on? he wondered.

'Do we ride on to the hall, my lord?' Rowena couldn't keep the eagerness from her voice. It was a wonder their cavalcade hadn't already been spotted and she didn't think she could bear any further delay.

Curbing his anger, Hugh nodded and gave the signal to continue. He would speak with Alain later. It looked as if his hope of having the keep-tower ready for habitation before winter set in was doomed to failure, unless he could find out what, or perhaps who, was responsible for the delay.

A rueful pang smote Rowena on seeing how well the palisade was guarded but as they rode into the courtyard a crowd quickly collected and her people's joyful shouts of greeting banished the uncomfortable memory from her mind.

'Father Wilfrid!' Rowena sprang down from her horse, all the frustration and weariness of their long, slow journey forgotten. Throwing dignity to the winds, she flung her arms around the old priest and hugged him tight.

'My lady!' A beaming smile split Father Wilfrid's weather-beaten face but it faded as he turned to greet Hugh.

His speech of welcome was both short and formal but Rowena heard the note of anxiety in his voice and a sudden chill descended on her. Glancing round, she saw the sullen stares and black looks being directed at her husband and all the other Normans.

Elgiva dismounted and came to stand next to Rowena. 'Something is wrong,' she muttered, echoing the uneasiness which was rapidly replacing Rowena's euphoria.

Rowena hushed her to silence but she knew that Elgiva spoke the truth. She hadn't expected the people of Edenwald to welcome Hugh and his men with any real warmth but this miasma of black hatred was unnerving!

'Organise the unloading of the carts, Odo.' Hugh was frowning again. 'Father Wilfrid, come with me.'

Rowena followed them into the Great Hall and let out an exclamation of angry surprise. It was filthy!

'Why have these rushes not been changed?' She rounded on the priest, her eyes flashing. 'They have not been sweetened in months.'

Father Wilfrid grimaced. 'There. . .there have been difficulties, my lady.'

'Somehow that doesn't surprise me,' Hugh said drily.

Rowena glanced at him sharply. He knew something. He had said nothing to her but all her instincts screamed that he had been expecting trouble.

'Tomorrow I shall set Aldith and all the other women to scrubbing,' she said tightly. 'Unless you have some objection, my lord?'

Unwittingly, her chin came up in the old challenging way and Hugh almost smiled. 'None whatsoever,' he answered briskly. 'But, for now, will you go and see how Robert is managing? We shall want supper soon and you will need to soothe his ruffled feelings if he thinks we should have given him more warning of our arrival.'

She was being dismissed.

Rowena clenched her teeth against the protest that rose to her lips. Only two weeks ago, on the night of their reconciliation in Winchester, she had promised him a truce. She would not embarrass him now by arguing with him before the priest but he had better have an explanation ready when they retired to her bower!

Dropping an obedient curtsy, she swept out to find the cook.

Supper was a subdued meal, although Robert had done his best to prepare dishes worthy to celebrate their homecoming. After the endless journey and the work of unloading the carts and storing away all the goods Hugh's men seemed weary and disinclined for talk. Her Saxons were equally quiet, confining themselves to eating, but an almost palpable air of resentment hung over their part of the hall.

The atmosphere wasn't much easier at the high table, Rowena decided. Gerard seemed to have difficulty in meeting her gaze and he replied in monosyllables to every attempt to draw him into conversation.

Glancing at Hugh, she caught a look of amusement on his face, although Odo was frowning. Perhaps he thought Gerard needed punishing. She could have boxed his ears for his silliness herself!

She was glad when it was time to retire. To her relief, Hugh announced that he would accompany her. He didn't look in the mood for drinking and she could only hope that weariness would lead his men to follow his example and seek their beds. Otherwise, she'd wager her best necklet that fighting would break out once the level in the wine-jugs dropped.

Her bower had shown the same evidence of neglect as the hall but Elgiva had been busy, restoring it to rights, and when Rowena and Hugh entered she hurried to light extra candles to show off her handiwork.

'Thank you, Elgiva. You have performed wonders. It looks like home again,' Rowena murmured gratefully before dismissing her with a smile.

'Oh, it will be good to sleep in my own bed.' Rowena

gave a little yawn as she sat down on the cushioned bench near the window. 'We seem to have slept on pallets of rock ever since we left Winchester.'

'You are tired. I will call Elgiva back to help you undress.'

'No, Hugh, don't. I want to talk to you.'

She was watching him closely and it seemed to her that he hesitated for an instant before coming to join her.

'What is it? Won't it wait until morning?'

'I don't think so.' Rowena smoothed a fold in her linen skirts. 'Ever since we arrived I have sensed trouble. It is my belief that there is something amiss.'

'Aye, with Gerard.' Hugh laughed. 'Pay him no heed. Your lack of interest intrigued him. He's always enjoyed great success with women but you turned him down. I imagine he feels offended but don't worry. He'll have forgotten his sulks by tomorrow.'

Rowena glared at him. Was he being deliberately obtuse? 'I am glad you are no longer jealous but I wasn't referring to Gerard,' she said impatiently. 'There is something seriously wrong here at Edenwald.'

'Your imagination is playing tricks on you.' Hugh shrugged, his expression carefully masking his anxiety.

'No! You know I am right. You have tried to hide it but you are worried, Hugh.'

'You are mistaken.' Hugh allowed his voice to carry a note of irritation. 'Now, shall we talk of pleasanter matters or. . .perhaps. . .?'

He stood up and, pulling her to her feet, drew her into his arms. 'Can you think of a better way than this to celebrate our return?' he asked, bending to kiss her.

The touch of his lips was as intoxicating as ever but even as desire rose in her Rowena experienced a flicker of indignation. It was plain that he did not wish to discuss the matter!

But why? Did he not trust her or had his talk of needing a helpmeet to partner him in running Edenwald been nothing more than a device to keep her sweet?

Rowena's resolve hardened. With his help or not, she intended to discover exactly what had been happening in her absence.

Fortunately for Rowena's other plan, the next morning dawned bright and clear. Much to Hugh's amusement, she donned one of her old gowns. The skirt was too short and the bodice strained to contain the curves she had developed since she left home but Hugh's laughter changed to respectful awe as she proceeded to turn the entire household upside-down in a frenzy of cleaning.

'Women!' Odo exclaimed in commiseration when Hugh sought shelter in the safety of the stables. 'They make such a pother about a bit of dirt.'

Hugh grinned. If the Saxon thralls had sought to annoy their temporary overlord with their deliberate slovenliness, they had picked the wrong man! He doubted if Odo had even noticed!

'How is Blaze settling in?' Hugh surveyed Odo's new horse, a recent purchase in Winchester.

'He'll do.' Odo gave a gusty sigh of satisfaction. 'What say we try breeding him with that mare of yours when the time's right, eh, Gerard?'

Gerard, who had come down to the stables to admire Odo's latest acquisition, nodded in a distracted fashion as he eyed his commander. Hugh looked to be in a good mood so he quickly decided to take advantage of this chance.

'My lord. . .my lord, may I explain about last night?'

Gerard felt his face must be turning red. 'I wish to apologise for my unmannerly behaviour——'

'Enough, Gerard.' Hugh waved him to silence. 'It is forgotten,' he said firmly. 'All of it.'

Gerard bowed his fair head, barely managing to restrain a huge sigh of relief, more grateful than he dared acknowledge. Disappointment at seeing all Rowena's attention focused on her husband had led him to behave like a fool at supper. But this morning common sense had overcome his fit of pique and he'd remembered that the beautiful Saxon was not for him.

Hugh dismissed the grooms. 'Now, let us have the latest news,' he ordered once they were alone.

Gerard's manner changed and became briskly efficient as he sketched in the details of the mysteriously dwindling supplies and odd incidences that characterised the slow, sullen opposition to the castle and the growing hostility to their rule.

'Every day men fail to turn up for work. When we go to find them they claim to be sick. We have wasted much time on such foolery.' Gerard snorted. 'It makes no difference if we beat them. They become ever more idle and slow.'

'Is the priest still interfering?' Odo enquired.

Gerard nodded. 'He harangues us to show compassion, saying that they do not understand our orders unless we speak to them in English, but there's more to it than that! Only last week one of our men-at-arms was nearly killed.'

'Explain.' Hugh rapped out the command, his black brows tugging together in a frown.

It transpired that the soldier had been supervising a party of Saxons detailed to unload a cart full of logs destined to become part of the stockade protecting the bailey. He had narrowly escaped serious injury when the heavy logs had crashed down, missing him by inches.

'But I have no proof that it was deliberate, my lord.' Gerard shrugged angrily. 'I had the men responsible flogged as a warning to the others but I thought it best to leave any further punishment in your hands.'

Hugh nodded thoughtfully but Odo burst out with an angry oath.

'These so-called accidents have got to stop!' he exclaimed, his heavy features twisting into a savage frown.

'Do they refuse to obey direct orders?'

'No, my lord, but it is my belief that they are clumsy on purpose,' Gerard replied. 'Their inefficiency makes it harder to check what is genuinely spoilt by mishap.'

'Perhaps it would be easier to keep an eye on what is being used if the supplies were kept in better order.' Hugh's tone was dry and Gerard flinched.

'Every time I get the site sorted out, something else happens to cause disruption. . .' He coloured hotly and faltered to a halt.

'But you haven't actually caught anyone in the act of stealing?' Hugh finished the statement for him.

Miserably, Gerard shook his head. Overseeing the building work was his responsibility, Hugh having deemed that Odo had enough to do with supervising the day-to-day running of the estate. The problems and frustrations had driven him almost demented and he longed to cry out that Alain was no help. The mason, who had come to England in William's wake like many others in search of rich pickings, spent all his time dreamily perfecting his plans and thought more of his drawings than practical matters.

Gerard was deeply ashamed of the lack of progress

but he would not lay the blame elsewhere lest Hugh should think he was whining. If circumstances prevented a Norman knight from carrying out his duty, then he must try all the harder to succeed!

'If I had caught them, my lord,' he said angrily, 'I would have known what to do!'

'Aye, hang a few of the bastards and the others would soon learn to work harder,' Odo growled in agreement.

'You are probably right,' Hugh declared. 'Still, I'll not take that course unless I'm forced to it.' His eyes turned cold. 'But they must learn to accept that I am master here. I will have order.'

Hugh's determination grew when he accompanied his lieutenants on an inspection of the estate. He said little but his black frown betrayed his anger.

Everywhere, there were small tell-tale signs of idleness and work skimped just short of the point where punishment would descend. His crops were more puny and thin than those in the adjoining strips which belonged to his peasants. His weeds grew thicker than anyone else's.

'Do they think I am a fool not to notice?' he demanded at last.

'I let Gerard take some men from the fields to help out at the castle.' Odo coughed apologetically.

'You can have them back as soon as haymaking starts,' Gerard offered hastily.

'You are missing the point,' Hugh snapped. 'This neglect is intentional. Someone is out to sabotage my rule here.'

He sensed a deliberate malice at work. Could there be one man controlling this silent rebellion? He didn't know but he was going to find out!

His unknown adversary didn't want a castle to rise

and dominate the landscape, a visible sign of Norman mastery, but, whoever he was, he was going to find out that Hugh de Lacy wasn't so easily beaten!

'But, Mildgyth, where has your man gone? Kenelm can't have disappeared into thin air.'

Rowena's tone was sharp but the middle-aged woman facing her merely hung her head and mumbled an indistinct reply.

'Mildgyth, look at me. Kenelm is a good shepherd. My father considered him the best in the shire. You've always received your dues: a fleece at shearing-time, milk and whey in the summer and a lamb culled from the flock ——'

'But that's just it, my lady.' Mildgyth's voice rose in plaintive interruption. 'Us never got our lamb this spring.'

She was a short, thin woman simply clad in homespun but her plain face, lined from a lifetime of hard work, wore an expression of stubborn dignity.

'When my man asked, that Norman bear told him only the high lord his master could grant such favours. He said our rights counted for nought.' She sniffed indignantly. 'Said 'twas only custom and not proper law, he did!'

Odo de Nevil, I could wring your neck! Furiously, Rowena wondered how to soothe the woman's offended pride. 'I shall look into the matter, Mildgyth,' she promised. 'If my lord agrees, I shall see to it that you are recompensed for your loss.'

From the way the older woman's eyebrows rose, Rowena could see that she didn't place much reliance on Norman generosity.

'But you still haven't answered my question. What

has happened to your husband? Surely he hasn't run off
and deserted you for another woman?'

'Nay, my lady! We are decent, respectable folk!' For
an instant it seemed as if Mildgyth's indignation would
lead her into saying more but then she shook her head
warily. 'I don't know where he is,' she muttered.

With a weary sigh, Rowena dismissed her. She was
convinced that Mildgyth was lying but there was no one
so obstinate as a peasant determined to keep silent.

A sense of disappointment flooded over Rowena.
Mildgyth did not trust her! Miserably, Rowena
acknowledged a truth she had been reluctant to face the
whole morning. Her people no longer counted her as
one of them! Yesterday's rapturous welcome had faded
to a distant uneasiness in her presence. No one even
wanted to become her page-boy!

Parents had avoided her eye when she had raised the
subject of training their children to serve in her household and hurriedly sought an excuse to scurry away.

It is almost as if they feared to confide in me, Rowena
though dismally. Do they think I have switched
allegiances? I married Hugh to save Edenwald; I never
dreamt that they would resent it and reject me!

'Father Wilfrid awaits you in your bower, my lady.'
Elgiva appeared at her elbow. 'Shall I bring some food
to you?'

Glancing up, Rowena was surprised to see the sun in
its noonday position. 'Thank you, Elgiva.'

Dismissing her maid, she picked her way through the
courtyard, which was littered with benches and other
furniture she had dragged out into the sunshine. The
wood glistened wetly and a small smile flickered over
her face. At least she had accomplished one thing this
morning!

The thralls had received a tongue-lashing they would not forget in a hurry. By nightfall, everything would be restored to its former glory. Already fresh rushes had been gathered to lay over the newly scoured floors and if the fine weather held tomorrow they would hold a long-overdue wash-day.

The anxious look on Father Wilfrid's face wiped away her smile.

'I fear I have bad news, my lady.' He hesitated and then added, 'It concerns young Ragge, the ox-herd boy.'

'What of him?'

'I think he is stealing your husband's cattle.'

Rowena sat down abruptly. Of all the crimes a peasant could commit cattle-thieving was probably the most heinous. Oxen and cattle were extremely valuable possessions and Rowena suddenly shuddered at the thought of Hugh's anger.

However, before she could question the priest Elgiva entered, bearing a tray laden with a loaf of barley bread, a jug of ale and a platter of cold meat. Demanding an explanation of her nursling's colourless cheeks, Elgiva exclaimed in horror.

'But where could he be disposing of them?' Rowena demanded when her nurse fell silent. 'No honest man would dare buy cattle from one such as Ragge! If it became known they were stolen, he would suffer forfeiture.'

'I do not know, my lady.' The priest looked grim. 'But the number of beasts in the pasture is short by three.'

'Then we'd best catch Ragge at it before the Normans do,' Elgiva observed with a grimace.

Rowena nodded slowly. She could not find it in her

heart to rebuke Elgiva. If he was guilty, Ragge deserved to be punished but she flinched from the thought of what Hugh might do to him. Norman justice was harsh.

'I shall speak to him myself,' she announced.

Father Wilfrid permitted himself a faint sigh of relief. He had wondered how much her marriage had changed her but it seemed she had abandoned neither her kindness of heart nor her duty to her people.

'Shall I send him to you, my lady?'

'No, that might attract comment. I shall seek him out tomorrow. Perhaps there is some innocent explanation.'

Rowena's fingers fiddled nervously with her girdle.

'I do not understand what is happening!' she burst out. 'Edenwald used to be such a happy place. Everyone took a pride in their work, even the thralls. They would never have let the hall get so dirty in the old days and Ragge's theft would have been unthinkable! It is as if a dark shadow has descended over the whole village.'

'Aye. Sullen faces at every turn and no one with a good word for anything,' Elgiva affirmed.

Father Wilfrid's gaze dropped unhappily to his dusty sandals. The seal of the confessional enforced his silence. Lady Rowena would have to discover the truth for herself. All he could do was pray. Pray his hardest that she would discover Edenwald's secret before it was too late to save them all.

Two busy days passed before Rowena found an opportunity to slip away unnoticed. It was a wet grey morning but the rain did not deter her as she made her way to the rough shelter out in the furthest pasture where the ox-herd boy lived, often for days at a time, while he tended the beasts.

'Ragge? Ragge, are you there? I want to talk to you.'

She peered into the smoky interior of the small hut. It was very dark inside. There were no windows to let in daylight but she could hear the sound of stertorous breathing.

Hitching up her skirts, for the earth floor was littered with filth, Rowena stepped inside. Her nose wrinkled in disgust at the stench but she could see a bundled form lying asleep in the far corner of the room.

'Ragge! Wake up! Wake up at once!'

Rowena shook him roughly by the shoulder, irritation bubbling up inside her. Blessed Virgin, he had no right to be snoring at this hour! Such laziness was as offensive as the filthy state of this dwelling.

In response Ragge's eyes opened. He regarded her blearily. 'What. . .what's the matter?' he mumbled.

Even in the dim light, Rowena could see that his eyes were bloodshot and when he yawned groggily she got a whiff of his stale breath. 'Faugh! You're still half drunk!' she exclaimed.

There was water in a pail by the door. Rowena picked it up and without hesitation flung it at his face.

Ragge gasped and spluttered, mumbling curses until his vision cleared and he recognised his visitor.

'My lady!' he choked, scrambling to his knees and hanging his head in apology.

'Get up!' Rowena made her tone sharp. 'I haven't time to waste. What have you been up to, eh? How long have you lain here drunk? Your mother will worry herself out of her wits if she hears of this.' She glared at him. 'You ought to be ashamed of yourself!'

He ducked his shaggy head, cringing away. Rowena experienced a desire to slap his pallid face but she restrained herself. Broad in the shoulder and well-grown for his fourteen years, he was a rather simple-

minded youth. However, in the past, his slow wits had
been matched by a placid, sunny disposition and
Rowena was puzzled by his sullen manner.

'Who were your drinking companions last night,
Ragge?'

Immediately his expression filled with fear and
Rowena let out a gasp of astonishment. He was afraid of
her!

'Ragge, what's wrong? You can trust me. We used to
play together when we were small. Don't you
remember?'

Until she was five years old Rowena had been allowed
to roam wild with the village children. Then the necessity of earning their keep had been forced upon her
young companions while she had begun her lessons with
her mother but she retained fond memories of those
early days.

'Aye,' Ragge muttered. 'But you have married the
invader and betrayed us, my lady.'

Rowena didn't stop to consider how oddly this embittered phrase sat upon his lips but exclaimed impulsively,
'That's a lie!' Taking a deep breath to calm himself, she
continued in a quieter tone, 'You must not call my
husband by that name, Ragge. He is lord of Edenwald
now and you must obey him in the same way you once
obeyed my father.'

He stared at her for a moment in confusion and then
nodded. 'Yes, my lady.'

'Now, were you drinking with Thurstan or some of
the other lads?'

'Nay. They. . .they were some men from over
Wynburgh way,' he mumbled.

His vagueness made Rowena compress her lips. Was

he being deliberately awkward? Deciding to try another tack, she said abruptly, 'Do you know why I'm here?'

He shook his lint-fair head.

'Because I've heard that three beasts you tend are missing.' She paused. 'Where are they, Ragge?'

His pale skin took on a greenish tinge.

'Answer me!'

'Who. . .who told you, my lady? Who else knows they are gone?' he stammered.

A dull weight seemed to press down on Rowena's temples. So, he was guilty!

'Oh, Ragge! Why did you do it? Why did you sell them?'

'I never!' Indignant colour surged into his cheeks. 'I wouldn't do a bad thing like that, my lady.'

'Then where are they?' Rowena demanded. 'What have you done with them?'

'Aye, lad, let's hear what you've been up to.'

Rowena whirled round.

Odo de Nevil's large, stocky figure filled the doorway and his frown made it plain that he had heard most of what had been said.

'Odo. What are you doing here?' Rowena switched to French, attempting a blithe unconcern, but her heart was banging against her ribs.

'It will not work, my lady.' He shook his cropped head. 'I understood what you said about the cattle.'

'You had no business following me here,' Rowena snapped at him angrily.

'My lord bade me keep a watch on you.' Odo's lip curled. 'But I did not expect to find you conversing with a traitor.'

The accusation in his gruff voice stilled Rowena's

protest and as she gazed at him in dismay Ragge
hesitantly touched her sleeve.

'What's he saying, my lady? I don't understand.'

From the fearful expression on his face, Rowena
knew that he sensed that he had been found out and his
eyes begged her to save him as Odo came forward to
seize him by the shoulder.

'Don't worry. Go with him now,' she instructed
Ragge. 'I'll think of something.' She tried to smile at
him. Odo dragged him out and Rowena followed them.
She watched them for a moment and then, picking up
her skirts, began to run.

'Rowena!'

Hugh de Lacy looked up in astonishment as his wife
came hurtling into the Great Hall, her skirts kilted
almost to the knees. Her cheeks were brilliant with
colour and her veil had fallen off.

Panting, Rowena strove to catch her breath. 'I must
speak with you.'

Hugh was seated at the high table with Alain, the
master mason. Spread out before them were several
parchments covered with drawings and figures and
Rowena belatedly remembered Hugh saying he wanted
to confer with the man.

'Now! It is important!'

Hugh's eyebrows soared at her tone.

'Please!'

'Very well.' Hugh nodded to the mason, who pains-
takingly collected his plans into a neat sheaf which he
tucked beneath his arm.

Rowena had to struggle not to hop from one foot to
the other but at last he was done and, with a low bow to
them both, quit the chamber.

The doors had barely closed before Rowena said urgently, 'I want to ask a favour of you.'

'Is that all?' Hugh grinned at her. 'I thought there must be a fire at least.'

'This is no time for joking!' Rowena felt she might scream.

Before Hugh could frame a reply, loud banging at the door announced the arrival of more newcomers.

'Enter!'

Odo marched in, dragging the boy at his heels.

'God's teeth, I swear this is becoming a market-place!' Hugh exclaimed impatiently. 'Did no one hear my order? I did not wish to be disturbed!'

'I ask pardon, my lord.' Odo gestured to his prisoner. 'But I think you will agree that this matter is worthy of immediate attention.'

'Go on.' Hugh waved him to continue.

'No! Wait!' Rowena gave a cry of interruption. 'Let me speak first.'

'By the Rood, what ails you, Rowena?' her husband demanded in exasperation. 'First you disrupt my meeting with Alain although you could see we were busy and now you seek to prevent Odo from carrying out his duties.'

Rowena clenched her fists at her sides. 'My request is more urgent,' she declared, feeling her temper beginning to rise. Had she run all the way by the shortest but most difficult path for nothing?

'By your leave, Lady Rowena, I beg to contradict you for I think you and I would speak on the same matter.' Odo gave her a shrewd look and Rowena flushed.

'With your permission, my lord?'

Frowning, Hugh indicated that he should continue.

'Is this true?' He turned to Rowena when Odo had finished, his mouth a taut line.

'Yes, but——'

'You would have had me promise mercy without letting me hear the full story?' Hugh interrupted her with apparent calm but everyone in the room could sense his rage.

Reluctantly, Rowena nodded.

'I see.'

Hugh's eyes were frozen ice and Rowena shivered, a wave of despair sweeping over her.

What had she done? In rushing to help Ragge, she had not stopped to think how her husband would feel once he learnt that she had tricked him. Cursing her impetuous stupidity, Rowena held her breath, anxiously waiting to hear him announce his decision.

'Take the boy and confine him for now in the old byre.' Hugh issued the order in hard, clipped tones. 'We will hang him at noon.'

'No!' Rowena's cry ripped apart the silence. 'You cannot! He is only a boy.'

'He is a thief and thieves are never too young to be hanged.' Hugh gazed at her coldly.

Rowena stared back at him in horror. Did she know this man? Had she ever really known him? She had lain in his loving arms but at this moment she felt he was a stranger.

Odo led the bewildered Ragge out. Rowena barely registered their departure.

'You may go.' Hugh stepped down from the dais.

His impatient order roused her from her daze. 'I am not a servant to be dismissed at your whim,' she retorted, recovering her fighting spirit.

'No. You are my wife,' Hugh agreed savagely. 'A wife who does not know her duty.'

Rowena's eyes widened at the cruelty in his voice.

'Was it so very wrong to wish to save him?' she cried.

'Wrong? The very fact that you have to ask proves how blind I have been!' A muscle twitched in Hugh's lean cheek. The disappointment he felt was crushing all his hopes to smithereens. He had really begun to believe she was happy with their marriage! 'Your loyalty should lie with me and me alone!'

'Have I ever given you cause to doubt it?' Rowena demanded through gritted teeth. 'You had no need to set your spy on me.'

'I ordered Odo to keep an eye on you for your own protection,' Hugh retorted hotly, forgetting caution. 'There has been a spate of strange accidents and I wanted to assure your safety.'

Rowena hesitated, trying to drawn rein on her temper. In spite of her fury she sensed his sincerity.

'It is not a question of denying you my loyalty,' she said more quietly, taking a step towards him. 'But Ragge is a simple-minded lad, little more than a child. Won't you show him mercy?'

'And have the rest of your Saxons rise against me?' Hugh shook his head. 'No, Rowena. You know as well as I that the man who holds this land must be strong.'

'Then punish him in some other way,' she begged, reaching out to touch his arm. 'I know he has done wrong—but to hang him!' She shuddered helplessly.

Hugh hesitated. The unshed tears in her eyes tore at his heart.

'What do you suggest?' he enquired drily.

Gulping with relief, Rowena said quickly, 'We could investigate further. I think someone must have put him up to it. He hasn't the wit to carry out such a scheme on his own.'

Hugh grimaced. The thought of hanging a simpleton was disturbing to his conscience. 'What of his family? Could they be his accomplices?'

'I very much doubt it. His father, Serle, was our ox-herd. He was lost at Hastings and his widow is a quiet, hard-working soul.' She shook her head. 'I'm sure Goodeth cannot know anything.'

'What of the rest of your villagers?'

'I would have sworn they were all honest.' Rowena shrugged in confusion. 'Perhaps Father Wilfrid might know something.'

Hugh frowned in concentration and the silence stretched Rowena's nerves. There was a sick feeling in the pit of her stomach and she gasped in relief when he nodded abruptly and said, 'Very well. I will speak to this Goodeth and the priest.'

'And then?' Rowena whispered.

'Then I will examine the boy but this time his story shall be judged in public.'

Rowena's lips parted in surprise and he smiled at her thinly.

'It is your custom to hold trial by ordeal, is it not?'

She nodded dumbly, afraid of what he was going to say next.

'So be it.' Hugh folded his arms across his chest and stared at her grimly. 'If Ragge denies he has stolen my cattle then he must plunge his hand into a cauldron of boiling water and pluck forth the hot stone as is demanded. And God shall be his judge, whether innocent or guilty.'

* * *

By nightfall the news of Ragge's imprisonment had spread throughout the village and as she helped Rowena dress for supper Elgiva asked anxiously, 'Is it true what they are saying my lady? Will Ragge have to undergo the ordeal tomorrow?'

Rowena nodded wearily. 'I could not prevent it. My lord would have had him hanged otherwise.'

Elgiva's plump face crumpled. 'Poor Goodeth. How will she manage by herself?'

'Elgiva!' Rowena pulled away from the ministering hands. 'We mustn't give up hope yet.'

'Unless his hand heals within the given three days he will be judged guilty,' the maid reminded her glumly. 'No one will deny Lord Hugh's right to hang him then.'

This gloomy forecast weighed heavily on Rowena over supper, destroying her appetite. Looking around, she saw that her mood was reflected in the hall, which was unusually quiet. No Saxon had come to dine at the long tables tonight.

As she stared at the empty benches, Rowena's thoughts drifted. In the old days, her father's hall had been a merry place with singers and tellers of sagas and verse-riddles to spice their meals. How she longed for that carefree happy atmosphere tonight! She doubted that such serenity would ever flourish in Edenwald again.

She cast a glance at her husband's hard profile and sighed inwardly. He hadn't spoken a word to her since they had parted that morning and she couldn't tell what he was thinking. Was he merely pretending to be calm, just as she was?

Toying with a dish of soft cheese, Rowena wondered if all marriages were so fragile. Since that night of decision in Winchester she had dreamt that they might be able to build a life together in harmony but in the space of a few hours it had all gone wrong.

Anger and suspicion had torn their delicate truce to shreds. She knew that Hugh was not as coldly indifferent as he appeared but his pride would not allow him to confide in her. She had hurt him by not trusting him.

Rowena's spirits plummeted still lower. Her attempt to trick him had been a stupid mistake. She longed to be able to apologise but the words stuck in her throat.

It is his own fault that I tried to deceive him, she thought with a flash of resentment. He promised to treat me as his partner but he is concealing things from me. I have a right to know what is going on!

Was his heart so cold that he could not recognise her distress at being treated like an irresponsible child?

Hugh desired her and he had taught her to revel in the delights their bodies could create but lust alone was not sufficient to heal the breach of the past and bind them together.

Her resentment faded and was replaced by a feeling of overwhelming sadness. Her hopes were nothing more than illusion. There was no base on which to build the settled future she longed for. They did not trust each other. How, then, could any true feeling ever grow between them?

Their marriage was a sham, doomed to failure.

CHAPTER TEN

'BRING out the boy.'

The command rang through the crowded hall and the coughing and shuffling abruptly faded to an eerie silence as Odo de Nevil appeared, one large, ham-like hand propelling the young ox-herd down the length of the room.

Hugh sat in solitary splendour on the dais. He was clad in a glittering silk tunic, his features a harsh mask above a jewelled collar. His chair was flanked by two men-at-arms standing to respectful attention.

He is the living symbol of the force that swept our world away, Rowena thought with a shiver. We are a beaten race.

She could feel the shame and humiliation filling the hall. Ragge's incarceration had fanned the flames of resentment and Rowena wondered if Hugh knew how angry they were.

More dirty and dishevelled than ever, Ragge was a pathetic sight. He hung back, his eyes swivelling nervously, seeking support from the crowd.

'Come on!' Odo gave him a shove that sent him sprawling, to land on his knees before the dais.

A low murmur ran through the hall. Rowena clenched her teeth and Father Wilfrid, who was seated next to her, reached over to give her hand a comforting pat. Their stools had been placed to one side of the dais so that they might have a clear view of the proceedings.

'Have you heard the boy's confession, Father?'

Hugh's voice was cool and he nodded briskly when the priest answered in the affirmative, adding that Ragge had also been given the Holy Sacrament.

'Then let the trial begin.'

At Hugh's curt signal, Odo dragged Ragge to his feet.

'You are accused of stealing three beasts from the pasture.' Hugh spoke in English but his tone was cold and clipped. 'How do you plead? Innocent or guilty?'

Ragge gaped at him open-mouthed, a shabby, gangling figure who tore at Rowena's heart.

Unable to bear his wretched misery a moment longer, she rose to her feet. 'He does not understand you, my lord,' she announced. 'May I repeat your words to him in an accent he is used to?'

All eyes turned to her.

'Silence!'

The tidal wave of muttering died down at Odo's bellow.

Hugh surveyed his wife through narrowed eyes. An angry pulse beat at his temple. She had dressed in Saxon fashion and Hugh wondered if it was to annoy him by flaunting her sympathy for the boy or whether it was a deliberately calculated attempt to soften his mood. Whatever her reason, the blue silk he had given her shimmered, highlighting her beautiful figure and deepening the wonderful colour of her eyes.

He hardened his heart. He would not let her work her magic on him this time. 'No, you may not. Sit down.'

Rowena paled at his curt answer but Hugh ignored her and transferred his gaze to the priest.

'Please put the question to him, Father.'

Ragge's blank expression mirrored his incomprehension of this exchange but he shook his shaggy head vigorously when the priest obeyed Hugh's order.

'I never sold any cattle.'

Hugh leant back in his chair, a frown tugging his heavy eyebrows together. He'd hoped the young fool would show sense.

'Since the beasts are missing I cannot accept your word, nor that of any other person here present given as a surety for your good character.' He paused to let this sink in.

Father Wilfrid had explained about the custom of oath-helping. If Ragge could produce several respectable people to confirm his statement on oath, then by Saxon law he would be cleared of the charge. But Hugh had refused the priest's request. He was determined not to listen to any well-meant lies.

'The evidence is against you. Since you persist in denying your guilt you must therefore undergo the ordeal.' Hugh signalled to one of his men and the great doors at the rear of the hall were opened.

Exclamations of excited horror rent the air as two of the kitchen scullions entered, staggering under the weight of an enormous iron cauldron. The steam rising from it revealed that it had only just been removed from the fire. Carefully, they set it down upon the large block of wood that Hugh had ordered to be placed close to the dais.

Ragge's eyes bulged as he stared at the blackened pot and he began to shake.

'At the bottom there lies a large stone.' Hugh's voice was completely toneless. 'You will plunge your right arm into the water and lift it out. If you fail to pluck out the stone or your hand festers, you will be judged guilty.'

At Hugh's nod, Father Wilfrid repeated the terrible command.

Rowena clasped her hands tightly together in her lap and strove to control the nausea rising in her throat. With apparent composure, she watched Odo grasp the boy by the shoulder and urge him towards the cauldron.

Ragge was whimpering to himself, his eyes darting among the throng in search of his mother. Rowena could see the tears pouring down Goodeth's face. Ragge was her only surviving child and her fear for him communicated itself in sickly waves.

Not ungently, Odo took Ragge's arm and rolled back the sleeve of his dirty tunic. His skin was very fair beneath the grime and Rowena gulped hard.

An intense silence fell upon the hall.

'My lord?' Odo asked, looking enquiringly at Hugh.

Rowena's eyes flew to her husband's face. His expression was as cold and remote as a statue's.

'Continue.'

Odo grasped Ragge's bare arm and held it over the steaming cauldron in spite of the boy's struggles.

Rowena flinched and shut her eyes, ashamed of her cowardice but unable to watch.

The thin high scream tore the silence to shreds and involuntarily Rowena's eyes flew open again.

To her amazement, she saw that with fear-crazed strength Ragge had pulled away from the burly Norman knight and flung himself down at Hugh's feet. His barely coherent cries for mercy were mixed with an admission of guilt.

'Father Wilfrid.'

The little priest ran forward and helped the sobbing boy to his feet.

Glancing across the room, Hugh encountered Rowena's stormy gaze. Her face was almost as white as the boy's and he sensed the fear which underlay her anger.

The hall was buzzing with alarm but order was rapidly restored and everyone waited in silence to hear judgement pronounced.

'I understand it is a Saxon custom to place a wergild price upon the head of everyone above the rank of serf.' Hugh spoke very slowly in a loud, clear voice. 'Ragge is free-born and thus his life has its price. It is my right to take his life for the theft he now admits. You all know this is so by Saxon as well as Norman law. Do any of you deny it?'

The villagers exchanged puzzled looks. What he said was true. But they had expected him to have the lad strung up without any further ado and this talk of wergild was bewildering.

Rowena stared at him. What was he planning in that wily brain now?

A sudden surge of hope filled her tight chest. Hugh was too clever to antagonise everyone at this difficult time if he could possibly avoid it. Was he going to make an example of the boy, as Odo advised, or did he seek another solution? He had always said he wanted reconciliation and peace.

When the buzz of speculation died down Hugh continued.

'Hear me, people of Edenwald. I, Hugh de Lacy, declare that this boy shall be set free on payment of a fine equal to the price of his wergild.'

He paused, allowing them to take the news in.

'Knowing that silver coin is rare among you, I am willing to accept goods. Father Wilfrid shall reckon the wergild and collect the fine. You may have one week in which to deliver payment. Until then, Ragge will be locked in the old byre and no one may visit him without my permission.'

'And if we cannot pay, my lord?' Nervously, Goodeth stepped forward.

'Then Ragge will be banished on pain of death, never to return.' Hugh spoke firmly but gently to her.

Removing his gaze from Goodeth's face, he looked up.

'The trial is over. Return to your work.'

He stood and signalled to the men-at-arms guarding the doors.

Odo, his face grim, took Ragge by the arm and led the dazed boy out. The rest of the soldiers and the noisily muttering crowd followed them.

Within a few moments only Rowena and Father Wilfrid remained.

'How shall I assess the boy's price, my lord?' the priest asked in a tone that betrayed his relief at this unexpected outcome.

'According to the usual custom,' Hugh replied drily, stepping down from the dais.

'Ragge comes from the lowest class. His wergild will not be enough to recompense you for the loss of your cattle,' Rowena announced with careful calm.

'I know.' Hugh gave her a wry smile. He rubbed at the muscles in his neck, apparently oblivious of her amazed stare.

Tactfully, Father Wilfrid requested permission to depart.

When they were alone Rowena couldn't contain her pent-up emotion any longer.

'You planned this. . .this farce, didn't you?' she accused.

He jerked his dark head in acquiescence. 'Aye. I

hoped he would break down and admit his guilt before it was too late.'

Rowena drew in a deep breath. 'I suppose it didn't occur to you to tell me?'

'You would never have managed to keep it secret.' He shrugged. 'They would have guessed from your face that you weren't truly in fear for the lad.'

Rowena seethed in silence for a moment and then gave a rueful little laugh. 'You're right. I am useless at pretending.'

A reluctant admiration for his cunning grew in her. He had managed to find a solution which had saved Ragge without endangering his authority. It had been a gamble but his reading of the boy's character had proved correct.

'I can show compassion when it does not run counter to necessity.' Hugh took a step towards her. 'Or did you imagine I meant to hang him out of revenge?'

'No! I never thought you cruel!' Rowena cried, startled into honesty.

'Does that mean you are no longer angry with me?'

Rowena dropped her gaze in confusion. 'I don't know,' she whispered in distress.

'It is time we talked.' Hugh stepped closer. 'There is something I ought to tell you ——'

'No! Not now,' Rowena interrupted him in panic. Desperately, she tried to slow her breathing but could not.

'Rowena, listen to me; why do you think I spared Ragge?' Hugh asked abruptly. 'Didn't you guess it was for your sake?'

She stared at him wide-eyed. 'I — I thought you did it to prevent further upset,' she faltered.

'Just for once, forget about Edenwald! Let me
explain——'

'No.' Again she shook her head. 'Please. I must have
time to think.'

Her thoughts were spinning so wildly that she wondered if she was losing her wits. He was looking at her
as if he loved her! Blessed Virgin, she must be imagining
it! He had never wanted to marry her!

'Very well.' Reluctantly Hugh gave way and Rowena
fled before he could change his mind.

Rowena stared at the contents of her strong-box spread
out before her. Night had fallen but she had sent a
message to Hugh saying that she would sup in her
bower. To have to sit at his side at the high table was
more than her nerves could bear this evening.

She had managed to avoid him throughout the long
afternoon. Now she half dreaded, half longed for his
return.

A rueful smile curved her mouth. She might have a
long wait. Judging from the noisy singing coming from
the hall, it seemed that her absence had given rise to a
rowdy drinking party.

Sighing, she forced her attention back to the jewellery
in front of her. The ruby-studded headband had been a
gift from Hugh but the rest belonged to the days before
her strange marriage.

She touched the bronze brooch fashioned into the
shape of two entwined snakes with a softly reminiscent
finger. It had been her father's gift to mark her four-
teenth birthday and she could remember her joy when
he had presented it to her. How grown-up she had felt!
Her future had seemed so clear and she had known
exactly what she wanted from life.

Rowena shook her head, impatient at herself. She was wasting time, sitting here awash with melancholy when she should be choosing something she could slip in secret to Goodeth.

'The past is dead!' she muttered fiercely.

'What? What did you say, my lady?' Elgiva jerked awake. She was dozing by the fire, a piece of sewing idle in her lap.

'Nothing. Nothing that matters, Elgiva,' Rowena sighed.

Recalling the past was even more foolish than trying to puzzle out the future! What could Hugh have meant? He had married her to please the King.

And yet. . . Rowena's pulse began to race. What if he told her he had learnt to care for her?

'My lady?'

Elgiva's concerned voice broke into her whirling thoughts and she found that she was gripping the brooch so tightly that it had left deep marks in her skin. Releasing it hastily, she picked up another piece.

'Do you think this might be suitable?' she asked, pretending a calm she was far from feeling.

Elgiva eyed the little ring. It was quite plain but it was good silver. 'It looks too fine to belong to Goodeth.'

Rowena bit her lip. Apart from a few strings of coloured-glass beads, there was nothing else remotely suitable. Even with the help from the other villagers, Goodeth might not be able to raise the wergild.

Her frown suddenly eased. 'What became of that length of linen I wove for my wedding-dress? Is it still in the coffer?'

Elgiva nodded and rose to fetch it. Carefully removing the layers of stored garments, she lifted out the roll of creamy cloth and brought it over to Rowena.

Rowena shook it out to examine it. She had woven it
on her own loom, intending to dye it a rich red with
madder. Her father's departure had put an end to this
plan and when Godric had failed to return she had
hidden it away out of sight at the bottom of the chest.

'Goodeth might have managed to hoard something
like this. I shall give it to her,' she announced with
sudden decision. 'It is time to forget what might have
been. At least this way some good will come of it.'

Elgiva nodded. It was a pity to waste such a fine piece
of cloth.

'And the money, my lady?'

Rowena hesitated. She had a few coins in the bottom
of her strong-box but Goodeth's eyesight was poor and
rumour had it she was growing forgetful.

'You could give them to Father Wilfrid,' Elgiva
suggested, knowing what her nursling was thinking.

Rowena laughed. 'The poor man would probably
faint! No, it would go against his conscience to conspire
with me in flouting my husband's authority.'

They sat in thoughtful silence for a while and then
Rowena shrugged. 'I shall give the coins directly to
Ragge. Father Wilfrid will probably guess where they
came from but he will turn a blind eye if we don't force
proof on him.'

'It will be easy enough to get the linen to Goodeth in
secret, but will my lord give you permission to see
Ragge?'

A sudden grin lit up Rowena's face. 'I won't ask.'

Jumping to her feet, she snatched up her darkest
cloak and pulled up the concealing hood.

'You're not planning to visit him now!' Elgiva
squeaked in outrage. 'You can't!'

'What better time than when they are all busy? Don't

scold, Elgiva. Remember I am grown-up and married now,' Rowena teased, stuffing the coins into a small purse.

Elgiva sniffed and then added fearfully, 'You will take care, won't you, my lady?'

'Of course. Don't worry, I'll be back before you have tidied this away.' She indicated the scattered jewellery with a careless wave of her hand. 'And don't forget to hide that linen in case my lord returns.'

'What shall I tell him if he asks where you are?' Elgiva gulped in dismay at the thought.

'Say I have gone to the chapel to pray for humility,' Rowena answered with a wicked chuckle, and escaped before her nurse could draw breath to remonstrate.

The thin moon gave Rowena a glimmer of light to aid her swift footsteps. Not that she needed its help — she knew Edenwald better than the back of her own hand.

Within a few short minutes she had reached the old byre. Her father had built a bigger one shortly before the summons had come from King Harold to attend him on that fatal march north, so it stood empty. Hugh said he intended to demolish it but he had found a new purpose for it.

Rowena's mouth hardened. She hadn't forgiven him for scaring her.

Yesterday's rain had softened the ground. Keeping to the shadows, she slipped silently past the yawning guard and made her way to the back of the byre. It was pitch-black here but she began to run her fingers over the time-scarred wood. Frustration made her curse softly and then all at once she found what she was looking for.

Long ago, when she had been just a child running barefoot with the other younglings, she had discovered a loose plank in the back wall of the byre. It had become a favourite trick to confound her playmates with her magical talent for disappearing during a game of hide-and-seek. The plank looked perfect to the casual eye and she had only confided its secret to one other person.

Hugh's command that Ragge be imprisoned in the old byre had brought the memory of this childish prank back to her and Rowena prayed that the trick would still work as she leant her weight in exactly the right spot to swing the loose timber inwards.

It moved and she breathed again. Thank all the saints that the plank had been hewn from a massive oak! There was still plenty of room for her to squeeze through!

The raucous singing pouring forth from the hall drowned out the creaking of the timber as it slotted back into place.

It was dark inside but a lamp had been placed on the rough earth floor near to where Ragge sat, his head slumped forwards on to his chest. Some straw and a rolled-up blanket were close by while a tray containing a couple of used dishes revealed that he had been given supper.

A little of Rowena's resentment towards her husband faded. He must have given orders that the boy was to be well-treated. Save for the thin chain around his waist, Ragge's condition was no worse than in his own hut.

Her gaze followed the chain to where it ended. It was fastened to an iron ring driven into the floor by means of a stake. Common sense told her that Hugh was right to prevent Ragge from trying to escape. If he attempted anything so foolish, Hugh would have no option but to hang him.

Suddenly, it occurred to her that her father might not

have been so lenient. Lord Edwin had dealt with offenders in a rough-and-ready fashion that admitted no subtlety. Hugh had enough trained soldiers to quell any uprising with brutal oppressiveness if he wished but. . .

Could he have really treated Ragge with clemency for her sake?

Putting this disturbing thought aside, Rowena crept forward. 'Ragge! Ragge!'

His fair, shaggy head jerked up and he gazed, bewildered, in her direction.

Emerging cautiously into the little pool of light, Rowena pressed her finger to her lips. Ragge's eyes followed her pointing finger and then he nodded as his slow wits grasped the need for silence.

Rowena knelt at his side. 'I have brought something to help pay your wergild price,' she whispered. 'Here.' She pulled out the drawstring-purse and handed it to him. 'Keep it safe until you can give it to Father Wilfrid.'

'Shall I tell him it came from you?' Ragge asked, tucking the purse into his tunic.

'No! This must stay our secret.'

Ragge nodded obediently and Rowena relaxed. He would do as she said. Her sudden appearance out of the darkness must seem almost miraculous to his simple mind and it would reinforce his respect for her instructions.

'What's that?' The sudden noise made Rowena jump in alarm.

''Tis probably the rats, my lady.'

Rowena grimaced in distaste. 'Ask them to leave you the lamp,' she said hastily.

He nodded and the sound came again.

The door was opening!

Rowena flung herself quickly to one side, rolling out

of the pool of light into the shadows. Her heart in her mouth, she heard the heavy tread of approaching footsteps.

The guard came into view. Rowena watched him bend to examine Ragge's chain and then pick up the tray.

'You are to keep the lamp, boy,' he grunted. 'My lord's orders. See you don't knock it over.'

Grunting a farewell, he went out again.

The closing of the door cut off the sound of singing once more. Rowena waited a few minutes and then scrambled to her feet and dusted off her skirts. It was time she went. She couldn't count on her luck holding forever.

'I must go, Ragge,' she said softly, moving back into the light. 'Don't worry. You'll be all right——' Rowena broke off. 'Ragge? Are you listening?'

He was staring beyond her into the darkness with a peculiar expression on his face.

'Ragge? Have you any message for your mother? Quickly now; I must go.'

He did not answer but another voice spoke out of the darkness.

'Rowena.'

An icy hand seemed to grip Rowena's heart and her scalp prickled with superstitious terror. Spinning round, she saw a figure emerge from the shadows and her hand flew to her mouth to hold in her scream.

'Godric!'

Rowena's eyes were enormous in her pale face and she stared at him, unable to believe the evidence of her own senses.

'I'm no ghost.'

His well-remembered voice convinced her that she wasn't dreaming. 'They said. . .they said you fell at Hastings,' she stammered, moving slowly towards him in a dazed fashion.

Closer, she could see the huge livid scar marking the left side of his face. He was also much thinner. His gaunt, hollowed cheeks and shabby garments made him seem a stranger.

'Godric, where have you been until now? What have you been doing?' She stumbled over the words in her anxiety. 'Does your mother know —— ?'

'Aye.' He interrupted her stream of questions with a rough jerk of his head and closed the distance between them. 'Holy Cross, but you turned into a beauty!' His eyes fixed on her face with painful intensity.

'Oh, why didn't you let me know you were alive?'

To her consternation, he ignored her question and pulled her into his arms.

'Wait. . .'

Before she could prevent it, his mouth came down on hers with an avidity that bruised her lips. His moustache prickled and his ill-tended beard scraped her soft skin but it was the deliberate brutality of the embrace that shocked her.

Choking for air, her ribs feeling as if they were being crushed, she beat her fists against him but he paid no heed to her struggles.

When he finally released her, she was furious.

'What kind of behaviour do you call this, Godric Athelstanson?' she choked.

'I suppose your fancy Norman friends have a daintier way of kissing.' The scorn in his voice made her recoil. He was looking at her as if he hated her! 'How should I treat a faithless slut who has betrayed me and all her people?'

Too stunned to defend herself, Rowena turned to Ragge. The embarrassment on his simple face told its own story. Her gaze flew back to Godric. 'Did everyone else know except me?'

'Those I could trust were told.' Rowena flinched from the anger in his eyes. 'You married one of *them*!'

Abruptly, his mood changed. The fierce glare died out of his blue eyes and he looked lost and bewildered. 'How could you do it, Rowena?'

Suddenly, he was the man she had always known and her face twisted with pity for his distress. 'I had no choice, my dear one.' She held out her hand to him.

'Don't lie!' He knocked her gesture of comfort aside with a violence that made her gasp.

'It's true! If I had refused, they would have locked me away in a nunnery.'

Rowena felt a cold trickle of apprehension down her spine. He was so angry! And he had always been such an even-tempered and gentle man. 'Can't you see? I did it because I wanted to keep Edenwald safe. Hugh de Lacy is a tolerant man ——'

'All Normans are oppressors.' Godric glared at her.

'Not Hugh. You do not know him.' Rowena's fingers curled into tight balls at her sides as she strove to keep her temper.

'Hah! I don't need to.' Godric shrugged her protest aside. He jabbed at the scar on his face. 'This was a gift from your friends.'

Rowena stared at his ruined cheek and a fresh wave of sympathy rushed over her. 'Oh, Godric!'

He had been her first love. They had grown up together and might have lived all their lives in sweet content but for the whirlwind that had swept their world away. There was nothing left of that inexperienced girl and her gentle young giant had turned into this angry and embittered man.

'Do you know how I got this?' Godric asked roughly. 'Shall I tell you about Hastings?'

Rowena backed away a step, shaking her head, but Godric merely gave a harsh laugh and carried on.

'We formed a centre round the King, holding our position on the ridge. It was a narrow marshy valley and they were forced to come to us. They fight on horse-back, your fancy Normans, afraid to stand on their own two feet like proper men. Did you know that, Rowena Edwinsdaughter?'

'Godric, please! I don't want to listen to this.'

He ignored her plea. 'You will hear me and then perhaps you will feel the shame which should have burnt your heart to ashes on the day you wed with that usurper,' he growled.

'They retreated time and time again in fear of our axes and the dead piled high. "Holy Cross! Holy Cross!" We yelled our battle-cry and they fled.' A remembered satisfaction coloured his voice but it vanished as he continued, 'Many of our warriors fell too. Our shield-wall held firm but the ground ran red with blood.'

'Blessed Virgin, will you stop? There is nothing to be gained from raking up the past!' Rowena clapped her hands over her ears in despair.

'Listen to me, woman!' Godric dragged her hands away, shaking her mercilessly.

'Sunset drew on and we were praying for darkness. We needed reinforcements. The men from the north had not arrived but we were winning, Rowena, winning!'

A deep sigh made Godric's huge frame quiver.

'Those damned Normans knew it and then their Duke, God curse his black soul, ordered his archers to fire on us.' He laughed bitterly. 'We couldn't return their arrows. Archery is a nobleman's sport. Most of our army were ordinary lads out to defend their homes and families.'

His grim amusement faded. 'We were distracted and confused, just as William wanted, for his final attack. Gaps began to appear in our wall and they forced their way through until they split us into small groups.'

Rowena shuddered. She could imagine how hopeless it must have been trying to fight men on horseback. There would have been no room to use their axes in that confused mêlée and no protection once the shield-wall had gone.

'Then Harold, my dear kinsman, fell and the heart went out of us.' Tears shone in Godric's eyes. 'We fought on but luck was with the Normans. The battle was theirs. I was brought down by a sword-blow to the head but I was lucky. Darkness was falling and my friends managed to get me away.'

He stared at her accusingly.

'Thousands of Englishmen died on that field, Rowena Edwinsdaughter. How could you have turned your back on their sacrifice and thrown in your lot with the enemy?'

'You fool! Why won't you try to understand?' Rowena hissed the words at him, aware of the need to keep her voice down in spite of her fury. 'Marrying Hugh was the best way to safeguard Edenwald. He is a good man.'

Godric's face darkened with jealousy. 'You speak as if you love him.'

Rowena opened her mouth to deny it but to her surprise the words stuck in her throat.

Her hesitation made Godric snarl and raise his hand. 'You little bitch!'

At the last instant, he deflected his aim and the blow missed her. He let his hand fall back to his side and his voice was raw with pain when he spoke again. 'All through those long weeks while I lay recovering I clung to your memory. It was my talisman when I left that safe hiding-place and began to make my way home. Days and days of living hand to mouth, so weak I was able to travel just a few miles at a time. I almost died but the thought that you would be waiting here for me gave me the strength to carry on.'

He shook his blond head in despair.

'I couldn't believe it when they told me you had left for London with the Norman usurper.'

'You have been back here all this time?' Rowena breathed.

'I went north to see my mother.' He shrugged irritably. 'But I couldn't settle there. My roots are here. So I came home again. Only to learn that you were married.'

'Why didn't you let me know you were safe? I would never have betrayed you.'

'Wouldn't you?' Godric sneered. 'My lands now belong to your husband.'

Rowena recoiled from the ugly implication in his words. She could hardly believe how much he had changed. Could his terrible experience have turned his wits? He was a bitter stranger with hatred festering in his heart!

'But I shall get Wynburgh back and he will pay. He will never raise that castle of his to lord it over our land.'

Realisation burst in on Rowena like a flash of lightning. 'You! You are the one responsible for causing trouble.'

He did not deny it.

'There are a few of us living in the forest now and they obey my orders. Soon I will succeed in persuading the rest of Edenwald to join me in throwing off this Norman yoke. I'll bring the bastards to their knees yet!'

Rowena wanted to weep. It was all so futile!

'Godric, you don't understand them. They won't just give up and go away! Your plan won't work. They are too strong. They will never let go!'

He glared at her and she moistened her dry lips nervously. How could she convince him?

'You must believe me. I know what I'm talking about. King William regards the whole country as his——'

'King?' Godric spat the word at her. 'Have you acknowledged him as your king?'

She nodded reluctantly.

Godric's nostrils flared. 'Traitor!'

Fear exploded in Rowena's tight chest. He looked demented with rage and in sudden panic she whirled to run.

She hadn't gone a yard before Godric caught her and clamped one huge hand over her mouth.

'Don't scream,' he hissed in her ear. 'I don't want to be forced to hurt you.'

Her eyes begged him to release her but he shook his head.

'I came here tonight to free the lad. He's been helping us and we heard he'd been caught. I remembered the secret you once told me so I thought there might be a chance of saving him.' He smiled sourly. 'It seems I needn't have bothered.'

'Take me with you, Godric.' Ragge spoke up suddenly, startling them both. They had all but forgotten him.

'Aye, lad.' Godric glanced in his direction and nodded.

'I wonder what your fine husband would pay to set you free?' His gaze returned to Rowena's face. 'You shall be my hostage, Rowena, but don't worry. I won't kill you even if he refuses to hand over a penny.'

A shudder of dismay racked Rowena's slender frame. The gloating sarcasm in his voice warned her that his love had turned to hatred. He held her in contempt but she had seen the burning desire in his eyes.

'Please me and I'll keep you for myself,' he told her softly, confirming her suspicions. 'Otherwise, I'll toss you to my men when I am done with you.'

Sickness rose in her throat at his threat and she felt herself start to grow giddy. Exerting every last ounce of will-power, she fought it off. She dared not faint.

Godric began to drag her towards Ragge, who got to his feet, an eager grin on his simple face, and Rowena realised that there was no help to be had from the boy.

In a few minutes it would be too late. She had to do something! She couldn't allow Godric to kidnap her.

Desperately, Rowena sank her teeth into the hand covering her mouth and tasted blood. Startled, Godric involuntarily relaxed his hold and she slipped like an eel from his grasp.

'Stop her!' Godric hissed the command at Ragge and whether by accident or design the boy jerked up the metal chain he was holding in his hands. It snaked taut, catching in Rowena's skirts as she fled for the door, and, taken completely by surprise, she fell headlong.

The hard-packed earthen floor came up to meet her and the world turned black.

Hugh awoke and rolled upright into a sitting position. A headache thumped unpleasantly behind his eyes and he groaned as he shrugged off his cloak and got to his feet.

Rubbing the stiffness out of his neck, he surveyed the hall. It was barely light and most of last night's revellers were still asleep. A faint grin touched his mouth. It had been a good feast.

He bent and shook Odo's shoulder.

'Come on. It's nearly dawn. There's work to be done.'

Odo opened one bleary eye. 'God's teeth,' he muttered but he obediently dragged himself out of the folds of his cloak.

By the time Hugh had roused the thralls and set them to cooking breakfast the rest of the hall was awake. Hugh flung open the doors and let in a blast of fresh air to blow away his headache and clear out the stale wine fumes.

'By all the Saints, it's a windy morning!' Odo exclaimed, coming to join Hugh.

'But a fine one!' Hugh felt his spirits rise. Last night, for a few hours, he had put aside his problems and enjoyed an impromptu drinking bout in the robust, uncomplicated company of his men. Now he felt relaxed and full of renewed optimism.

Yesterday, he had taken the first step in the manoeuvre which might bring him closer to the people of Edenwald. He had been more than generous to Ragge and he hoped that they would see it as a sign that he meant to keep his promise to be a fair master.

His heartbeat quickened. With any luck, Rowena would have also realised the truth by now. He hadn't been exaggerating when he'd said that his clemency was for her sake. He wanted to please her even more than he wanted to reconcile the villagers.

She had kept aloof from him for too long! Surely she knew how he felt? He had tried to show her in every way he knew. Words of love had never come easy to him. He was a man of action, not a poet, but, if necessary, he would make her pretty speeches. Anything to get her to listen to him!

Did she care for him? He must have her answer. He had given her enough time. He couldn't go on like this, not knowing whether he stood a chance or not. It was driving him mad!

'I'll wager it'll rain before noon,' Odo predicted as they sat down to eat. 'It's always raining in this damned country.'

'Nonsense,' Hugh said cheerfully. 'Come on; let's saddle up and go and see how Alain is getting on. Gerard, you are in charge. Make sure this place is thoroughly cleaned before my lady sees it.'

Hugh flung down the rest of his oatcake and sprang to his feet, energy fizzing in his veins as he issued brisk orders to the rest of his men. Odo lumbered after him, full of glum predictions about the weather as they headed for the stables.

The discovery of yet another mishap at the castle brought the frown back to Hugh's face.

'You should flog them,' Odo growled.

Hugh shrugged the suggestion aside but his light-hearted mood vanished and he was silent on the ride back.

A grey drizzle began, echoing the tenor of his thoughts. It seemed he had been too optimistic. He had hoped they would see sense but nothing had changed.

Now he would have to pursue Ragge's accomplices and show the stubborn ones that his leniency was no mere weakness!

The heavy weight of his position suddenly seemed to bear down on Hugh and a desperate urgency to hold Rowena in his arms filled him. She would understand his mixed feelings and he longed for the comfort of her body.

'My lord! Oh, my lord!' Elgiva came running up to them as they rode in, her plump face wet with tears.

Hugh leapt down and summoned a groom to take his horse.

'What's wrong, Elgiva?'

'It's. . .it's my lady. She's gone!' Elgiva stumbled over the words in her haste. 'Disappeared! I've looked everywhere for her but I can't find her.'

Hugh felt a cold hand squeeze his spine. 'When? When did you last see her?' he snapped.

Hot colour flooded into the maid's face. 'Last night,' she whispered. 'She went to see Ragge after supper. I meant to wait up for her but. . .but I fell asleep.'

She hung her head in shame, praying that he would not ask if she had been drinking. Anxiety had led her into taking a second cup of wine and then a third, and the next thing she knew it was morning.

'She didn't come back, my lord. Her bed hasn't been slept in.'

'Send for the man on guard outside the old byre last night.' Hugh gave the command to Odo in a tightly controlled voice. He suspected there was more to this tale than Elgiva had confessed but right now he wasn't interested in anything but Rowena's whereabouts.

He strode into the hall, beckoning Elgiva to follow him.

'Here. Drink this.' He thrust a beaker of ale at her with rough sympathy. She was shaking like an autumn leaf.

The guard arrived. When told that Lady Rowena had visited his prisoner last night he vehemently denied it.

'Nay, my lord! I let no one pass. It was a very quiet night. The boy gave us no trouble. He was still asleep when I looked in on him this morning.'

Hugh believed him. 'Then how. . .?' He thought for a moment and then turned to Elgiva. 'Is there a secret entrance?' he demanded in an incredulous voice.

She nodded. 'My lady found it when she was a child.'

'You will show me.'

'I cannot. I don't know the trick of it, my lord. I only know she said she could get in and out of the byre without anyone seeing her.'

Hugh dismissed the guard.

'Come. We will take a look. Maybe Ragge will know something.'

When they got there, the new guard was about to take in a tray of food.

'Give me that.' Hugh took it and the man opened the doors for them to pass inside.

It was very gloomy but as his eyes adjusted to the darkness Hugh made out the sleeping form huddled beneath a blanket. Something about the boy's posture made him frown. With a sudden oath he leapt forward, dropping the tray. It landed with a clatter but the sleeper never moved and Elgiva gasped in astonishment when Hugh snatched the blanket aside to reveal a roughly fashioned human figure.

'They made this from his bedding.' Hugh kicked the straw man aside, his expression livid.

Elgiva stared around helplessly. 'I. . .I don't understand,' she faltered in bewilderment.

'Someone came to rescue Ragge. Rowena must have interrupted them.' Hugh's tone was impatient. 'Don't you see? They must have taken her too.'

'But who would do such a thing, my lord?' Fresh tears began to pour down Elgiva's face.

Hugh wasn't listening. A dull gleam amid the straw had caught his eye. It was part of the metal chain that had bound Ragge. It had been snapped in two.

His brows tugged together. Whoever had done this possessed almost supernatural strength.

A sudden shiver of apprehension ran through him. Where could his wife be?

CHAPTER ELEVEN

ROWENA sat huddled beneath an oak tree. It was starting to rain and she was cold and hungry. All around her shabbily clad men sheltered under the trees. They were chewing on bread and slices of bacon but no one offered her any breakfast and her stomach twisted at the appetising smell coming from the cooking-fire.

She had recovered consciousness to find herself bouncing against Godric's broad back. He had slung her over his shoulder as if she were a haunch of meat and for all the heed he paid to her protests she might as well have been. It had been a pitch-black night, the moon lost as soon as they were under the trees, but Godric seemed able to smell the way back to his camp.

Rowena hadn't the faintest idea of where she was. The journey had seemed to take hours and she'd been too busy trying to protect her face from the twigs and bushes. Her arms were covered in scratches and she had lost her veil. All she was certain of was that this clearing must be somewhere in the depths of the forest.

Cautiously, she stretched her cramped limbs and someone immediately turned his head to watch her. Rowena froze. After a while the hard eyes looked away and she breathed again.

No wonder Godric had not bothered to tie her up. He had merely tossed her a blanket and left her. Luckily, the June night had been mild but Rowena had felt a dozen curious eyes drilling into her and knew that there was little chance that she might escape.

Pondering over her dilemma, Rowena realised that
even if she did manage to win free of the camp there was
still the problem of finding her way out of the forest.
Even worse, it was all her own fault!

No one knew where she was and, tired and miserable
after the long sleepless night, Rowena was beginning to
think no one would care.

Tears gathered at the corners of her eyes.

Stop it! Rowena gave herself a mental shake. She
abhorred self-pity in others and she wasn't going to give
way to it now! Her situation was dreadful but crying
wasn't going to help.

'Here.'

She looked up and saw Godric standing there, holding
out a piece of bread. She was temped to tell him what he
could do with it but resisted. She had barely eaten any
supper last night and she felt hollow with hunger.

He watched her swallow the dry crust, chewing it with
difficulty.

'Not what you're used to, is it? Never mind, you'll
soon get accustomed to less fancy fare.'

She ignored the taunt and said calmly, 'My throat is
parched. Can I have a drink?'

Godric signalled to one of the men by the fire in the
middle of the clearing and the outlaw brought her a cup
of ale. Rowena drank it down quickly and handed the
empty cup back. 'Thank you.'

The man coloured and backed off.

'Don't try to charm them, Rowena. It won't do you
any good. They are loyal to me.'

She shrugged. She had recognised a few men from
Wynburgh and she thought she'd glimpsed Kenelm
from Edenwald but she'd already guessed none of them
could be persuaded to help her.

'Do you really intend to ask a ransom for me?' she asked abruptly.

Godric laughed merrily, throwing back his head on the strong brown column of his throat, and for an instant she caught a glimpse of the man she had once known.

'Perhaps. You are a rich prize.' His eyes lingered over her figure. 'And then again, perhaps I won't.'

Rowena blushed. She could not help it. He made her feel uncomfortable. 'Don't!'

'Why? You used to want me once.' There was an awkward urgency in his voice and he dropped down on his haunches so that their faces were level. 'Rowena, look at me. Does my scar disgust you that much?'

'No, of course not!'

'I'm glad.'

Rowena stared at him in confusion. Last night he had seemed a stranger, a cruel and bitter monster. She had hardly been able to recognise him. Today. . .

She shivered. His moods were unpredictable. She had heard that wounds to the head could change a man and make him act strangely. Dared she trust his present affability?

He held out his hands to her. 'Walk with me.'

Cautiously, Rowena allowed him to haul her to her feet. Her joints creaked in protest but after a moment the stiffness went away.

When they were out of earshot, Godric spoke again.

'Last night, I was wild with anger. Will you forgive me for accusing you of being a traitor?'

She nodded cautiously and replied, 'I am still a Saxon. I want the best for my people.'

'Then join us. Forget the Norman. They made you marry him.' He gave her a shy smile. 'You and I belong together. Let me make things as they were.'

Rowena's pulse quickened in instinctive response but
then she shook her head sadly. 'Godric, the past is
dead.'

He reached out to touch her uncovered hair. 'I can
make you love me again,' he whispered.

'It's too late.' She drew away from him. 'We have
both changed too much.'

Disappointment clouded his face and her heart
twisted with pain. 'I'm sorry,' she murmured.

When had she begun to realise that her love for
Godric had faded into a gentle memory? Looking back,
she saw that Hugh had taken his place in her thoughts
even before she had been sent to St Etheldreda's.

She had loved Godric truly but her feelings for him
had been those of a young, immature girl. Now she was
a woman and it was Hugh de Lacy who held her heart.

How could she have been so blind as not to realise it
until now? From their very first meeting, he had aroused
a fierce response in her. She had tried to tell herself that
it was hatred but she had been deceiving herself.
Godric's unexpected reappearance had shocked her into
at last acknowledging the truth. Hugh was the man she
loved and only foolish pride had kept her from admitting it.

'The Norman has bewitched you!' Godric exclaimed
angrily.

Too late, Rowena realised that he was watching her.
'No! You are wrong. I care nothing for him,' she lied
desperately, cursing her expressive face.

'No matter. I shall kill him and take over Edenwald.
Then you will be mine again.' Hot blood suffused
Godric's fair skin and his eyes shone with the manic
light she dreaded.

'You'll never get away with it. Oh, Godric, give up

this crazy plan of yours.' Rowena tried to inject a note of calm into her voice but she was trembling. 'You must leave here. Hugh will come to find me and when he does he will punish you.'

His burst of harsh laughter interrupted her. 'Don't talk like a lack-wit. How will he follow us here?'

'I don't know but he will find a way!' Rowena pushed a loose strand of hair off her hot forehead. She couldn't explain her conviction but she knew Hugh would not desert her.

A strange flash of happiness shot through her distress. Hugh would come, she knew it, and the knowledge gave her the courage to ignore Godric's black scowl and say, 'You will never defeat the Normans. If you stay here you will only destroy yourself.'

He laughed mirthlessly.

'Please. I don't want to see you hurt. You could build yourself a new life away from Norman influence. Saxons are welcome in Denmark——'

'I won't run away,' he growled at her but the anger was fading from his eyes.

'Or you could go to Byzantium,' Rowena persisted doggedly. 'I know for a fact that other Saxons have gone to seek service with the Emperor there. It isn't running away. It's showing sense.'

'Do you think I am some useless dotard? Would you have me sit safe by the fire?' He shook his head at her. 'No, Rowena. This is my home whether or not you still wish to be my woman,' he said with simple dignity. 'I won't seek safety at the cost of honour. I am a warrior and I shall die fighting.'

An icy despair gripped Rowena. He would not listen to her. All she could do now was pray!

* * *

'There is someone here who wishes to speak to you, my lord.'

Hugh looked up from his untouched supper. For a moment he had difficulty in focusing on what the man was saying and then he nodded.

'Show him in.'

The guard returned a moment later and held aside the leather curtain that shielded off the private quarters from the rest of the hall for the visitor to enter.

To Hugh's surprise, it was Goodeth.

'Well, woman? What is it?'

It had been a long day. His anxiety and frustration had mounted with each passing hour but for all their efforts they had found no clue which might lead them to Rowena.

'I've brought you this, my lord.' Timidly, Goodeth came closer.

Hugh stared at the scrap of silk she held out. A pulse began to beat at the base of his throat. 'Where did you find it?' he asked thickly, taking the torn veil from her.

'In the forest, my lord.'

Hugh lifted his eyes to her lined face. 'When my men questioned you this morning you told them you didn't know where your son was.'

She shuddered. 'Aye, I did.'

Controlling his impatience by a supreme effort of will, Hugh waited.

'You've been good to us, my lord!' Goodeth wiped the sweat from her brow. 'You could have hanged Ragge but you spared him. He's a young fool but he's my only son.'

'Tell me what you know and he shall have my pardon for running away.'

Goodeth let out a sigh of relief. 'Father Wilfrid told

me I should come to you,' she breathed. 'But I was afeared.'

'There is no need. All I am interested in is my wife. Help me to get her back, Goodeth, and I will see to it that no one but her abductor suffers for it.'

When she had gone, Hugh sat back in his chair and pondered over what she had told him. It was little enough to go upon but it confirmed what he had suspected for some time. The woods surrounding Edenwald were harbouring dispossessed Saxons and their leader was vowed to the destruction of Norman rule.

It was the man's identity that surprised him. Godric Athelstanson. The man to whom Rowena had once been promised.

A cold fear clutched Hugh's heart. Had she gone willingly?

He sprang to his feet, overturning the small table and sending dishes flying. A goblet of wine crashed to the floor, the red liquid spilling like a pool of blood.

Odo came running at his shout.

'What is it?' he demanded, alarmed by Hugh's pallor.

'Find me the priest. I am going to get to the bottom of this mystery,' Hugh grated. 'And when I do, I want men ready to search the woods.'

'But we've already combed them.'

'Then we will begin again!' Hugh stared at him, his eyes icy. 'My wife is out there somewhere. I mean to find her. Now go!'

He paced up and down in a restless fever until a quiet cough announced the priest's arrival.

'Where is the outlaw's camp?'

Father Wilfrid flinched at the directness of Hugh's attack. 'I do not know, my lord.'

Hugh glared at him. 'Your robes will not save you if I find you are lying.'

'I wish I could help,' the priest retorted. 'I love Rowena as if she were my own child.'

Hugh sucked in a deep breath and strove for calm.

'Does anyone else have the information I need?' he asked in a quieter tone.

Father Wilfrid wrestled with his conscience. He could not betray the secrets whispered to him in the confessional but Rowena might be in danger. In his right mind, Godric would never harm her but who knew what a man driven by the demons of grief and rage might do?

'Godric has been visiting Edenwald in secret for some months,' he replied slowly. 'He has never approached me but I know he has spoken to several of the other men.'

'Then someone must know the way to his camp.'

Hugh nodded thoughtfully. Peasants were a stubborn breed. He would lose much valuable time if he tried to force information out of them. 'Would a reward work, do you think?'

'The right one might.' Suddenly, Father Wilfrid smiled. 'The people fear you mean to take away their ancient privileges, my lord. If you could reassure them, they would have no need to listen to Godric Athelstanson's blandishments.'

Hugh raised his brows. 'You would have me compromise my authority, priest?'

'Nay, my lord. All I ask for is justice.'

Hugh came to a decision. 'Very well. Present your claims to me and I will consider them.'

Father Wilfrid bowed his head. 'Lady Rowena told me you were a man who desired peace. Thank you.'

'Don't thank me yet.' Hugh smiled at him thinly. 'Our

bargain depends on finding my wife. Give me a man who can lead me to Athelstanson's camp and I will honour my promise.' He paused and added softly, 'But, I warn you, if one hair of her head has been harmed, my vengeance will be both swift and terrible. The people of Edenwald will rue the day they conspired against me.'

Father Wilfrid blenched. The devil lurked in those icy eyes! Without doubt, Hugh de Lacy meant every word he said!

It was barely light when they left Edenwald. Hugh would have started out even sooner but the man who was to be their guide, Alric, warned that the going was tricky.

'It will be difficult enough as it is, my lord. If we make too much noise, Godric will suspect something. I know the password so I can get you past his look-out but once they realise I'm not alone they will fight.'

Hugh had nodded to show his understanding. Ordering his men to wear dark clothes and muffle their weapons, he wished he could have allowed them to don chain-mail to protect themselves. But this wasn't a full-scale battle. It was a surprise attack and they would have to be ready to run and dodge between the trees. Armour would only hinder them.

The rest of Edenwald still slept but Father Wilfrid stood waiting by the gates to see them off. 'God go with you, my lord,' he said, raising his hand in blessing.

'Stay in peace, Father,' Hugh replied, his tone dry.

He was relying on the priest to ensure that no one tried to take advantage of their absence. Every single one of his men was needed for this rescue attempt and for the first time since their arrival Edenwald stood unguarded. A perfect opportunity for rebellion!

Hugh slammed a shutter closed in his mind. He could not afford to worry about a possible uprising now! Pray God it would not happen but, even if it should, Rowena's safety came first. If he lost her, then nothing else mattered anyway.

He forced himself to concentrate only on the task of placing his feet quietly and carefully on the path. All his men had been warned to stay silent and they flitted between the trees like a band of ghosts.

He risked a glance up at a patch of sky showing through the trees. It was growing lighter. They must hurry or the camp would be wide awake and their best chance of surprise lost.

'We are almost there, my lord,' Alric whispered and Hugh signalled his men to a halt.

Alric whistled a few notes, a clear, distinctive sound that broke the silence.

After a moment, it was echoed by an answering whistle and Alric heaved a sigh of relief.

'He's heard me. He'll let me through.'

Hugh had located the source of the look-out. 'Are there more of them?' he asked in a whisper.

'Nay. Godric hasn't got enough men to mount sentries all round the camp. He relies on being hidden. Up to now it's worked.' Alric shifted uncomfortably, his expression miserable.

'Remember he is holding Lady Rowena prisoner,' Hugh said sharply. 'You swore you would help us.'

'Goodeth is my sister. I promised her I would bring Ragge home if I could,' Alric replied with a rough shrug.

'And I'll see you are rewarded for your loyalty.' Hugh laid a hand on the shorter man's shoulder and smiled at him.

Alric blinked, taken aback, and then he nodded. He didn't owe Athelstanson anything. The man was crazed! His scheme to disrupt work at the castle had brought nothing but misery and hardship to the village and he for his part didn't want anything more to do with it!

Hugh beckoned to Odo. 'I'm going to deal with the look-out. Be ready to move the men into position.'

Odo nodded but as Hugh turned to go Gerard spoke up in an urgent whisper. 'Let me deal with him, my lord.'

Hugh raised his brows at him but before he could issue a reprimand Gerard grinned and said, 'I'm in practice at climbing trees. Are you?'

Hugh shook his head. 'Very well. But take care. If he screams, our plan is done for.'

Gerard's eyes gleamed. 'He won't make a sound.'

He slipped away and a few minutes later they heard a muffled thud.

Gerard returned. 'The way is clear, my lord,' he reported, wiping his knife-blade clean.

Alric swallowed hard. 'Follow me,' he muttered, wishing it were all over and he were snug at home.

The shouts of alarm jerked Rowena from her uneasy sleep and she sat up hastily, blinking in the pale light.

'Rowena! Rowena!'

She heard Hugh calling her name and leapt to her feet, her heart hammering.

'I'm over here,' she screamed.

The camp was alive with men rushing to seize their weapons. Stools were overturned and bedding went flying in a confusion of noise and hurtling feet. In the middle of it all, Godric roared commands.

'Stop her!'

His cry of rage lent wings to Rowena's feet as she sped across the clearing. Someone caught at her cloak but she twisted like an eel and slipped from his grasp.

The clash of weapons rang in her ears and she shrieked with terror when she ran headlong into a tall figure who erupted from the trees.

'Rowena.' Protective arms wrapped themselves around her and held her tight. 'You're safe now.'

'Hugh!' She sobbed his name, almost incoherent with relief.

'My lord.' Odo's voice was urgent.

Hugh nodded and released Rowena. 'Take care of her. Get her back to Edenwald as fast as you can.'

'No!' Rowena resisted Odo's attempt to steer her away and clung to her husband's arm. 'I will not run away and leave you.'

There was no time to argue.

'Where are you, de Lacy?' Godric's bellow tore the dawn apart. 'Come. Are you afraid to fight me?'

He was standing in the middle of the clearing, his head held high. 'I see you, Norman.' He let out a roar of scornful laughter. 'Are you going to hide behind a woman's skirts?'

Hugh put Rowena gently aside. Stepping forward, he raised his voice. 'Choose your weapon, Saxon.'

'We have them beaten, my lord. There is no need,' Gerard spoke up quickly.

Glancing swiftly around her, Rowena saw that he was right. The raid had been successful. Only Godric remained free and unharmed.

Hugh's eyes met hers. 'There is every need,' he said softly and Rowena shuddered.

Waving his men back with a sweep of his arm, Hugh strode into the middle of the clearing.

Godric let out a yell of glee. 'Welcome, Norman cur. Let's see how you fight without your horse!' In his upraised hand, a sword glinted wickedly in the early morning sunlight. The long, double-edged blade was stained with blood.

Rowena sucked in her breath. Hugh was a tall man but Godric topped him by several inches and his massive bulk made even Hugh's broad shoulders seem insignificant.

'Let us begin, Saxon.' Hugh lifted his own sword, his voice ringing out with clear confidence.

A rush of pride surged in Rowena's breast and she called out, 'Take care, my husband.'

They began to circle each other, seeking an opening. Then Godric lunged forward with a yell of triumph. His blow would have sliced Hugh in twain if Hugh had not leapt nimbly aside at the last second.

A baffled grunt escaped Godric and then he swung again with greater ferocity.

Watching Hugh parry the attack, his blade moving so swiftly it dazzled the eye, Rowena bit her lip. If Hugh let Godric close with him, he was done for. Godric had the reach on him in height and strength. Digging her nails into the soft flesh of her palms to contain the fear that threatened to swamp her, Rowena prayed that her husband might possess the edge in skill.

Round and round they went, Hugh always managing to elude the slashing blows aimed at him.

'Stand still and fight, you conniving bastard!' Godric roared, infuriated by his opponent's unusual method of combat.

Hugh didn't answer. He was too busy saving his breath. His only hope of winning was to goad the bigger man into carelessness. Godric would hack him to pieces unless he used his wits and he was damned if he was going to die now, not when he had at last seen Rowena smile at him with love in her eyes.

'Curse you, Norman! Fight like a man!' Godric's blows were becoming wilder as anger began to rob him of judgement.

Shrieking a battle-cry that sent shivers of horror racing down Rowena's spine, he hurled himself at Hugh, slashing fiercely in a frenzy of uncontrolled fury. Twisting and turning, Hugh managed to elude the attack but sweat poured down his face and he was gasping from the effort.

At her side, Rowena heard Odo mutter uneasily, 'Rot the bastard! He isn't tiring fast enough.'

'Why?' Rowena demanded anxiously, without taking her eyes off her husband.

'Because his is in the grip of an insane fighting rage, the berserker fury which robs a man of his senses and drives out normal fear,' Odo explained tersely.

Hugh had also recognised the manic light in Godric's pale eyes and he silently thanked God that the Saxon was not armed with one of those great battle-axes he'd last seen in use at Hastings or he wouldn't stand a chance of surviving this encounter.

Summoning all his reserves, Hugh grimly persisted with his tactics and his skill and determination began slowly to bear fruit. Godric was finally tiring. Hugh knew that the hard life and poor diet of the last months must have sapped even his mighty stamina. His breath started to come in great gasps and the sound was sweet to Hugh's ears.

They fought on with bitter doggedness, their laboured breathing loud in the tense silence.

Godric lunged once more and a cry went up as he

missed his footing in a patch of mud caused by yesterday's rain. He went sprawling and in an instant Hugh's sword was at his throat.

'Yield, Saxon!'

Godric glared up at him, his face a mask of sweat and spittle. 'Never!'

Breaking away from Odo, Rowena ran forward.

'No, Hugh! No!' She dropped to her knees, her arms stretching out in supplication. 'I beg you spare him.' Tears began to pour down her cheeks. 'Mercy, good my lord!'

Involuntarily, Hugh's gaze was drawn to her tear-streaked face.

With a yell, Godric seized his chance. Careless of its sharp cutting edge, he grasped the blade held to his throat and wrenched it aside with a force that wrested the sword from Hugh's hand and sent him skittering backwards.

Hugh recovered his balance in an instant but Godric was on his feet and advancing towards him, his teeth bared in grin of savage triumph.

'Die, Norman cur!'

Rowena screamed and, scrambling up, she flung herself in his path, shielding her unarmed husband with her own body.

'Get out of the way, Rowena!' Hugh shouted at her desperately but she would not move.

'Godric! Please!'

Godric paused. The burning glare died out of his blue eyes as he stared down at her and his expression clouded with bewilderment.

'Rowena?' The uplifted sword trembled in his grasp.

The flight of the arrow made a singing note in the air as it winged its way across the clearing to lodge with a dull thud in Godric's massive chest. For a moment, he remained standing, a look of bafflement on his face, before he crashed to the earth like a fallen oak.

Rowena stared in disbelief at the end of the quarrel protruding from his dirty tunic. Swinging round, she beheld the crossbow in Odo de Nevil's hand.

And began to scream.

It was sunset. Rowena could see the western sky burning from the tiny window of her bower. With a sigh, she closed her eyes wearily and hugged her mantle closer about her cold body.

They had carried her home half swooning and left her to Elgiva's anxious ministrations. When she had recovered, she had bathed and changed her clothes. Elgiva had tried to coax her to eat but she had refused. The afternoon had dragged on. Finally, Rowena had refused supper and sent her nurse away, in spite of Elgiva's protests. She had got ready for bed but, unable to rest, she had moved to the window to wait.

But still Hugh had not come.

A slight sound made her open her eyes and she turned to see her husband enter. He closed the door quietly and Rowena moistened her dry lips. Unable to speak a word, she could only gaze at him, her eyes burning darkly in her pale face.

He looked as tired and worn as she felt but he moved with the same lithe pride as he came towards her and she felt something strange and wonderful stir in her heart.

'Rowena.' He spread wide his arms and she flew to him, burying her face against his chest with a little cry of relief. He held her tightly as if he would never let her go and Rowena was content to rest against him in silence.

After a long moment, he turned her face up to his and wiped her tears away. Then he kissed her with a tender passion.

'I love you,' he said simply.

Rowena's heart skipped several beats. She hardly knew how to answer him.

Hugh saw her confusion and smiled gently at her. 'Come; we must talk.'

She shivered. He had said the same thing to her after Ragge's trial but so much had happened since then!

They sat down side by side on the bench and Hugh said, 'I should have told you of my feelings long ago. Our marriage was at my request. I asked William for your hand. Oh, your dowry was important, I don't deny it, but I wanted you for my wife.'

'I thought you married me solely for my lands.' Rowena spoke softly, avoiding his gaze. Her fingers played nervously with a strand of her loosened hair, which glittered about her shoulders in the candlelight.

A wry grimace touched Hugh's well-cut mouth. 'William believed that was my motive. He knew I found you beautiful but I didn't dare tell him the whole truth. I would have asked for you if you had been penniless, my sweeting.'

Rowena closed her eyes, a swift ecstasy flowing through her veins, warming her weary and chilled limbs. 'I told myself I was marrying you to save Edenwald, but — oh, Hugh, I think I had already begun to love you!'

A fierce joy lit his face. 'Say it again!' he demanded, pulling her close.

Rowena was happy to obey. 'I love you, Hugh de Lacy,' she murmured, lifting her face for his kiss.

The touch of his warm mouth on hers dissolved the past. All the tension and unhappiness of the last few months faded to insignificance. She loved him and she was loved in return!

'I hoped that once we were wed you would lose your aversion to my Norman origins,' Hugh explained when at last he raised his dark head. 'After our wedding night I thought I stood a chance of success.'

Rowena blushed. 'I didn't know you cared so deeply but I liked your loving,' she admitted shyly. 'I wanted us to become friends and learn to live together in harmony.'

'But then we quarrelled and I allowed you to think I cared for Judith. I was hoping to make you jealous but it was a mistake,' Hugh said ruefully.

'I hated her!' A little sigh escaped Rowena and she snuggled closer to him.

Hugh's arms tightened around her. 'You seemed to hate me! You wouldn't respond to my attempts to mend our quarrel and I don't think my pride would have allowed me to persist if it hadn't been for Gerard. Seeing you together that night made me so angry I knew I had to do something to break our stalemate.'

'I couldn't bear the idea of being sent away from you.' She smiled up at him.

He dropped a kiss on her forehead.

'Why didn't you tell me that rebellion was fomenting at Edenwald?' Rowena asked a moment later.

'I wanted your homecoming to be a happy one and I was worried that it would spoil our truce if you knew. I thought you might take their part against me.'

Rowena swallowed hard. He deserved an honest answer.

'I went against you to help Ragge,' she admitted. 'I suppose I was trying to prove that I hadn't deserted them. I was away too long! If I had been here, they wouldn't have listened to Godric or disobeyed my instructions to keep the peace.'

She gave a little sigh. 'I left to seek security for them. But when I returned they no longer trusted me.'

'Because you had married me,' Hugh observed.

Rowena nodded. 'But you didn't seem to trust me either and I resented your treating me like a witless child. It made me angry,' she continued frankly. 'But I should not have tried to see Ragge without your knowledge. It was both foolish and disloyal of me.'

He ran his forefinger gently down her cheek in response to her admission. 'I was at fault too. I should have had the sense to explain my reasons,' he conceded. 'However, I did guess you would aid Ragge one way or another. You have a tender heart, sweeting.'

He paused and then added quietly, 'I must thank you for saving my life.'

'You have no need to thank me,' Rowena replied swiftly. 'My feelings aside, I owed you a debt. You once rescued me from being crushed to death and I always hoped to repay you in some way.'

Hugh nodded, remembering that dangerous Christmas coronation, but he frowned suddenly as he recalled the risk she had taken for his sake.

'When you ran out in front of me my soul despaired! I thought I was going to lose you!'

'It was my stupid folly which had exposed you to danger. If I hadn't been so stubborn, you wouldn't have had to rescue me. Then, to crown it all, I distracted you when you were on the point of winning!' Rowena's fingers clutched his sleeve convulsively at the memory. 'Godric nearly succeeded in his ambition to kill you!'

A deep shudder ran through her and, sensing what she was thinking, Hugh placed his hands on her shoulders and looked deep into her eyes. 'You have nothing to blame yourself for, my beloved, nothing at all.'

Rowena shook her head but Hugh continued firmly, 'You must not hold yourself responsible for what happened today. We would have routed that outlaw camp in the end. Their behaviour could not have gone unchecked.'

'But Godric——'

'Athelstanson brought death upon himself,' Hugh interrupted her swiftly. 'The man was half out of his senses.'

His words eased a little of the guilt that had haunted Rowena all day.

'He was so changed,' she said sadly. 'He thought me a traitor to my own people.'

'Grief can make a man too bitter to see the truth.' Hugh tried to comfort her. 'No matter how many revolts William has to put down he will never let go.'

'Godric didn't understand that.' Rowena sighed. Her eyes met his squarely. 'He couldn't accept that you have won.'

Hugh held his breath and waited. Was she about to acknowledge Norman victory at last?

'You are the masters now. There is no one strong enough to defeat William,' Rowena continued in a low voice. 'Men like Godric may continue to deny it but I cannot. Perhaps women are better at admitting the truth. Life forces us to be practical.'

Her eyes flashed with sudden fire. 'But if I had been King Harold I would have retreated and tried again when I had rallied more men to my standard. What use was his bravery when he left us with no leader worthy of the name?'

'A king must defend his honour,' Hugh reminded her, startled by her outburst. 'War is the natural solution to such quarrels.'

'Aye, and women must weep because of it,' Rowena retorted bitterly.

They sat in strained silence for a moment and then Hugh said quietly, 'Harold is not the one you should blame. I once saw him rescue two soldiers from a quicksand in Brittany at considerable risk to himself. He was a good man. He did his best. . .and deserved a better end.'

He hesitated, aware of her surprise. 'William is my liege lord. I would die for him but this time I think he was wrong.'

Hugh's conscience had always troubled him about that oath at Bayeux. Harold's face had worn a look of astonishment when the holy relics had been disclosed but William had been smiling. . .

'Hugh, what are you saying?' Rowena's heart began to beat very fast.

'I do not wish ever to speak of this again, Rowena, but between ourselves here and now I admit there was no real justification for William's behaviour. His claim was no stronger than Harold's.'

A faint sigh escaped him.

'A crown should be given by God and the people. No matter what he had said earlier, at the end King Edward named Harold, not William as his successor and your Witan whole-heartedly approved that choice. Harold was duly anointed and crowned. But my lord refused to accept it. He had boasted of his pretensions and he felt insulted when they rejected him.'

Hugh shook his dark head.

'England was too great a prize for him to resist. It was

worth tricking Harold, worth cajoling the Pope, worth risking an invasion to gain his desire. I still think him a great man but I no longer admire him as I once did.'

His light eyes met hers with naked regret.

'Greed was William's real motive and luck, not God, decided in our favour.'

A strange tingling sensation ran down Rowena's spine. 'You trust me,' she breathed. 'You must to admit such thoughts to me!'

'With my life.' Hugh's tone was dry. If William should ever learn of this it would cost him dear but Rowena deserved to know the truth.

'Edenwald is mine only by right of conquest,' he continued, painfully aware of the implications of what he was saying. 'In God's eyes, it still belongs to you.'

Hugh's unexpected honesty filled Rowena with delight. She knew how he had always dreamt of owning his own land. The very fact that he was willing to make such an admission dissolved the last lingering traces of resentment which had poisoned her feelings for him.

'You have another claim, my lord. You are my husband and all I have is yours,' she announced, smiling at him with pride in her eyes.

'Are you sure, Rowena?' he asked with a trace of uncertainty that caught at her heart.

'Oh, Hugh, let's forget the past. You are here and I love you. That is all that matters now,' she whispered, laying her head against his shoulder. 'It is no longer a question of who was right but of making the best of what we have together.'

His doubt allayed, he laid his lips against her hair and held her tight.

Rowena wanted this precious moment to last forever

but at last she steeled herself to ask what would become of Godric's men.

'The threat to Edenwald is over. I am willing to forgive those who want to live in peace. But this is the last time I will show such unwarranted mercy. If I am to be lord of Edenwald, then they must accept my rule and not even your tears will prevail if any Saxon transgresses against me again.'

While Rowena had lain recovering, Hugh had called a meeting of the whole village. When everyone had assembled, Godric's band had been brought into the hall. Hugh had spoken briefly of his desire for peace and Father Wilfrid had relayed his terms. Kenelm, Mildgyth's missing husband, had been the first to swear fealty and the rest quickly followed.

Rowena rejoiced to hear this news but knew the matter could not be laid to rest so easily.

'What would you have done with Godric if Odo hadn't taken things into his own hands?' This question had tormented her and she couldn't keep the anguish from her voice. 'Would you have hanged him?'

'What do you think?' Abruptly, Hugh released her and stood up. He took a few hasty strides about the room before returning to the bench and saying gruffly, 'I would have had no choice and you know it! He had made a complete fool of my men, totally disrupting the work at the castle and causing havoc everywhere else. Even those cattle Ragge stole went to feed his band. If I had pardoned him, I would have been a laughing stock!'

Taking a deep breath, he sat down again and continued in a more moderate tone. 'Odo is my friend. He acted to save our lives. I had told him to take care of you and he thought you were in danger.'

Her expression remained troubled. Hugh waited for a

moment and then broke the silence with deliberate harshness. 'Godric was a worthy opponent. You shouldn't hate Odo, Rowena. Odo saved him from swinging at the end of a noose, a fate he would have despised.'

Slowly, she nodded her golden head. Godric died fighting, the way he would have wished. He would never have submitted and it would have been intolerable for everyone if Hugh had been forced to mete out a sentence of death.

Maybe in time she would learn to forgive.

'Were you still in love with him?' Hugh asked quietly.

'No! At least not in the way I love you.' A tiny sigh escaped her. 'My feelings for Godric were all bound up with my love for Edenwald and the happy days of my girlhood. He was part of my past.' She lifted her eyes to Hugh's face. 'I didn't want him to be part of my future.'

Hugh's jealousy died. Until this moment he had been so afraid that she might have gone willingly with the Saxon! The big man had been impressive and they had shared so much in common. In spite of Ragge's awkward attempt to explain what had actually happened in the old byre, Hugh had hardly dared believe that Rowena might prefer him.

He reached out to stroke her silken hair.

'I think I began to fall in love with you on that Christmas Day at West Minster. You were so soft and fragile in my arms but I knew that you possessed a core of steel. I tried to tell myself you were merely a child but I could not forget you. Your image remained in my mind no matter where I went.'

A sudden grin lit his face. 'I was as surly as a bear! It wasn't until I saw you again at Winchester that I realised what was wrong with me.'

Rowena stared at him in wonder. He had just described her own feelings exactly. A fierce bright joy flowered in her heart. Their love had already survived many tests. With God's help, they would learn how to live in peace together and bring happiness back to Edenwald.

Hugh stood and drew Rowena to her feet. He glanced towards the window. 'The day is done,' he said softly. 'Will you come to bed, beloved?'

Rowena melted into his embrace and, lifting her into his strong arms, Hugh carried her to the bed. He set her down gently and slipped the cloak from her shoulders. Beneath it, she wore only a thin shift and he caught his breath at the perfection of her lovely body.

Pinching out the candle, Hugh joined Rowena beneath the coverlets. Rowena wound her arms around his neck and they clung together for a moment in silence. Then Hugh kissed her gently, his lips warm and tender.

'Oh, Hugh, I love you so!' Valiantly, Rowena fought to conceal her exhaustion. She wanted him but she was so tired!

'Go to sleep, my little Saxon,' he murmured, smiling down at her. 'There is plenty of time for our loving in all the years ahead of us. When we wake it will be a new day for us and for Edenwald.'

Rowena nodded sleepily, a warm glow of contentment stealing over her. 'I will love you tomorrow. And tomorrow and tomorrow,' she promised, laying her head upon his broad chest.

'What I have, I hold. Forever,' Hugh murmured, kissing her golden hair before they fell asleep in each other's arms.

LEGACY of LOVE

Coming next month

HOUSE OF SECRETS
Sally Blake
Penzance 1858

Bethany Leighton's situation was not happy. Left destitute by her parents' deaths, she had no choice about becoming a companion to widowed Mrs Evelyn Harcourt of Truro, a difficult employer.

It was not surprising that she should listen to Justin Carlyon's proposition, outrageous though it seemed, that she impersonate his cousin Georgina. But what seemed straightforward soon became complicated. Bethany knew she ought to extract herself from the consequences of that fleeting moment of recklessness—but could she leave Justin?

ELEANOR
Sylvia Andrew
Regency

Briefly in London for a family wedding, Miss Eleanor Southeran was intrigued to meet Mr Jonas Guthrie. He was more forthright than the polished gentlemen she had been meeting, which she enjoyed. But then she discovered he was being ostracised by the ladies of the *ton*, and, finding out why, she was confused. This interesting man surely couldn't be guilty of such accusations!

Still, once she was home in Somerset, she wasn't likely to meet him again…

LEGACY *of* LOVE

Coming next month

BRADEN'S BRIDES
Caryn Cameron
Australia 1835

Before Abigail Rosemont even arrived in New South Wales, her life of adventure had begun—with Duke Braden's searing kiss at sea.

But this was a land divided—by rich and poor, injustice and strife. Abigail lived in the opulent world of her cousins, but she dared to join courageous station owner Duke—only to become trapped in a raging feud. Could Abby's courage meet the passionate challenge of this proud land and gain Duke's love?

THE GENTLEMAN
Kristin James
Montana 1888

Stephen Ferguson had arrived in Montana to search for his father and brother...not for a bride. Until Jessie removed her hat, and he saw her long braids, he'd had no idea she was a woman, but somehow this tomboy touched him.

Jessie hadn't cared what men thought of her—until Stephen came. Now she wanted to be a lady, but how—and would it make a difference to Stephen?